All Of My Firsts

Meghan Hollie

Book Cover by Coffin Print Designs Ltd (Paperback and eBook only).

Book Cover by Kylah Cover Designs (Hardback only).

Copy and line edit by Sarah Baker @ Word Emporium.

Proofreading by Sophie @ Iris Peony Editing / Lisa Hine.

Formatting by Atticus.

Published through KDP Publishing Amazon.

1st edition 2023.

Blurb

Ten things to improve my life...

And he was not meant to be one of them.

New year, new me.

Total cliche right? But when I did something completely out of character just before new year, I realised I needed to shake up my life.

Hence my list.

Except nowhere on that list did it say, *"fall in love with Grayson King."*

He's irritating, he's infuriating and devastatingly gorgeous.

The only problem is he doesn't want forever, he's only after right now, and for some reason he's hell bent on helping me complete my list.

But with every task we complete, the more I start to fall for his charms. I'm playing into his game, and I don't know that I can resist him anymore.

How is my heart supposed to cope when I know there's only one way this can end?

Dedication

For the readers who always want the FMC to have it all together... she doesn't because no one does.

Foreword

Please be aware there are a few sensitive topics discussed during this book.

Content warnings:

Childhood trauma & healing. (Parents divorcing and arguing).

Sexual content intended for 18+ audience and explicit language.

Just like *All of My Lasts*, this book is also written in British English.

Playlist

Therefore I am – Billie Eilish

34+35 – Ariana Grande

I Like Me Better – Lauv

Kiss Me – Sixpence None The Richer

Talking Body – Tove Lo

Cupid (Twin version) – FIFTY FIFTY

Crazy in Love – Sofia Karlberg

Ruin My Life – Zara Larsson

3:15 (Breathe) – Russ

Don't Blame Me – Taylor Swift

I Guess – Saint Levant

The Only Exception – Paramore

Howlin' For You – The Black Keys

Until I Found You – Stephen Sanchez

This Is Me Trying – Taylor Swift

Prologue

October - Grayson

My body feels weighed down. And I'm hot, like really fucking hot. Sweating even. Can I smell cupcakes? brownies? My flat definitely doesn't normally smell this sweet. My bed isn't anywhere near this soft either.

Fuck.

My eyes snap open and I blink a few times to try to focus. A heavy groan rumbles around the room. *Wait, was that me?* Fuck, no. I look down to see dark hair splayed across my chest and an arm and leg wrapped around me, like a baby koala.

It takes a second, but then memories of last night flood my brain. This cute little firecracker let me fuck her in a plethora of positions, and had multiple orgasms from my tongue, my fingers, and my dick... my dick, which is currently twitching to wake his new best friend up for another round. Last night was... well, I want to do it again this morning, evidently, which is weird because I'm not one for sleepovers, let alone a second round. *The fuck is that about?*

I shift my arm around Nora's petite frame and adjust the shoulder that she's sleeping on, which in hindsight is a bad move because that wakes her up.

"Oh, fuck!" her raspy voice breathes against my skin as she jolts herself upright. I smile because I don't know if I've ever heard her swear before. Her big brown eyes blink owlishly at me before she closes them and then rubs them fiercely, as though I might disappear when she opens them again.

"Morning, shorty," I say, leaning towards her to brush her hair from her face, wanting to pull her in for a kiss but instead, my hand lingers in the air between us. *This is weird. What am I doing?*

"Oh, fuck..." she repeats. Her eyes become wild as she surveys the bed and my naked chest. "You... and me... last night... we..." She's struggling to get the words out between her panting breaths, which I understand because before last night we were... friends? Maybe, frenemies? I don't know, but now I've seen her naked and I'm not sure how to stop picturing it.

"Had sex," I finish for her. "Several times."

I might be grinning because those sweet memories of her falling apart beneath me are playing on a loop in my head. My dick twitches again. *Yeah, I could definitely go another round.*

She isn't smiling, though; in fact, she looks like she might burst the pulsing vein on her forehead. My smile slips and I hesitate for a second. "Wait, was last night not good for you?" I have to ask even though I'm already 99% sure she enjoyed herself. No, actually, I *know* she enjoyed herself. I never disappoint, and she was extremely vocal with her approval.

Her eyes connect with mine, that vein still popping on her forehead. "Last night was... a mistake," she says sternly.

I can't hide the disappointment from my face. For whatever reason, her words hurt more than I thought they would. I mean, it wasn't like I didn't expect this. She kept saying it was just sex and only one night, muttering about self-control and boundaries—but all women say that don't they? And then they change their mind when they wake up. That's usually when I bolt because those heart eyes freak me the fuck out. But Nora isn't giving me heart eyes. She looks disappointed. Well, fuck. This *is* a first.

I school my face and tell my semi-hard dick to calm the fuck down because what I want clearly isn't going to happen. "Okay, no biggie. You want breakfast?" I mask my disappointment at her reaction as I climb out of her bed and stand to the side, completely naked.

Her eyes eat up every inch of my bare, inked skin like she's reconsidering her decision to not go another round. I'm confused by her mixed signals, blaring red lights shifting to green, in the space of a second, leaving me with so many questions. Does she want me? Does she want to disappear? *Who the hell knows?* So, I do what I do best and what our whole *friendship* has been built on until now; I revert to teasing her. I sway my hips, swinging my still semi-hard dick back and forth. "Like what you see?"

Nora's cheeks pink slightly before she leaps up from her bed, grappling at her bedsheet to keep herself covered. "Grayson..." she groans with a frown, but I interrupt her again.

"Don't get your knickers in a twist. I'm getting dressed. Eggs for breakfast?" I sigh as I locate my boxers across the room, ignoring the weird feeling in my chest. I pick up my black shirt and push both arms

3

into the sleeves before tugging on my now very crumpled black chinos and walking downstairs.

The first thing I do in her kitchen is search for the kettle. I've only been here a few times and I have no idea where anything is. When I spot it resting on the worktop, I flick it on to make a coffee because, now I'm upright, I realise how exhausted my body actually is from last night.

I rifle through cupboards in search of mugs. Just as I close one filled with plates, Nora appears on the other side of the kitchen island wearing some tiny sleep shorts and an equally tiny vest top. I let my eyes scan over her petite, toned body, her shoulder length dark–almost black–hair, her full lips that I had wrapped around my... *fuck no, I need to stop*. I clear my throat. "Coffee?" I ask, turning away from her.

"Please, mugs are up on your left," she replies, just as her phone rings. "Jess? Why are you whispering?" As she walks out into the hallway to talk to her sister, I make the coffee, not really sure how she takes hers, so I opt for milk and no sugar for now. Nora paces back and forth past the door as she chats to Jess. Trying to stop myself from watching her body move and unable to wait any longer for food, I go on the hunt. When I find the little wooden house that clearly says 'eggs' on the worktop is empty, I sulk.

"What self-respecting household doesn't have eggs?" I shout loud enough that Nora stops in the hallway and shrieks 'No' down the phone. I smile as I open the fridge door, knowing full well she's going to be scowling at me.

"This is the saddest fuckin' fridge I've ever seen," I say, closing it and opening another cupboard that's filled with all sorts of fancy pasta. "And why do you have so much pasta?" I close the cupboard door, feeling the fury Nora is directing at me without even looking at her

4

and I'm right because when I finally do lock eyes with her, her cheeks are red, and her lips are tightly pressed together with rage.

Scowling, Nora gets my blood pumping. Fuck, she's hot.

"Don't be ridiculous," she squeals, slicing her finger across her neck as if she'll kill me if I make another sound. It's too cute, so I just smile smugly at her, throwing her a wink for good measure.

"A guy puts out and you can't even provide eggs?" I say far too loudly given how closely we're standing now, only the island separating us. She turns and ignores me, but I'm just not having it. My need to push her buttons is far too strong because it's safe territory for us, it's what we do. My favourite pastime is winding her up because she bites. "Nora!" I call out.

She spins back to face me, her face alight with fury, as she presses the phone against her chest. Her pointy finger comes and is aimed straight at me as she steps forwards. "Oh my God, shit for brains, stop talking." She huffs out her annoyance and returns the phone to her ear as she walks away.

My grin couldn't be wider. She makes it way too easy to get under her skin. This, I can handle, the back and forth we have that's familiar whilst she gets more and more annoyed with me until she explodes. This is what our relationship has always been. From the moment I met her, when Liam started dating Jess a couple months ago, I wanted her, but she kept me on my toes, until last night when she put me on my back. So, I don't know what to do with this fascination my dick seems to have with her now because this wasn't supposed to be what we do. Oh, and would you look at that? Right on cue, he's chubbing back up. *Down, you horn dog.*

I distract myself and my dick and after a few minutes of searching, I've found some bacon, and it's cooking away in front of me when

Nora comes back into the kitchen. "Jess doing okay?" I ask about her sister, knowing she's having family issues, although Liam hasn't told me everything, I know that's why I've been covering for him at work this week. Honestly, I don't mind. I'll do anything for my best mate and boss, but I definitely don't want to piss him off... maybe last night was a bad idea.

"You're such a dickhead. But yeah, she's going to be okay." Nora sits at the island, distracted as she sips her coffee. "Listen, I need you to not say anything to Jess or Liam about this." She points between us, obviously talking about last night. "He's your best friend, but he's also your boss. Jess is my sister... they've not long been back together. It's probably the worst time to tell them about this."

I turn down the heat on the bacon and face Nora, crossing my arms over my bare chest. Her eyes track my movement and stay glued to the huge Lion tattoo that covers my chest. "Are you embarrassed that you slept with me?" I ask, not sure I want to hear her answer.

"Embarrassed, no. Ashamed, a little," she says meekly.

My frown deepens as I ponder her words. She's ashamed. Fuck that feels... I don't even know, but I'm not going to dissect it before I've eaten. I can't think on an empty stomach. I school my expression and try to distract myself by popping some bread in the toaster as she continues.

"I know you sleep with a lot of women, Grayson, like a lot. And there's nothing wrong with that. You do you. But if Jess finds out about last night, she'll marry us off, and that's just not what this was. They'll make it a huge deal, and what's worse is, if we tell them it was just one night, then she'll probably kill you for sleeping with me. We both knew what we were doing last night and that it would only be a one time thing and that's fine. It was just meaningless sex."

"Fucking great, meaningless sex," I guffaw, turning off the heat to the bacon.

She shrugs as she stands and reaches for her phone charger, plugging her phone in, avoiding making eye contact with me. "I mean... it was okay." Her lips twitch at the side.

What the fuck. I want to rip that charger from her hand and fuck her against the counter. I have this sudden, desperate need to remind her just how 'okay' she thought it was last night. If she really thinks it was mediocre, then I have something to prove, deciding there and then that this will absolutely not be a one-night thing because last night was sure as fuck, better than okay.

The toaster pops and I'm distracted for a second and when I look up again, she's disappeared, and I hear the shower turn on upstairs.

Fucking okay sex, my arse.

It's game on.

Chapter 1

Nora – Three months later

It's 7:15am and London has been awake for a while, with commuters racing to get to work, but our street always seems peaceful. The frosted trees sparkle like the Christmas lights everyone took down last month, and the wide pavements look like ice skating rinks.

January has been in full swing for almost three weeks now, and my life has remained the same. I go to work and I come home. Lather, rinse, and repeat.

My sister, Jess, got engaged on New Year's Eve and I'm so happy for her, but if I'm being honest, something snapped in my brain after it happened; I realised that I'll never get anything different from my life if I keep doing the same things.

I've always been the good girl, the reliable one, the one who didn't drink too much, who made the right choices (well most of the time), the one who coloured inside the lines, but that life, I am quickly realising, is incredibly boring. The only thing it's left me with is a re-virginised vagina, no good stories to tell, and no one throwing rocks at my window in the middle of the night to sneak in and ravish me, because isn't that the foundation of every love story? Spectacular declarations that sweep me off my feet? It's never happened, so I wouldn't know. But from what I've seen in my parents' perfect marriage and Jess and Liam finally finding something special together, I feel... left out somehow and I hate that I feel like that.

I've spent my whole life playing it safe. The lack of risk taking and the absence of fun is frankly, depressing. For Christ's sake, Jess and Liam got engaged within four months of finding each other again, but it took me almost four months to decide which sofa was best for my patients. I'm not impulsive in any way. The most unpredictable thing I've done recently is sleep with Grayson, which was a huge mistake for many reasons, and one I will not repeat. Because there are risks and then there are really bad ideas. Despite the fact that all I do is dream about the soft touches he peppered over my skin, the way he made my head spin with ecstasy and my body thrum with desire for him. But it's not going to happen. He doesn't want forever; he wants right now and we've already done that. Case closed.

All I want is to be the ooo to someone's aahh, the hum of appreciation when someone lays eyes on you–I'd fooled myself into thinking it could be Grayson but we've hardly spoken since that one night, which is entirely my fault. I may or may not be avoiding him because I can't trust my body around him. I deserve to be someone's everything. Which is why I decided at stupid o'clock this morning that I am damn well going to change things.

Which also brings me back to the notepad I've been trying to write in since the dawn of time. The no-pressure-bucket-list that I've somehow managed to give myself writer's block over. The list that I promised or convinced myself would push me out of my comfort zone is currently... blank.

'Knock knock.'

"Come in," I croak and clear my throat of the early morning start and lack of coffee lacing my voice.

Jess' petite frame comes into view. She's dressed for work in her dark silk blouse and cream chino trousers. "Morning babe, can I borrow your gold hoops today? I can't find mine," she asks, walking over to me with a steaming mug of coffee.

I gratefully take it, letting the sweet earthy smell invade my senses, and nod towards the jewellery box on my white chest of drawers. "They're in there."

"Do you have a day off today?" She eyes me in the reflection of the large mirror as she places the hoops in her ears.

"Just a half day." I sip my coffee, appreciating the way the warmth trickles down my throat, heating my stomach.

"That's nice. You've been working so much lately, I feel like I've barely seen you."

I sit up straighter on my reading chair. "I have to work hard to keep a solid client base, and even though I've been doing it for five years, it still takes so much effort. Especially in a city where there's a therapist on every corner. Getting people to trust you and share intimate details of their lives takes time, so I'm focusing on that right now." I don't mean to sound grumpy and I'm not sure who I'm trying to convince–me or Jess. I love my job, but I know I've been using it to escape too.

"I know, sweetie, and I'm so proud of you. I just don't want you to be lonely. When was the last time you had a date? Was it that guy last summer?"

I cringe at the memories of that fling, that never really flung, with Freddie. He was so dull and boring that he made *me* look like a daredevil and my ideal night involves a crossword puzzle and a cuppa. He only ever had missionary sex with the lights on, I shudder at the memory of how dull it was. Okay, the first thing I need to add to my list is *have better sex*.

"I'm not lonely," I reassure her. "I don't have time to be. Besides, bringing someone into my life right now would only complicate things. Not everyone understands that work comes first." Which I think is half my problem; I'm serious about work and needing to achieve the goals I've set myself, but that also means I'm not as fun-loving as I could be. It's a catch-22 but one that I'm determined my list will solve.

Jess' shoulders slump as her eyes stay locked on mine. "Just promise me you won't put your life on hold for work. You still need to take time for you, Nor." She softens her stare. *I know, I'm trying*, I think to myself. "You know I love you, and I'm only looking out for you."

"I know. I love you too. I'm just... trying to make it all work.. I mean, as well as my own clients, we also have the charity clients now too. And whilst that's relatively quiet just now, I'm trying to figure out a balance. I promise I'm good. Just busy."

"Okay, well, I'm here to talk whenever. You know that, right?" I nod, smiling up at my cousin-turned sister-but always my ride or die best friend. Jess glances at her watch, her eyes widening when she notices the time. "Liam and I will be back late tonight. I've got a winter wedding on today and because he is now my fiancé, I've roped him into helping me with the end of night tidy up." She wiggles her engagement ring in front of her face as she smiles at it.

"Liam agreed to helping?"

"He doesn't know he's helping yet."

"That sounds about right." I laugh lightly. "I'm going to the gym later anyway, so I'll be home late too."

"Okay," She smooths down her chinos. "Do I look okay?"

"You look awful, truly awful. You shouldn't go out in public today," I deadpan.

Jess mock laughs and sways her hips as she walks out of my room.

Once I'm alone again, I consider Jess' comments. I haven't lied to her. I'm really not lonely. I just want to find a balance between work and creating a life that I love and that was the point of this list. The expectation of having that fun-filled social life in your twenties is fading before it ever really got started. My twenty-seventh birthday is creeping up on me and making me feel like I've been adulting wrong all this time. Objectively, it isn't that old; I know that, but no matter how much I tell myself that I am an independent woman who doesn't *need* to have all the things that the world of social media brags about—Husbands, wives, kids, golden retriever, big houses... there is a still a part of my brain that feels like I'm lacking. *Sigh.*

My Instagram feed is full of book boyfriends and videos of kids saying things like, "Just in case you need to hear it, you're amazing." *Like they can actually read my mind because yeah, I did need to hear it, okay?*

Truth is, I don't *need* a man's attention; I don't *need* the white picket fence and kids, but I'd like it. I'd like to think that one day I can bring someone to their knees. To be worshipped the same way Jess is by Liam. Lately, the only men who bring me to my knees are fictional and whilst my imagination is full of gorgeous, tall, muscled men with huge dicks, my reality is very far from that.

I am ready for a new balance in my life. I let the thought sit for a second. Finding undiscovered parts of myself feels exciting. The 'new year new me' vibe sounds cliché, but I don't care, I need this.

Just write one thing down, Nora. You're not writing a bloody novel. I think, my pen tapping against my lip. I write one thing which came to me earlier–*have better sex* and then I'm stumped again. I pull out my phone to Google a few bucket list things and I'm surprised to see that 'sex pact' isn't on any of them. Oh well, I'm not removing it. I need to push myself to say yes to more things that are outside of my realm of control–which I seem to be far too comfortable living in. I want fun, adventure, love, excitement. I want to *feel* more because I don't want to become a spinster or a robot.

I'm in a slump and I need to get out of it.

An hour passes and I give up and begin to get ready for work, pulling on my black pencil skirt and white blouse, tucking it into the waistband. Like a predictable ticking clock, I grab my trainers and shove my feet into them and pack my heels separately for the office. I walk towards the nearest tube station, get on the same tube... How do I know this? Because this train has a hole in the seat nearest the doors on carriage five, which is the one I always get on, and I stare at the same torn fabric every day. When four stops pass me by, I walk up the same escalators and head to the same coffee hut outside the station.

"Hey Nora, you here for the usual? You're late today, missed the morning rush." The coffee guy, called Matt, smiles at me and I smile robotically back at him, distracted by my sour mood.

"Less work is always good, right?" I say emptily because less work implies more play – which has not happened.

Matt makes my coffee with a shot of vanilla and I pay and wish him a good day, like always. Hamster meet wheel.

The office is quiet when I arrive and I'm grateful for that. Although my day is a blur of clients, note writing, and follow up phone calls. Even when I'm on my way home at 7pm, I'm still in a bit of a funk.

Deciding to forego the gym, I stop at my usual Thai takeaway, where they know me by name too. As I stand, waiting in line, I let out an annoyed sigh because I need to just get a grip. My new life isn't just going to magically appear. I need to take action.

Marching back down the darkened street to mine and Jess' townhouse, with my food in hand, I decide I'm going to eat and then I'm going to plan. Maybe I'll eat *and* plan. *Woah, Nora, don't get too crazy.*

I slip off my trainers and jacket as soon as I'm in the house and then plonk myself at the kitchen island. I eat my Massaman chicken curry and rice so fast that I end up feeling like I've got a bowling ball as a stomach. So I take my overfed self into the living room and relax onto the sofa with my pen and notebook.

Okay, you've got this Nora. It's just a list. A list to make you have more fun. I read what I wrote earlier:

1. Have better sex – must be mind blowing.

Yes, I still agree with this – I'm feeling good, giddy even. Maybe that's because I ate, but I don't pay it much thought because I've got my first thing. Okay, let's go for another. I think back to my Google search this morning, remembering a few things on other people's lists.

Conquer one fear.

I hate lifts so maybe I'll start there. Not crazy about spiders either, but I don't know if I'll ever be over that irrational fear.

RIDE IN A LIMO.

Who doesn't want to ride in a limo? It's wholly unnecessary, which obviously makes it necessary for this list.

GO TO A CONCERT OR FESTIVAL.

Zoey might be my hype girl for this. She lives at festivals in the summer.

DO KARAOKE.

This one won't be my favourite. I hate singing. I'm not good at it but for one night, I'll be someone's entertainment.

BE KISSED UNDER THE STARS.

I have to try and get some romance in somehow.

GET A TATTOO.

I hate to admit this, but Grayson might be the best person to help me with this one. From what I remember, the man has a fair few tattoos. Not that I sit and imagine them. Well, not that often. Once a day is healthy, right?

SAY YES FOR A WHOLE DAY.

I'll need to figure out someone to help me here and push me outside of my comfort zone. Otherwise, I'll be asking myself lame questions like: 'do you want to stay in and do a crossword puzzle? Why yes Nora, I do'. Like I said, lame.

FALL IN LOVE... FOR THE FIRST TIME.

That's a big one, and not one I think I'll achieve any time soon but it's there and it'll happen, one day.

I can't think of another one yet, I hate leaving the list on an odd number, but I'll have to come back to it.

Now I just need to actually do the things on my list.

Nora's New Year list

1. Have better sex – must be mind blowing
2. Conquer one fear
3. Ride in a limo
4. Go to a concert or festival
5. Do karaoke
6. Be kissed under the stars
7. Get a tattoo
8. Say yes for a whole day
9. Fall in love for the first time

Chapter 2

Grayson

"**M**ate, that office contract for the new construction company over in Chelsea? I heard that Killian Harris' company was after that one too, but you've just swiped it from under their noses. Sneaky fucker. You've got the first draft contract drawn?" Liam asks as he fusses around the kitchen looking for water glasses. In his defence, he's only recently moved in with Jess and Nora, so he probably still doesn't have any idea where things are.

"I have, and it's signed already. I met with the owner, Ethan, yesterday and he signed there and then." I metaphorically puff out my chest, pleased that I landed such a big deal.

This contract is my first big score since working for Liam and getting my promotion at the end of last year. I met Ethan on a night out a few months ago when he told me about his construction company, and how they were looking for a space to rent in central London. So I wooed him and swooped in last night with my fancy tequila and company credit card. By the end of the night, he agreed to a deal and before I knew it, I had secured a five million pound lease with him.

Thank you, Don Julio, for the assist, but I'll take the credit for this one.

Liam slaps my shoulder as he congratulates me. "Yes mate, you fucking shark. I knew you were made for this."

He's right. I'm good at my job but it's because of him. Liam taught me everything I know in the corporate real estate business. He's been born and bred with this company, his dad starting it in his home office, and now it has clients all over the UK, and more recently, internationally.

We've been friends for years now. Liam was there for me when other people weren't. He helped me get my life on track when I was a lost kid who struggled to hold down any kind of friendship, let alone a relationship. My parents divorced the year I met him, and they both left London when I was nineteen. I spent the best part of my childhood being a pawn in their marriage. It made me bitter, and I hated everything and everyone. My dad moved up north to be nearer his brother, whilst Mum went across the pond to America to be nearer her newest boy-toy.

But me? I didn't want to leave London. I had my whole life here. So, I dug my heels in, refusing to follow either of them. They left me with enough money to see me through a year's worth of London rent, which, of course, I blew on booze, food, and whatever the fuck else a nineteen-year-old boy wants.

A few months later, I met Liam, and the rest is history. He took me in five years ago, forced me to be his friend, gave me a job and a place to stay. I owe him a lot.

A blur of brunette hair whips past my shoulder, snapping me from my thoughts, and pounces on Liam. This is Jess, Liam's fiancée, the one responsible for the hearts in his eyes. For real though, he's happy and I'm happy for him. Jess has been good for him. Anyone with eyes can see they're madly in love.

The other Scott female, Nora, is a very different story. She isn't my biggest fan. Well, she was that one night, but since then we've barely spoken. Despite my plan to chase after her, I remembered that I don't do relationships, and I talked myself out of it. It's probably better for my ego that we don't say much to each other anyway. Sex has always been a transaction for me, to scratch an itch and I can't offer more. She's the only woman who has ever told me that sex with me was 'okay' and yeah, I'm still pretty sore about it. I now hate the word *okay* and refuse to use it anymore because I feel hot rage building in my stomach if I even think about saying. As petty payback, I beat her at a few games of *Uno* around Christmas time and then *Monopoly*. Liam warned me that I would've been better off letting her win, but me being me, I couldn't. My pride needed the boost.

I did learn that my competitive side seems to piss her off, which, of course, I love. Although she didn't seem to mind that night when I made it my personal mission to make her see stars over and over again. But I'm actively *not* thinking about that because it was just 'okay'. *Ooof, there's that little ragey feeling again. Chill the fuck out, man. You're a sex-champion and you know it.*

Speaking of Nora, she rounds the corner into the now slightly crowded kitchen, freezing when she sees me, her big brown eyes zoning in on me, her full, pouty lips pursing at my presence. But just like that, the rage I've just been feeling about our 'okay' encounter dissipates the second I see her, which is really fucking confusing.

"Oh," she blurts out flatly.

Not exactly the warmest greeting, but not the worst either. She's been known to scoff at my presence before, so, this might be an improvement. I haven't seen her for almost three weeks... not that I'm counting or anything, and she's a sight for sore eyes.

"Hey shorty," I reply, letting my lips tip upwards into a smirk that I know infuriates her.

Her eyes narrow as she looks at me, little sparks of fury form in her caramel irises, sending a hit of serotonin straight into my veins. "You're here... for dinner?" Her tone is almost accusatory as her arms cross over her body, accentuating her breasts beneath her thin blouse. The masochist that I am, I can't help but sneak a peek. My deviant mind wanders back to that night and how it felt stripping her out of a blouse very similar to that. The way her back arched when I bit her rosy nipples. Her tight grip in my hair as she begged for more... Oh fuuuuuck, she's so hot. I clear my throat, which has become thick with need.

"That's the plan. Unless you've got something else I can eat." I let my eyes devour every inch of her body, licking my lips equally as slowly, pushing her buttons in my favourite way. But also torturing myself because now I'm fighting a semi at the memory of her.

Watching her squirm and blush always makes my blood pump faster. I like the fact that she resists me; she makes me work for it, not giving into me easily. Even her snarky comments turn me on.

She's not afraid to tell me what she thinks of me It's kind of like foreplay, but instead of getting to kiss it all better, like I got to do that one night, I'm usually met with her prickly side. She's like a cactus, and I'm the idiot who likes to see how spikey she is but, no matter how much it hurts, I never learn not to touch.

"Nope. Not today, Satan." She pops the *p* when she says nope, as she stomps to the fridge and pulls out a bottle of water. She opens it and downs the contents, and I watch with intrigue as her throat bobs and my dick perks up again, remembering exactly how it felt when she swallowed down every drop of me. *Fuck, I need to get my mind out of the gutter.* I blame my lack of sex for these horn dog thoughts occupying my brain.

Don't get me wrong, I love a naughty sex daydream, but they shouldn't include her. The one person who all but threw me out of her bed, insulting my sex skills.

Besides, I don't want a relationship, I have no interest in marriage or monogamy and Nora screams 'I want to settle down', with her sensible pencil skirts, perfectly styled hair, shoes without a single scuff, and a personal planner (who even uses them anymore?) that's stuffed full of lists and all sorts of boring relationship things, I'm sure.

That's enough of a reason for me to stay clear, but there is also the fact that the one person I never want to push out of my life happens to be her future brother-in-law, so, it can only ever be that one night.

"So, dinner, shall we order in?" Liam suggests as he opens his phone to a delivery app whilst simultaneously burying his face into Jess' neck as he continues to talk. "Chinese, Indian, Italian, Thai... someone stop me when I say something they want."

What I want is to not have a front row seat to your canoodling, I think to myself. *But we can't all be picky. Especially since I'm not planning on paying for dinner tonight.*

"I could eat pizza," Jess announces, and I watch Liam nibble her neck and she giggles as a frown forms on my face.

"Will you two stop eating each other for one second, please?" Honestly, seeing two people so in love is pretty foreign to me at the best of times. My parents were the least touchy-feely people. It didn't help that they hated each other for the majority of their marriage, either.

Liam carries on like he hasn't heard me, but throws up his middle finger in my direction. "Okay, baby, pizza it is," he kisses her mouth quickly and asks what toppings Nora and I want. When we both say *meat feast*, Nora shoots me a glare as though we're not allowed to like the same pizza.

"I've got some meat for you, shorty; we can share that too." I'm dying to add that she already knows what my meat tastes like, but I stop myself. I did promise not to tell Jess and Liam. But watching her face colour while she seems to silently fluster over my words is all the satisfaction I need.

"Yeah, meat you'd share with me and half of London's female population. No, thank you." She turns to face Liam as she begins to back out of the kitchen. "Actually, I think I'll have the vegetarian pizza. The thought of meat is making my stomach turn." She looks directly at me as she leaves the room.

She really is extra prickly tonight.

A few minutes later, I leave Liam in the kitchen eating Jess' face. There are only so many times you can break those two apart before you know it's time to leave them to it.

When I step into their living room, I see Nora sitting on their cream two seater sofa. Her dark hair is now tied up into a ponytail and she's staring intently at a book like it holds the holy grail. I move towards the space next to her, letting her sweet scent drift over to me as I sit. Dipping my head sideways, I read the title of her book. *Pleasing Mr Parker.* Well, I don't know who this Mr Parker is or why he needs pleasing but colour me intrigued.

"You're staring," she whispers as she keeps her eyes firmly on her book, shifting in her seat.

I *am* staring. Partially at her, the way her legs are tucked underneath her tiny frame, making her look smaller somehow, which is a feat because she's pretty much an entire foot shorter than my six-foot-four body I'm watching her eyes scan over the words, not missing the infrequent lilt of her mouth when she obviously reads something she likes.

There's no denying that she intrigues me, although I wish to hell she didn't. I like the disdain she throws my way, but I like that I'm getting to glimpse a different side of her like this; quiet, less quippy, more... her. I'm drawn to her, and I can't figure out why – is it because she's forbidden fruit? It can't be because I've tasted her, and fuck, is she the sweetest fruit. But I still can't explain why I have this desire to be around her. I've not seen her properly for a while and seeing her now is like getting a drink of water on a hot day.

"What'cha reading?" I ask, scanning the front of her book before she can reply. "Dude is ripped on that front cover."

Her laugh is light, almost as though she could find me funny. The noise settles in the air around us. "He is, huh? Do you need to use him for inspiration?" she mocks and fuck, here I go again, getting a buzz in my veins for her snarky arse. Her gaze leaves the book, and her caramel eyes darken as they trawl over my body it shouldn't get me hot, but it does. It feels like she's undressing me without touching me, and my entire body burns for her.

"I don't need him for inspiration, shorty. I know you remember what's under the hood," I say confidently, as I pull up my t-shirt, revealing a sneak peak of my abs. My grin only grows wider when her breathing stutters and she pulls her book closer, hiding her face from me entirely, leaving a hot ripped guy on the cover of the book facing me. "Why *is* that guy naked anyway?"

She lowers the book, turning it to look at the cover herself. "This is a romance book, so the guys are sometimes shirtless on the cover, to… enhance the contents of the novel…" She drifts off, regret pouring into her expression as she looks at me, probably hoping I don't catch on but it's too late.

My eyebrows shoot upwards to meet my hairline. "You're reading porn," I shout a little too loudly.

Her eyes widen like saucers as she pins me with a look that could burn, fumbling through the words erupting at speed from her mouth. "It's not porn. It's a contemporary adult romance book. Keyword there being *adult,* something you'd know nothing about."

"Oh, shorty, I know plenty about being an adult. I'm a fully grown man and I know plenty about pleasing women, too. C'mon, I know you haven't forgotten." Because I sure as fuck haven't. "If you ever need to put your books into practice, I'm all yours." I wink, watching as the crimson spreads across her face, lighting her up like a goddamn rocket. Judging by the deep set of her brows and fury pooling in her eyes, I'd say that she's about ready to blast off.

"More like man-child," she mutters angrily under her breath, but I hear a hint of desire in her tone. Of course, me being me, I want to push more.

"So, tell me more about what makes you hot. Aside from me, of course."

Her eyes snap to me again as she slaps her book shut. "You know you're incredibly annoying."

Yes. Yes, I do. I revel in her annoyance. This is what I live for, her reaction to me, because she bites, every time. *This* is why I'm drawn to her; the challenge.

"Come on, tell me about your smutty books. I want to know your kinks."

"Oh, my God." She buries her face into her hands and the flush on her face peeks out from behind her fingers. *I love it.*

"Don't be shy now, Nora."

"Please stop. I'm begging you," she pleads, keeping her head buried.

"Okay, begging is a kink I can get on board with. I know you liked—"

Her head snaps up, a few pieces of hair have escaped her ponytail and whisp around her delicate face. "Don't finish that sentence. We are not taking a trip down memory lane." Her eyes glaze over for a second and I know I've got her thinking about that night. God, what I'd do to reach out and kiss the living shit out of her right now. I almost do, but then she adds. "I'd rather not remember that night." Her voice wobbles and has absolutely no conviction whatsoever.

"Oh, c'mon. I'll tell you mine if you tell me yours," I offer, hoping she'll take the bait. Instead, she picks up her book and continues to ignore me, not an ounce of amusement on her face.

"I don't want to talk to you anymore. So, if you are going to sit there, please be quiet."

I grumble. I like annoying her. It's kind of like annoying your teacher at school, and they continually get irritated with you until they either ignore you or send you to detention. Well, if Nora reads smutty books, I think I'm interested in her version of detention.

"Actually," she says, abruptly snapping her book shut. "You know what, now you're obviously not leaving me alone, we need to talk."

God, she really is being a grump today. Maybe I've pushed her too far, or maybe not enough–maybe she's about to crack and give in, and that annoys her. I have no idea. I should be annoyed at her cockiness, but I'm more turned on than anything else.

"Oh yeah? Finally going to admit you want me again?"

She scoffs, "that's cute," and then bops my nose. "No, I was hoping to get a head start on the planning for Jess' hen do. But I wondered if we could end the evening in the same club or something."

"If this is just an excuse to spend more time with me—"

Nora interrupts me by pushing two fingers to my lips, the contact making me tingle all over. "I'm going to stop you right there. They're our best friends and I want to do this for them, with or without you. So, tell me now if you want to help."

I chuckle. "Okay fine, I'll help. What do you need?" I shift my legs so one of them is on the sofa between us. When my leg catches hers, she locks onto the contact and bites her lip. I almost outwardly groan, because that action sends me a little crazy and I want to be the person to bite that lip. When our eyes meet, I know she feels it too. Her cheeks flush, her breathing is shallow, and she's got the same desire filled look she had *that* night.

The moment is interrupted by Jess and Liam walking into the room. "What were you two talking about?" Jess asks. "Nor, you look so shifty over there."

Nora swallows and flicks an unsure look at me. "Well, we were actually talking about your hen party."

Jess and Liam share a look that tells me this whole thing might be dead in the water. "We were actually thinking about having a joint one," Liam says.

I shoot him a look that says, 'Dude, what the fuck?' but he just ignores me.

"I mean, we're getting married in a few months so, planning something big isn't really an option. Plus, we don't want big. We want to spend it together. We've spent enough time apart," Jess says. It's true, they spent ten years apart and I can see why they want to do more things together, but still, there go my dreams of watching Liam freak out in a strip club.

Nora tucks a strand of her dark hair that's fallen from her ponytail, behind her ear. "Do you still want me to plan it?"

"We wondered if you and Grayson wouldn't mind doing it together?" Liam replies. "If you want to, that is. There's really no pressure."

Oh, now we're talking.

"I'm good with that. You are too, right, shorty?" I ask, earning an unmistakably flustered look from Nora.

"Uh, yeah. Of course, if that's what you both want. We'll do it together," she answers robotically.

"This is going to be so much fun," I say, rubbing my hands together. In my head, I'm thinking strippers, cigars, booze...

"You look like you've just been given the keys to Willy Wonka's chocolate factory. I'm scared." Nora raises an eyebrow, sensing my scheming plans.

I wink at her. "You have no idea baby."

"Well, I'm good with whatever, so long as I get to take you home at the end of the night," Liam murmurs, pulling Jess closer to him. Glancing over at Nora, I find her watching them with a longing expression on her face. But when she catches me looking, it disappears.

"Okay, so Grayson and I will get planning then," she says with a grimace.

This is going to be fun.

Chapter 3

Grayson

"**W**ell?" Her brown eyes are wide and furious with me, for fuck knows what. It's like I'm supposed to read her mind or pay attention, neither of which I've ever claimed to be good at. Plus, I've been here for maybe fifteen minutes, four of which she's rambled on and on about something I definitely wasn't listening to. I might've been too distracted by her lips, and it freaked me out that I was imagining her *again*. I've never slept with any woman twice, and the more time I spend with Nora, the more I think about sleeping with her for a second time... and maybe a third and it's messing with my concentration.

"Well what, shorty?" That gets me a serious scowl. With a look like that, I feel like I've accomplished everything I needed to for the whole day just by pissing her off. If I can't sleep with her again, I may as well settle on getting a rise out of her any way I can.

"Don't call me that, it's awful," she glares at me with the fire of a thousand suns. I grin and resist the urge to bop her nose, like she did to me the other day. "I'm serious. Cut it out. We have work to do here."

She's serious? Newsflash, she always is. There is a fun version of Nora that I've seen a few times. My favourite was when she let loose at a Christmas Eve party last year. She was absolutely hammered and dancing around like she was auditioning for a strip club; it was highly amusing and hot as fuck.

My head shakes away the memory before it travels down to my over-eager dick. "Let's just get on with this for the lovebird's sake, yeah?"

Nora's eyes roll. "I've only been saying that for the past twenty minutes," she mumbles as she opens her huge planner that's already full and we're only in January.

"So, I already have a spa planned for the morning and then a pamper session at Jess' favourite salon. She's agreed to spend that amount of time away from Liam, at least. So, the area I'm not very experienced in is clubs." Her eyes land on mine at me as she taps her pen on her planner, obviously expecting me to carry on the conversation.

"I know a few places where we can hire a VIP area. They have stripper packages for events."

Her gaze narrows as she leans her elbows onto the kitchen island and I resist the urge to try and look down her blouse, when it's all I *want* to do. "Do I want to know how you know that? Also, do we want strippers?"

"I think the answer is yes, we want strippers. It's a stag party."

"And a hen party. Maybe we don't want to be around a bunch of men getting lap dances."

"I've got friends who like to go to these clubs. There are male and female dancers. They're not sex clubs but they're also not-not sex clubs, if you get me."

Her eyes narrow even further as her anger towards me intensifies. "I do not get you at all. What about me screams 'I've been to a strip club'?"

I laugh. "There are female and male dancers, strippers if you want to call them that, but also, some of those strippers can be uhhh." I suddenly feel hot all over trying to explain to Nora what this place is. "They can be other entertainment for the evening. For a price."

"It's a brothel, then?" Her nose scrunches up. "Grayson, that's illegal. Wait." Her face falls. "Have *you* slept with the girls at this club?"

I scratch the back of my neck where I now seem to be sweating too. "I mean..."

"Actually, I don't want to know." She closes her eyes tightly and turns away from me for a second.

Fuck, I've made this so much worse.

"Nora..." She doesn't turn straight away, not until I see her shoulders deflate and she spins around to face me again. I instinctively reach for her hand and a zap of electricity travels through our connected hands, making us both flinch and her pull back. Her eyes widen as she looks at me, but I go for her hand again. "I've gone about this all wrong. The girls offer private dances. They don't include sex. But maybe they include heavy petting. That's all. It's not seedy. Most of the girls there are actually just there to earn money for university or whatever."

"And you'd know this because..." Her voice is quiet and unsure, I open my mouth to speak, but she stops me. "No, wait, don't answer that. If you say it's fine, then just book it. I'm moving into my 'ask

31

fewer questions era' with you." Her hand moves from mine as she sighs, looking deflated. "If Jess hates it, it'll be on your head."

"I'll call now." I stand, ignoring the need to reassure her and reach for my phone in my pocket to make the call.

Five minutes later, it's all booked. "Okay, booked for the same day, which is lucky because that's all that was available until Spring. He said he would throw in a free drink for us all, too."

Nora's head snaps up from where she's been scribbling notes in her planner. "Okay, great. So that's sorted. Shall we pick somewhere to have dinner too? We'll be at the salon until 5-6 at the latest."

"How about the new place over on Southbank? Pretty sure they do pizza and have a decent party section. It's not too far from the club either."

"Oh, you mean Fiori's? Yeah, that would be great. I'll book it. I'm sure you can book online, too."

I watch her as she makes a few more notes and gets out her phone to Google the restaurant, all the while she's muttering to herself.

"Don't look at me like that, Mr King." She says without even looking up.

An involuntarily rumble erupts from me, heat bubbling inside me as my eyes all but roll in my head. "Call me Mr King again..."

"No."

"C'mon, please?" I whine.

"Absolutely not." My eyes are dutifully drawn to her lips. She wants to smile. I can tell by the way her mouth twists, her plump bottom lip pouting just a little more than normal.

"You're no fun. Also, how do you know how I'm looking at you? You aren't even watching me."

A slow, reluctant smile builds on her perfect mouth. "Because I can *feel* you looking at me and I can practically hear your thoughts."

"Oh yeah? What am I thinking?" My voice is filled with lust as I let my tongue leisurely lap along the seam of my lips to make sure she sees it.

She lets her own tongue peek out, as though it's searching for mine as she wets her bottom lip, and it triggers a memory of her doing exactly that on her knees. My blood turns to fire as it pumps faster around my body, heating up with arousal. This is dangerous territory. Her eyes lift from my mouth to meet my stare, and something must flash over my face because she smirks at me.

"Tell me honestly, were you thinking about me just now?" she asks, her bravado wavering briefly.

"You can't answer a question with a question, shorty. It's not fair."

"Okay, then let me answer you. That night we spent together, you gave me that look you just had plastered on your face, so I'm willing to guess that you were thinking about me or that night just now." I'm surprised she's brought that night up. We've been avoiding it for so long and each other that it feels like a dream. But her acknowledging it, does something to me; it makes me more desperate for a repeat.

"Can you blame me if I was?" I ask, whilst wondering if she thinks about that night as much as I do.

She lilts her mouth into a playful smirk. "I mean that night was alright..." She trails off, suddenly distracting herself by putting pieces of paper back into her planner.

Again, with the mediocre. She's giving me a complex and I hate it. Just as I'm about to argue my case for my performance that night or remind her just how good it was. A piece of paper flutters out of her planner directly in front of me. I pick it up and read the title '*Nora's*

New Years List'. My intrigue trumps my need to argue about how amazing my dick is.

"What's this?" I ask before I read on. The way her eyes bug out has me tightening my grip on the paper.

"Oh, my God. Give that back," she squeals, leaping around the kitchen counter, her hands grab frantically for the paper. *Well, this is interesting.*

I move swiftly, holding the paper high out of her reach, enjoying the perks of being tall. "Tell me what it is first."

Her grabby hands are completely useless around me. There's no way she'll reach the paper, but it's fun to watch her tiny five-foot-four self *try* to reach it. Her palm lays flat on my chest as she attempts to propel herself towards my hand. Even if I wasn't six-foot four, she wouldn't ever reach it with my hand in the air.

"It's nothing, just something for work." She huffs from exerting herself.

I raise an eyebrow, waiting to see if she's going to tell me the truth because I can sense there is more to it. Lowering my hand, I open the paper and see a list. Reading through it quickly, my smile grows. "This isn't for work, this is for you." My eyes flick back to hers.

She buries her head into her hands. "Oh, my God. No, no, no. This isn't happening," she curses to herself.

"Nora?"

"I don't expect you to understand," she says flatly.

I approach her, wanting to give her a hug, wanting to figure out more about her, maybe why she's so hot and cold with me but instead I use the side of my index finger to lift her face to mine feeling our connection again. "So, help me."

She searches my face, and just when I think her pause is her shutting me down. "My life needs more balance, okay? I work a lot and my social life is... dull. The most exciting thing I've done in the last year is well... never mind. I made this list because I promised myself that I would do more things that scare me, or finally get around to doing the things I've always wanted to do but haven't got around to." She looks at the list thoughtfully but quickly masks her face as if she's dismissing whatever emotion she's feeling. "It's stupid really."

"I don't think it's stupid. I think it's cool. You want to take charge and make changes. I respect that," I say, honestly. I see how tightly wound she is, and I think this will be good for her. Fun Nora is in there somewhere and I like it when she comes out to play. It's like spotting a hummingbird in the middle of London; a very rare occurrence.

Then the need to tease her overtakes me like a fever, but not because I want to piss her off, because I want to earn a smile from her more than anything right now. "If you want help with anything, I'll happily oblige. Especially that first one, have mind blowing sex? Pff easy, I'm your man."

She drops her head into her hands again, groaning but there's a smile I see peeking out from beneath her hands. "Please leave."

I chuckle as she begins to try and usher me out of the kitchen. But it's futile because she's tiny and I'm, well, I'm not. "We're not done with the planning, and now I have a much more exciting reason to stay."

"You really don't."

"I really do."

Her hands fall to her sides, as she finally gives up trying to push me. "Grayson, if you're going to be more of a pain in my arse than usual, then I need you to leave. I'll sort the rest of it out another time, but right now I'm this close." She uses her finger and thumb to show me a tiny amount. "To losing it with you." When I step closer to her, she twists her mouth to try and hide a smile and I grin, hoping it'll bring out her own. When it does spread across her face, I feel triumphant. "Stop making me smile," she slaps my chest playfully.

I catch her wrist on the rebound and place it back on my chest, she stiffens from my bold move, but I don't miss the way she licks her lips quickly. "I like making you smile." I say, reaching up to tuck a lock of hair behind her ear. I freeze, just before my fingers touch the soft dark strands, the affectionate move catching me off guard. I redirect my hand to land on her shoulder instead. "Plus, I don't think you're thinking clearly, I can help you with this list."

"Say *list* one more time I dare you," she whispers, her voice raspy and lustful. It makes me wonder if she wants me to take her up on the dare and what would happen if I did...

A smirk passes over my mouth at the thought of her daring me to do something. She has to know that it's near enough impossible to give up the threat of a dare, especially when she's involved. But I let it go just this once. "So salty. Fine, if you're too chicken..." As I start to walk away, she grabs my hand and quickly releases it like a hot potato. Both of us track the connection as she steps backwards.

"I'm not...." her fingers strum her sides. "You know what, I'm not biting."

"Well, that's a fucking shame in itself. I happen to love seeing my teeth marks all over you."

"Grayson!" she squeals. "Please leave," she requests for the second time, But this time there's a lot less push and far more desire in her eyes and her body, her nipples peaking beneath her blouse.

"You're always so keen to kick me out."

"Maybe because you're the most irritating person to walk the planet." She huffs, placing the list on the worktop with a groan.

"I don't think you've always found me so irritating. Have you?" I give her my best 'come fuck me' look because right now, I'd love nothing more than to fuck her.

She loses the annoyance in her eyes and replaces it with something else, something that heats me up even more as she leans towards me, giving me a glimpse down her blouse that's the perfect V-shape, pointing to her beautiful breasts that I want to play with again. I can't help but let my eyes travel the length of her delicate neck and imagine that it's my tongue and not my gaze. She reaches out for me and grips my chin to force my eyes to hers. Her smile has an air of evil. Damn it's hot.

"My eyes are up here."

Her attitude has me licking my lips. "I know. I wasn't looking for your eyes, shorty." I'm not ashamed she caught me looking at her. She's got a great body and my dick definitely remembers that right now. Which still makes my head spin.

My phone buzzes, breaking our connection, and she grabs the list from my hand, the look on her face triumphant. "My list, not yours."

"Oh, you're so wrong, shorty."

Chapter 4

Nora

"Tell me about your mother?" I ask my thirteen-year-old patient who sits across from me on the soft grey sofa. We've been playing this game of avoidance for the last thirty minutes, and now she only has ten minutes of her session left.

"I don't know what to tell you. She's a bitch."

"Okay, how do you feel right now?"

Her eyes almost roll back into her head. "What's that supposed to mean?"

"Ella, I'm simply asking how you feel at the moment. Do you have any emotions you'd like to share with me?"

Again, with the eye roll. "Not really."

This is our fourth session together, and she's definitely a tough egg to crack, but I always get there in the end. I lean forwards onto my thighs. "Can I tell you how I feel?"

She nods shyly and I smile at her, excited that I might be getting somewhere. "I'm a little annoyed because it's raining right now, and I know I have to get the tube home later and, in these shoes, that means my feet will be wet, so that's why I feel annoyed."

A small smile appears on her face, which is progress from her scowls and eye rolls, so I'll take it. She shuffles in her seat, as if she's preparing to say something.

"I feel confused." *Yes, I got her.*

"Tell me more."

She shrugs. "I don't know why I have to come here and talk to you; I know that my dad died, and my mum is struggling, but I'm fine. She's the one who needs help. She's been such a bitch since he died, so I'm confused why isn't she here?"

Hmm she definitely isn't fine, but I'll bite.

"Ella, your mother is seeing another therapist in the building. I assure you that her behaviour is not your fault and I'm sorry you feel as though she isn't treating you fairly. Maybe I can arrange a joint session so we can all talk together?"

Ella looks down at her hands and fiddles with her cuticles. "Okay," she says quietly.

"Okay. I will talk to her therapist, and we will set something up. Does that sound good?"

She shrugs again. *Ah, we're back to that.*

"Great. I'll see you next week for your usual session. Take care Ella." She picks up her school bag and walks out of the door as I deflate further into my chair.

I love my job, but sometimes, *just sometimes*, I have days that are difficult. But I remember that it's worth it because that little girl in my office a second ago needs me, and if I can help, then that's what I'll do.

As I stand, waiting for my tube, my feet are as wet as I expected they'd be and I'm officially grumpy, which seems to be a default mood for me lately. I hear the telling *whoosh* of the tube just before it arrives. As I step through the doors, I decide to stand near the exit, to avoid the rush hour madness.

I glance to my left, and I catch sight of a familiar face. Grayson. He is sitting, scowling at his phone. *Shit. He has a car. Why is he on the tube? I only saw him yesterday. Do I need to see him again right now? Why does the universe hate me?*

As though he heard me thinking about him, or more likely, felt me staring at him, his gaze lifts and connects with mine. The way his face lights up when he smiles in my direction is pure porn and should be illegal. He isn't allowed to be so stupidly handsome when I look and feel like a soggy wet dog.

His grin grows wider as he stands to make his way towards me, all swagger and big dick energy that's blazing my way. *Holy shit, I need to chill.*

"Fancy seeing you here," he says in his deep, raspy voice that makes me want to throw myself at him.

"Don't you have a car?" I say, hoping and praying that I don't sound as breathless as I feel.

The tube jolts us to a stop, and I stumble towards him, my palms connecting with his chest. His very hard, very muscly chest. *Oh great*, I'm actually throwing myself at him and it's doing nothing to stop the dampness of my underwear, that has nothing to do with the rainy London weather.

"Oh shit," I curse. "I'm sorry. I didn't mean to manhandle you there." I right myself and grip onto the pole I should've been holding onto in the first place.

When he leans towards me, my whole body stiffens. "You can manhandle me anytime." His hot breath brushes against the skin behind my ear and everything clenches in memory of the last time I felt him against my skin. My body desperately wants to arch towards him and give in to every carnal desire racing through my mind, but I somehow manage to stop myself.

I suddenly feel awkward as he moves away from me. His steely eyes assess me, probably waiting for my quip back like I usually do, but the truth is, I'm a little flustered and I don't trust myself not to fall onto his dick again with the way he's licking his lips.

"I have wet shoes," I blurt out with the least amount of finesse. *Shit, good one, Nora.*

His eyes crinkle at the sides, his hand moving up to cover his mouth, which is already threatening a smirk. "Wet shoes?"

I nod frantically like I'm trying to disconnect my head from my shoulders. "Wet shoes," I repeat, pointing down because apparently, I like to embarrass myself.

Grayson chuckles, showing me his devastating, cheeky grin that sends all the butterflies fluttering all around the world, or maybe that's just in my chest. "When we get to your house, I can dry them for you if you want?"

My lips curve into a small smile, not really taking in what he said.

Wait, did he say get back to my house?

My eyes widen. "My house?" I squeak.

"Oh yeah, Jess invited me for dinner tonight," he says casually. Meanwhile, I keep thinking about the last time he was at my house and the list he found. The embarrassment rivalling how I feel right now. *Jesus, I'm roasting.*

"That's great. Dinner. Yay!" My hands fly out to my sides and do a little jazz hand wiggle. I haven't done a move like that since my mum forced me into taking dance classes. I hated it. I was more elephant than ballerina. Those jazz hands are once again going to cause me trouble though because the tube jolts forwards, catapulting me directly into Grayson's chest for the second time tonight. *I'll ask again, why does the universe hate me?*

"Woah there, tiny dancer," he laughs, catching me by my waist and tugging me towards him. I'm immediately met with his scent mixed with fresh rain and coffee. I inhale, relishing the tight grip he has on my waist. I like it. A little too much. Our eyes briefly connect, and I swear, energy zaps around us.

No, Nora, this is bad, bad, bad. Do not let your lady-bits tingle for him. Why is my body suddenly so hot for him? Is it the proximity, the fact I've seen him more than I have in the last few months, or is it am I just incredibly weak around him? I need to chill out.

I push away from him, desperate to take back control of my wayward feelings and I wince as the wetness of my feet rub against the rigidness of my heels.

"Your feet bothering you?" he asks.

"Yeah. I usually wear trainers for commuting, but I was in a rush this morning."

"I could always hike you over my shoulder and carry you out of here. Your stop is next." He nods towards the board where it says, 'Victoria Park'.

I flush, my poker face well and truly exposed to him at the thought of him throwing me over his shoulder. An awkward laugh erupts from my mouth. "Oh no, please don't do that. I think I've done enough to embarrass myself tonight."

"My personal favourite was the jazz hands," he says with that low raspy voice that seems to be a form of foreplay for me tonight.

I slap his chest playfully, whipping those rock hard pecs again, giving myself just the right amount of touch that I crave from him. "Years of training went into those bad boys."

"I could tell." He grips my arm protectively as the tube judders to a stop. I look down at where he's touching me as a hot inferno ignites at my nipples and shoots down to my desperately needy sex. He chuckles. "Purely preventative, so you don't fling yourself at me again. Unless you want to do that, in which case I can let go."

"Probably best you hold on tight," I smile, wondering at what point I'm going to stop picturing him naked tonight.

Chapter 5

Nora

My alarm beeps incessantly on my bedside table. My hand flies out, desperate to stop the stupid guitar music that I thought would wake me up peacefully every morning. It does not. The thudding in my head tells me that I definitely do not want to be awake right now.

Once Grayson went home after dinner, I couldn't sleep. I was far too turned on from our train journey and then dinner with Jess and Liam, so I spent most of the night obsessing over every tiny detail of Jess' hen do to make sure it was extra special because I'm a perfectionist. But right now, I hate that about myself because, ouch my head. I need more sleep.

I groan into my pillows before I force myself to sit up against my headboard and rub my face, hoping to bring some life back into me. If I can't have sleep, then I need coffee. Slipping on my silk robe, tying my hair into a messy bun, my feet trudge downstairs to make the nectar of the God's.

The buzz of London waking up slowly filters in through the ajar window in the kitchen as I flick the kettle on and pull out my favourite giant mug.

I hear a faint knock on my front door. Stretching my body before walking out through the kitchen to the hallway to answer it, I suddenly realise that I'm wearing a barely-there silk robe over my barely-there pyjamas. I wonder for a second if I should be answering the door wearing this, but I'm too tired to care right now.

As I pull the heavy door open, I'm met with familiar swirling grey eyes and an all too familiar smell of bergamot. Grayson. He looks far too sexy for this 7am wake up call, dressed in his signature all-black suit and white trainers.

Questions buzz in my head about why he's here, but they die on my lips when I notice him openly staring at my bare legs. I try and cover myself up with my arms but realise that it's completely pointless, and he's seen me naked anyway, so I wrap my body as best I can and try to form words to talk to him. Although, remembering the fact he has seen me naked only serves to increase my body temperature to scorching, because right at this very moment my brain has decided to project in full 4K clarity the face he makes when he came down my throat.

He lifts his eyes to meet mine and thrusts a coffee cup at me, totally unaware of my raging hormones. "Relax, shorty, I just brought you a coffee. You were texting me to-do lists until 3am for a stag party you're only half organising. So, I figured you might need a decent coffee to help you this morning." He smirks, sipping his own coffee and gesturing to my outfit, or lack of. "You, uh, you always answer the door in your underwear?"

"This isn't my underwear. These are pyjamas," I reply croakily as he scans me over once more. My head shakes whilst I try to piece together this thoughtful side of Grayson I've not seen before. "Wait, you came all the way here to bring me coffee... just because?" I take the cup tentatively and sniff it just to make sure he hasn't slipped something into it.

He scoffs, "I'm not a bad guy, Nora. I have a meeting not far from here this morning, so I just..." He pauses and looks at my face, which I'm sure has a suspicious look on it, "you know what, forget it." He turns to walk away which is exactly when I realise, I don't want him to leave.

"Wait." I grab his arm, and of course this is the moment my robe flies open. "Shit," I shout as I drop his arm and cling to the edges of my robe, knowing full well that he saw pretty much everything. Heat spreads up my neck like the ivy growing outside my house, while Grayson stares at me with eyes full of heat. He swallows hard, his Adam's apple bobs up and down, and he gently bites his lip. *God, why is it so hot when he does that? Why is everything he does so hot – he's buying me coffee and I'm inner monologue swooning.*

"I'm more annoyed that you just gave me *and* your neighbours a show at the same time. Next time you strip, make it just for me, yeah?" He winks and smiles another one of his charming smiles that always make me weak, but my expression is quickly schooled. I can't fall into his quick wit and charm like I did in the past. That was just a minor blip in the road. One night of blips.

"Rude. I was going to invite you in for breakfast, but now I don't think I will." My stubbornness (and maybe weakness for him) side taking over, as I go to push the door closed but his foot springs out, stopping me.

"Well, now I want to know what's for breakfast." He nudges past me, his arm brushing against mine, sending an involuntary shiver down my spine. "Anyway, you need me. You need help with your list thing and I'm not taking no for an answer. I thought about it all night."

I follow him into the kitchen, hoping he'd forgotten my bucket list. When he didn't mention it at dinner last night, I was hopeful. I decide to play dumb and pray I can deter him. "You're helping me do what, exactly?"

"Tick stuff off your list."

My arms cross over my chest. "I thought you were joking," I lie, because I have thought about his offer to tick off number one on the list—have mind blowing sex—in the last fifteen hours since I saw him, but I still don't trust him, or myself for that matter. "Why?" I ask. "What is this really? Do you need sex? Is this a booty call? Aren't they usually at night?" I ask, not taking a single breath.

He shrugs. "Because I want to help you."

"Because you want to help me," I repeat, not fully believing his motives.

He nods with a great big cocky smirk that tells me he's messing with me. "And I'm not going to say no to sex if it's on the table, but that's not my motive here." That smirk of his will be the death of me, I swear.

"Sex is *not* on the table." I try to be snarky, but it just comes out breathless. Meanwhile my vagina is shouting *Liar, liar, pants on fire* in my shorts. I step towards him, wiggling my index finger accusatorily. "You know, you'd be more convincing if you didn't smirk like that. The jokes on me. I almost believed you were genuine for a second." I walk past him to start breakfast, ignoring the fact he smells far too good this morning.

Motto for today – Ignorance is bliss.

"I am being genuine." He stands directly behind me, so close I can feel the heat from his body scorching into mine.

"Right, of course." I reach up to get two bowls out of the cupboard. "I have a hard time believing you at the best of times but when it's me, or us, it's always just jokes and banter," *and sex and foreplay, so much sex...* "So, what am I supposed to think?"

He exhales loudly, his breath tickling my bare neck as I place the bowls on the counter and roll my shoulders back with a shiver.

Ignore it. Ignore it.

"Fine, don't believe me, but I'm helping you. C'mon, aren't you even a little curious?" he says darkly, and it makes my skin pebble at his question because yes, I am curious. Very.

"Not really," I say, stepping away from him while I make breakfast and hope he can't hear the lies in my words.

"Thank you." He takes a bite of the yoghurt and granola and groans. "Oh, this is good. Did you make it?"

I nod, crunching into my own bowl, loving the sweetness of the honey and oats on my tongue.

He chews his food, then swallows, never taking his eyes off me. "You don't have to believe me, or even like me that much, but I'm helping you. My mind is made up."

I choke at his insistent tone. "Oh right, so I have no say in this anymore, despite it being *my* list?"

He snorts, and it takes all my willpower not to drown his stupid handsome, smirking face in yoghurt. "It was *your* list before I saw it. It's *our* list now." I keep my scowl firmly in place as he exhales, his voice taking on a softer edge. "Look, don't overthink it. I know how to have fun, and you wanted more adventures, right? Well…" he taps his chest hard like a gorilla beating his chest. "I'm your man."

I bark a laugh. "You are not *my* man," I say loudly, trying to convince myself and him that this is the exact definition of a bad idea. But with him being here, bringing me coffee, and looking… like that, it's scrambling my usually smart brain.

I watch him as we sit in silence, both eating our breakfast. It's peculiar because even though I'll never admit it to him, I feel a connection, a pull that I can't name or pinpoint. I'm also not sure I'm ready to give into it yet either.

But he *does* know how to let loose. He might be a playboy, but he's also spontaneous and adventurous. He *could* help me. *Oh, my God, why am I even considering this?*

"Fine, I'll let you help me." My mouth opens with the words before I can fully talk myself out of it. My determination is pathetic around him.

When Grayson fist pumps the air I know I've made a mistake. "Oh God, what have I just done?" I mutter as my head drops into my hands.

"It's okay, shorty. I've got you. We're going to need to work on that list and make it more fun. Where is it?"

I shake my head, regret pouring into my poor decisions. "I've changed my mind."

"Nope, not happening. I'm in it to win it now. Where's the list?" He bounces around like a puppy – I don't think I've ever seen him so happy. It's adorable to see him this excited, which of course makes my tummy flutter, but now is not the time to assess that. I shake my head as he searches through some papers stacked next to him on the counter, throwing his hands up when he can't find what he's looking for. "You know what? Fuck it, we'll write a new one."

I slam my hand onto the paper he's about to start writing on. "Wait, I'll get it." Reaching into my handbag on the kitchen counter, I pull out my planner and the elusive list. I stretch my hand out to give it to him, then snap it back quickly. "I'm doing this for me, not you."

His broad smile shows off his perfectly straight teeth and full lips in a way that makes my body react in a way I wasn't expecting. I'm excited too. His enthusiasm and goofy smile actually have me feeling lighter than I have in months.

"Got it." He leans in quickly and plants a chaste kiss to my cheek and my whole world explodes, except I'm frozen in a moment that felt so *normal,* which is strange because we've never done normal together. I run my fingers over the same spot his lips were seconds ago, and my entire being shivers. He's blissfully unaware of my swooning, and thank God, because I'd probably never hear the end of it.

He opens the list, and taps his chin with his finger, but keeps his face neutral, which is arguably more unnerving and endearing at the same time. "These are great, but mind if I add a few?"

I throw my hands up in defeat when in reality I feel like I gave up control the minute he acted like a cute puppy. "Why not... I'm already making a deal with the devil. Why not just let him run the show, too?"

He laughs but doesn't look up, holding out his hand for the pen that I pass him. Then his eyes dart to mine. "All the things on the list... they're all new things, right? You've never done them before?"

I nod sheepishly.

"Except the mind blowing sex, which obviously you've already had with me. I'm willing to press replay any time, too."

Replay? Sure. How about now? Because all I can think about is having your fingers inside me, curling and pumping in and out of me while I

scream your name as your tongue... Oh shit, I'm daydreaming again.
Stop that right now, Nora.

When I look at him again, he's focussed, scribbling God knows what on my list, or *our list* apparently.

"There," he announces confidently, sliding the paper back to me.

Nora's New Year List

1. **Have better sex - must be** Music to my ears, shorty, but I know you've already
   mind blowing had mindblowing sex with me.

2. **Conquer one fear** You'll have to tell me your fear, but I'm really good at helping. Promise.

3. **Ride in a limo** Also have sex in said limo (I know a limo guy).

4. **Go to a concert or festival** I'm behind this 100% concerts, festivals are the most fun.

5. **Do karaoke** Only if you let me video it.

6. **Be kissed under the stars** too cliché.

7. **Get a tattoo** I also know a guy or girl actually.

8. **Say yes for a whole day** This is going to be my favourite.

9. **Fall in love for the first time** You're on your own for this one.

10. Remember that this list shouldn't end here. I don't know a single savage person who would leave a list on an odd number.

My eyes scan over his notes.

"I am not having sex in a limo, Grayson."

He waves his hand, dismissing me. "I said I know a guy, trust me." His eyebrow quirks, and I sigh. I have a feeling I'm going to get myself into trouble doing this list, but I can't bring myself to tell him I can't do these things with him.

"Why is it cliché to be kissed under the stars?"

"Because it is. If it's a memorable kiss you want, then where it happens shouldn't matter." He pauses as he moves closer to me, the grey in his eyes flickering brightly, as they run over every inch of my face and settle on my mouth. I lick my lips without a second thought, mirroring his intense stare. He drops his voice to a low whisper that sends shivers all over my skin. "I think you want the type of kiss that makes you hot and cold, that makes you see stars. The kind of kiss that re-writes your DNA because suddenly everything and nothing makes sense." He tucks a strand of my hair behind my ear as I swallow throatily. "That's what I think you mean."

My breathing is shallow as I stare at him, trying to piece together what just came out of his mouth. Because he's right, that's exactly what I meant when I wrote that. And the scary thing is that he is probably the only person that has ever got me close to that.

The blood in my body has decided to heat up a few thousand degrees and travel at warp speed, making my heart race. I clear my throat and wrap my arms around myself, praying that he doesn't see the effect he's had on my nipples.

His eyes stay locked on mine, burning his gaze through all my defences. "Say yes, Nora." His voice is low and gravely, making me want to burst into flames. *Why am I panting?*

"Yes," I say, without a second thought, although I'm not entirely sure if I'm saying yes to the kiss, to the list or yes to him. I'm so worked up; I'd let him do anything to me right now, and that is not a good idea.

He smiles, his eyes dropping to my lips again. But then he exhales and breaks the spell cast around us. "Fuck," he mutters as he turns away, running a hand through the dark, messy curls on top of his head.

From my peripheral, I watch him put his bowl in the sink behind me, but when he appears behind me my body freezes, and my knuckles whiten as I grip the counter.

"I've got to get to work now, but if you're free tonight, I can come by again." His thick fingers ghost down my arm, making my head loll to one side, igniting something deep within my belly. I want to see him again and soon, but I need to get my body under control before later. I nod, then it dawns on me.

"Oh, shit." I twist my head to look up at him.

"What?"

"I have a date tonight. I forgot that Zoey set it up. I can't cancel."

He stiffens, but then instantly releases the tension from his shoulders. "No big deal. I'll call you."

As he walks off, I realise I'm barely breathing, so I force myself to fill my lungs. My body is tingling, but I can't figure out if it's because I'm relieved he's gone or sad.

Chapter 6

Nora

I'm trying very hard to act interested as Brandon, my blind date, sits opposite me talking about his work. He's attractive with his sandy blonde hair and big green eyes and he's successful, but I'm bored. I find myself nodding when I think he wants me to and I hum when he says something that should be interesting, but it isn't. Usually, I'd try harder to actually listen, but if he talks about spreadsheets and data or anything else equally dull one more time, I swear I'll be falling asleep on the table.

It's a shame because the date started out so well. He was on time, and he looks cute in his striped shirt. It's giving a little grandad vibe, but I'll give him the benefit of the doubt. He looks like he's in great shape, which means he takes care of himself. Another tick. He has this soft, caring presence that should be so appealing, but tonight, it's falling flat, and I can't figure out why. Something must be seriously wrong with me if I don't find this guy attractive.

The restaurant is beautiful and the food... God, the food has probably been a highlight, especially when I tasted the lobster linguine, which is when I realised that I'm really not enjoying the company as much as I should be.

"...so yeah, the input I had for this year alone was staggering. We managed to combine two departments, which means more revenue..." He continues as I nod with wide eyes and a polite smile. He's mostly having a conversation with himself at this point, and I just feel guilty for not being interested.

My mind drifts to other things like what I'll wear to work tomorrow, the report I need to file for the new clients from Jess' charity who are now having regular sessions. The organisation of my desk, my office, my wardrobe. Anything except what this man is saying in front of me. His lips are still moving, but it's all Greek to me.

"...don't you think?" He ends his sentence, making my stomach drop suddenly because I honestly have no idea what he is asking me. My face flushes a shade of red that makes Louboutin's look pink. "Uhh, you know I'll be right back." I excuse myself to the ladies' room, hoping he won't want an answer when I get back.

Finishing up in the toilet, I check my reflection and top up my red lipstick. Well, it's Jess' but since she steals most of my things, I decided to do the same tonight because that's what sisters do. I should give the guy a chance. I should be getting to know him. My dating life has been non-existent for well over a year, and yet I don't feel anything for him. I promised myself adventure and excitement and sadly he isn't it.

Maybe it's because you keep thinking about a certain playboy.

No I'm not going there. It's platonic, two friends, helping one another. I can't let myself think about him naked again, or his toned abs, the contrast of his tattoos on his olive skin, how he made me feel so safe when he caged me into his strong arms. Brandon should be exactly what I want. He has a great job (not that I can remember anything about it) probably has a house somewhere in Richmond waiting for his future wife to fill it with kids. That white picket fence life that I so thought I wanted; he could be the guy. Except he really isn't. My body deflates as I face myself in the mirror and decide that the date is over.

After paying the bill secretly, I walk back to our table and sit back down, finding Brandon on his phone. When he looks up again, he grabs my hand and kisses the back of it. "You're beautiful, Nora," he coos.

"Thank you," I say politely, like I'm thanking someone for letting me go ahead of them in supermarket line. I subtly move my hand and tuck it under my thigh out of his reach. "I've had a lovely time, but I should probably get going."

I see the moment his shoulders deflate in disappointment. I feel bad for a second and then the feeling is gone, and relief floods my mind. He gestures to the waiter for the bill, but I interrupt, "Oh, I've already settled the bill. Please, it was my treat."

His mouth gapes open when he realises what I've done. "You didn't have to do that."

I'm guessing he's not used to many women paying for dinner. "Oh no, honestly, it was my treat." It definitely wasn't a tactical move on my part so I can leave, especially as my phone pings telling me my Uber is here.

I stand to leave, and he follows my lead, offering me my jacket like a gentleman and I slip my arms in. I chastise myself one more time, wishing that this date worked out. The guy is attractive; he has the kindest eyes, and that therein lies the problem. He is safe, not exciting, and right now, I need a little more excitement in my life.

As we walk into the cool night, London traffic rumbles past us. Wanting to be polite, I turn to embrace my date as he awkwardly tries to kiss me, ending up planting his lips on my eyebrow. It's probably not the worst thing that's happened to me on a date, but that's another story entirely.

"Thank you for a lovely evening, Brandon. Take care." *Take care, the most British way to say, Please, kindly fuck off now.*

I barely register him talking behind me as I open the door to my Uber and duck inside, the safety of my getaway car soothing my fraying nerves.

I pull up my phone and text Jess telling her I'm on my way home, considering it's only 10pm, she'll know exactly how my date went.

When I get home, I haven't heard from Jess, and the house is quiet. Wondering if she's at work still, I slip off my coat and toe off my heels, relishing the feeling of the cool wood on my bare feet. A loud rumble of laughter has my ears perking up. It sounds like it's coming from the kitchen. I'm not entirely used to having another person living with us yet, even if it is Liam, who we've known forever (minus a ten year hiatus). I'm not sure how I'm supposed to resist Grayson when Liam is his best friend and boss, and now he's helping me with the list. He's going to be everywhere, and I need to figure out how I feel about that, without input from my sex drive.

My tired feet pad slowly towards the door and when I open it, I see Liam and Grayson sitting at the table, drinking beer.

"Oh, hey Nor. I thought you were out tonight?" Liam asks.

Grayson tips his beer back in that stupidly attractive way that men do, as his eyes crawl over my body. I'm used to him checking me out; the man thinks with his dick, but I'm not used to the way my body suddenly decides to respond to the attention. Ignoring the hammering of my heart and the sudden need between my thighs, I shuffle over to the kettle and flick it on. "I was on a date."

"With Brandon?" Grayson asks, his voice low and deep. The way he says his name has a hint of something lacing it.

I nod, not turning around. "How do you know his name?" I ask trying to remember how much I told him this morning.

"Jess told us earlier on the phone," Liam says, interrupting us.

Warmth suddenly floods from behind me, and I smell the familiar smell of one Grayson King. "The date went badly?" he whispers. I turn to face him. His dark hair needs a trim. It's getting a little long, although running my fingers through it wouldn't be... no, I mean it would be a bad thing. *Christ, Nora.*

"The date was boring. He wasn't... anything. It was a bust." The bubbling kettle behind me takes my attention away from a smirking Grayson in front of me, and I'm grateful for the distraction. "Do either of you want tea?"

"Nah, we're good. Actually, I promised Jess I'd pick her up from work after the wedding she's working tonight. I'd better get a move on. See you later, Nor. Grayson, see you at work."

Liam leaves, and the silence that fills the room is deafening. The tinkling of me making my tea is the only sound echoing around the room. In truth, I'm grateful for the moment of quiet. The thought of yet another failed date under my belt grates on my nerves. I inhale and exhale deeply just as I see Grayson put his beer on the side next to me.

"You wanna talk about it?"

My head jerks to where he's now leaning against the kitchen worktop, his tattooed arms crossed over his body. I see swirls of black ink underneath the sleeve of his t-shirt, which I know is an extension of the lion tattoo on his chest. His King of Hearts tattoo peeking from the underside of his forearm is probably my favourite. It has a crown sitting off the edge of the card and an ace slotted behind it. The worn looking card intertwines with the other images. He flexes his forearm as if he can sense me staring, rippling the tattoo and snapping me out of my trance.

"Not really," I reply flatly. "There's nothing to tell."

"Is that why you're grumpy?"

I side eye him, huffing under my breath, "I'm not grumpy."

Grayson unfolds his arms and shuffles an inch closer to me. "You are. Why?"

I turn to face him, not realising how close we would be; our toes are almost touching. I take a step backwards just so I can breathe a little better, but I'm hit with the edge of the worktop at my back.

"I'm done with dating. I'm fed up with it being dull and boring. It's become a chore that I don't want any part of. I seem to only attract boring men and maybe it's because I'm a little inexperienced or maybe it's just how it is. I'm bound to end up an old spinster at this rate. Someone buy me a fucking hundred cats and I'll be fine." My chest heaves with my outburst. My pulse flickers wildly in my neck. I blink, the room coming back into clear focus after my mini meltdown. "Sorry, that was a bit much, wasn't it?" I awkwardly feel my face heat from Grayson's unreadable stare.

He takes two measured breaths before placing his arms on the counter either side of me, trapping me. My traitorous body reacts immediately to his familiar masculine scent. My eyes flicker to his lips. They're plump for a guy, and the memory of how well he knows how to use them flares in my mind, making my nipples harden. "I'm adding to your list," he whispers.

My head shakes lightly, not enough to protest, and I immediately feel dizzy from the onslaught of this man on my senses. "Wh-what?"

"I'm taking you on a date. Tomorrow. I'm going to show you what a good time looks like."

I feel myself pale and then my unwavering desire to sass him takes over in an instant. "I don't need you to pity date me. I don't want you to help me like that." I place my hand on his chest to shove him back, but it's met with too much resistance, and I can't actually push at all.

"Don't be stubborn, Nora. I'm trying to help," he says, letting his gaze drop to my lips.

I huff, lowering my hands from his wall of muscle. "Well, you're not. You're offering me a date because you think it'll make me feel better, but it won't. In fact, your charity date makes me feel a thousand times worse. The only people I want to go out with are those who are actually interested in me and find me attractive. Not playboys whose only agenda is to inflate their own ego."

"Don't mince your words there, Nor. Jesus." He turns away from me, letting me finally inhale fully, but in a split second he's back in the same position, making my breath hitch. "I don't do *charity* dates. I was genuinely trying to help," he snaps, as his eyes roam over my face. "And I do find you attractive. I think you know that. In fact, I think you're the fucking bomb, but what do I know?"

"I..."

"Don't bother apologising. We both know you meant what you said. I understand why you feel grumpy and are acting out, given the bad date tonight, but lucky for you, I don't give a shit. What I do *want* to know is if you're going to get over yourself and go out with me, despite what you think you know about me."

My mouth opens and closes in quick succession. Words aren't coming, so I snap it shut before I say something I regret. The nearness of him is making me light-headed, messing with my brain. His full lips are far too tempting and the warmth radiating off his hot, sculpted body is sending me a little feverish. A part of me wants to throw myself at him for calling me out and still being there for me, despite my mardy attitude. But I'm confused because my anger is mixing with something much more dangerous, and I can barely control it.

"Good talk. I'll pick you up tomorrow at eight, shorty."

And then he's gone.

Chapter 7

Grayson

Waiting outside her house, my leg jitters up and down, as my fingers tap the leather steering wheel. I hate waiting, but this is more than that. I have this weird pit in my stomach reminding me this is probably a terrible idea. I don't date because I've never had a relationship or met anyone I wanted to date. I refuse to fall into the trap that my parents endured and made me endure along with them. My dad's voice echoes in my head constantly. '*Don't get married, son. Women will break your heart.*' But despite all my apprehension, Nora looked so fucking sad last night that I had to do something. I couldn't let her think that men are all boring shitheads who don't know how to treat a woman.

Her front door opens, and she steps outside wearing a dress that makes my pulse pick up. It's red, knee-length, and clings to every curve on her body. As she turns to lock the door, she gives me a full view of her perfect arse, which makes me want to bite my hand to stop the overwhelming need to bend her over and bite her. There's no doubt about it; she looks stunning. As she walks to my car, my gaze trails up to her face and I notice a light dusting of make up, which is exactly *her*. Her dark hair falls poker straight around her perfectly delicate face and neck, and I'm definitely ogling.

Fuck me. This was a bad idea.

I climb out to open her door, and she stops and looks at me, surprised. "Opening doors for women, Grayson? Careful, you'll lose that playboy title you covet."

I'm still unable to form a full sentence as she gracefully climbs into my car. I hadn't thought this through. Now I'm going to have to sit next to her and opposite her all night while she looks like a fucking snack; no, a whole damn meal. And right now, I'm also remembering everything about my night with her. Her taste, her moans, the feel of her body in my hands, the way her walls tightened around my dick as she came dragging me toward my own release. My dick swells and I take a few deep breaths as I round the car again, trying to ignore the feelings that this woman stirs up in me.

Walking into the restaurant, I bypass the front desk and head to the private area where another desk sits dimly in the corner. I'm not sure I'll get used to having money and connections. Liam has plenty and uses them with ease, but I still feel like a bit of an imposter sometimes. Most people wouldn't realise I feel like that, but then again, not a lot of people know me that well. They only know Grayson King, the playboy.

"How can I help you?"

"Grayson King, reservation for two."

"Ahh yes, Mr King. Your table is waiting for you upstairs. The rooftop restaurant is best accessed via the lift over here." The waiter points to a small set of aluminium doors just to the left of us.

I nod, placing my hand on the small of Nora's back, guiding her forwards. Her breathing stutters as we wait for the lift. I'm not sure if she's just nervous about this whole evening or it's something else. We step inside the lift, and she clamps her hands together and closes her eyes, breathing through her nose and out through her mouth.

"Are you okay?" I ask. Her eyes snap to mine, wild and dilated as we travel up to floor 40.

"Fine," she breathes heavily. I want to ask more, but she doesn't look at me, she just breathes deeply. I don't push the subject again, and we ride the lift with the only noise being her deep breathing. When the doors finally open, she walks, no runs, out. I'm guessing she wasn't that comfortable, but was it the lift or me?

Taking a second, I look around the exclusive setting. Dimly lit and simply decorated with clean lines and Nordic style furnishings, the place is stunning and modern. The waiter immediately appears and guides us to our table. Nora sits opposite me, thanking the waiter as he hands her a menu.

"Have you been here before?" she asks, obviously wondering how I managed to get us a reservation here.

I nod. "I know the owner."

"Is this where you bring your dates?"

I shake my head. "I don't date."

Nora mindlessly picks up the drinks menu whilst keeping her eyes trained on me. "But you're here with me... on a date."

"I am."

A beat of tension passes between us.

Her deep caramel focus solely on me, as if she's seeing my vulnerability for the first time. For a heartbeat I wonder if... and then I stop myself because those thoughts about Nora can never end well. Deciding not to overthink things, I silently vow to myself that I'll show her the good time that I promised her and hopefully make her smile.

Nora

Being here right now isn't awful. Except for the lift, which was borderline terrifying, but thankfully it was a short ride and I used some of the techniques I teach my clients and I'm still alive to tell the story. I'm going to partially and tentatively tick that one off my list. I'm on my way to conquering one fear.

The restaurant feels... exclusive and luxurious. Wholly unnecessary for a little date with me. "Grayson, this place is fancy," I whisper as I lean towards him.

"You don't have to whisper. But yeah, it's nice here. Liam recommended it. He's apparently brought Jess here a couple of times."

"Why would you pick this place just for me?" I ask quietly.

He cocks an eyebrow at my question. "What do you mean, just for you?"

I look around the table we're sitting at, searching for something to distract my nerves. "I mean..." Suddenly, emotion clogs my throat, preventing me from saying that I'm confused as to why I feel special when I'm not special to *him*.

"Nora?" He says my name with an intensity that makes my legs clench together. His hand finds mine across the white linen tablecloth, the roughness of his fingertips on my skin makes me tremble. "I brought you here because I wanted to show you that dates can be fun, so you realise that you are special enough to deserve more than you've had before."

I can't stop staring at him as I process his words. I can see why women fall at his feet. It goes beyond looks, of course, his tattoos give him sex appeal, his hair is perfectly messy, his eyes fire up a storm and manage to be all kinds of warm and icy at the same time, pinning you in place, like he's the big bad wolf and you're little red all alone in the woods. But what has really blindsided me is seeing this softer, more caring side that he obviously doesn't show everyone.

His tattooed hand reaches out and the very tips of his fingers brush across my forehead, taming some flyaway hair, and my eyes flutter from the contact. Heat swirls around us like potent, untamed energy as my heart attempts to escape my chest. I can't help but wonder if he's doing this because he's showing me how I could be treated or because he wanted to touch me and couldn't help himself.

"Are you both ready to order?" the waiter asks, dissipating the energy between us.

Grayson looks at me, silently asking me if I'm ready, and I nod. "I'll have the scallops to start and the Blue Grey beef for my main."

"I was going to order the same." He looks at me for a beat too long, as though he's trying to figure something out, but I have no idea what. When he turns his head to look at the waiter, I hate the way I miss his eyes on me. "And whatever wine you recommend for the beef."

The waiter nods and leaves. And I have to remind myself that this date is to make me feel better about dating, not feel *more* for Grayson.

An awkward silence now fills the space between us. The small candles on the table barely flickering–probably because there's no air of any kind in the room right now. I shift on the leather seat beneath me and glance up at him, sitting so casually; calm and collected, while I feel like I have a wild storm whipping around inside me.

I break the silence. "So how does Grayson King *do dates?* Tell me how you're going to show me all your dating swagger. Besides the fancy black BMW and the fitted black suit you're wearing..."

He pauses in thought before smiling. "I don't date many women in reality."

"Are you telling me I'm special again, Grayson?" I mock a surprised look, but there's a secret part of me that wishes that I was someone special.

A flicker of a blush traces across the tip of his nose before it vanishes. He reaches for my hand, letting his fingertips draw patterns over my skin and my body reacts dutifully with goosebumps. "Do you want to be someone special, Nora?"

Just as I find myself leaning towards him like a gravitational pull whilst simultaneously sinking into the depths of his eyes, I snap out of the trance he's put me in. "That's good. A plus for that move, you almost had me." I shake the shiver off before it gives me more goosebumps.

He sits up straighter, a wicked grin in place. "Yeah? You like that one?"

I ignore the confusion building inside me. "What else? Show me your moves."

"Well, there's one move I don't think you'll like..."

"Okay…"

His thumb travels across my jaw, burning a fire in its wake until it rests on my chin, popping open my mouth. His eyes are entirely focused on my lips, which makes me feel like I'm the only person in the room. He's giving me his full attention, and it's intoxicating.

My mind wonders to *that* night. I'd had a heavy day at work. He came over to pick something up that Liam left for him when I was two glasses of wine in. We talked for a while, he was being his usual flirty self. Then suddenly we were kissing and undressing… *God, is it hot in here?*

"You thinking about kissing me?" he rasps.

Once again, I have to snap myself out of the spell I've fallen under. "Actually, I'm thinking about what my work day looks like tomorrow," I lie.

A roguish smile creeps across his lips, as his thumb brushes over my bottom lip making me gasp. "Sure you were. I think you want to kiss me…"

You have no idea.

When he sits back in his seat, I curse my body for missing the heat of him. I watch as his thighs fall open as he rests one arm over his chair *Fuck. Me. He looks hot.* I want to jump his bones and teach him a lesson right now, but that would definitely be crossing a line. One I'm not willing to cross with him… again.

"I'm just going to powder my nose," I say, standing from my chair, while I chastise myself as my desire thuds between my legs.

As I walk back into the rooftop restaurant, Grayson is staring at me, and I swat him when I reach the table. "You aren't even trying to be subtle about checking me out. It's gross. Please stop."

It's not gross. It's the biggest ego boost, but I'll not tell him that.

He shrugs as I sit down. "I know you wore that dress to torture me, so I'm allowed to stare."

"Maybe I did wear it to torture you. This dress does look great on me."

"Trust me, Nora, it's not the dress that makes you look great."

I blush hard. Embarrassingly so. "Compliments coming from you? I'm flattered."

He licks his lips. Like he's remembering what I taste like.

Gulp.

"Seriously, stop looking at me like that." I wave my hand to break his heated gaze.

He doesn't stop staring and I don't stop blushing. Instead, he leans forward, so he's a few inches away from my face and whispers. "I like teasing you because I like seeing how much you want me." His warm breath ghosts over my cheek, sending my mind into a spiral of memories. Hot kisses being peppered all over my body, my hands pulling him closer, his own gripping my skin...

He chuckles disrupting my daydream. I hate that he thinks he can best me because I blush when he says things like that. Well, he's wrong if he thinks he's the only one who can show exactly what it's like to date, then he's also wrong. I have some moves of my own.

Before I can stop myself, I'm leaning towards him, over the small round table and placing my hand on his leg. Running my palm firmly but slowly up his inner thigh, as far as I can reach, loving the way he's vibrating from my touch. "You're cute. Also, not the only one who can tease."

Chapter 8

Grayson

I t took all my restraint not to grab her hand and show her how hard I am right now. I had to force myself to stop thinking about pinning her down and fucking the sass right out of her on this table. So, I thought about puppies, kittens, unicorns, fucking anything that is not Nora and how she would taste if I moved forward and collided with her lips.

Everything about her is irresistible. She likes messing with me. I can see it in her eyes. She makes me hot with her comebacks and those curves that should be illegal. She's the best combination of curvy and petite. I could easily throw her over my shoulder, like I offered to on the tube last week, carry her home and spank her until she has my handprint on her arse, and die a happy man.

But she also intrigues me. She shows me a vulnerability occasionally and then this brave, spicy side makes me think there's more to her. Add that to her list and her need for adventure. She's much more than just a fuck, and I'm stupid for thinking one night would be enough. There are so many sides to her, some I haven't even explored yet, but I want to bring them out, help her explore herself. I think Nora Scott is looking for something to excite her. And boy, do I wanna be that something.

Her scent invades my space. It's warm and subtle, but sweet too. It reminds me of the moment you bite into a hot brownie. My mouth waters at the memory of her being this close to me, and it seems I can't convince my dick that she and I won't happen again.

Our waiter arrives with the wine, taking what feels like years to open it and let me taste it. When I nod, he fills both glasses and leaves. Clearing my throat, I sip my drink before I look at her. I think about her list and how I can get her to let loose and then it comes to me, a plan, an idea, one that just might work.

"So, I was thinking, on your list you have a 'say yes the whole day'," I pause, sipping more of my drink. "Will you actually stay true to that?"

She nods her head, then knocks back a gulp of her drink too. "Yes."

"Good girl. You're all mine on Saturday then."

Her body stiffens at my suggestion. Before I can work out if her reaction is a good or bad thing, our starters arrive, and we eat for a while in silence. After I swallow down a delicious scallop, I ask Nora about work. I like watching her face light up when she talks. It's evident how much she loves her job and how dedicated she is. Other women I've spent time with, usually in bars and never on dates, are not as willing to talk to me, they want me for what I can do to them in the bedroom (or wherever really), and conversation quickly dries up. But not with Nora. It's refreshing to talk to someone who understands the pressures of achievements and wanting to meet the goals you set yourself. I've always been goal orientated and I like the fact Nora seems to be as well.

When we finish our starters and the plates are cleared, leaving the table empty for a second. I pour her another glass of wine and then refill my own. "Thank you," She smiles and we cheers.

"So, tell me something no one else knows about you," I ask, wanting to know more about her.

"Okay... when I was at university, I tried my hand at musical theatre. I had to make sure that therapy was it for me by testing out other things. I used to take plenty of risks back then." She looks thoughtful for a second, a ghost of a sad smile tipping the corners of her mouth. "Turns out, I was definitely meant to be a therapist and listen, rather than sing, dance, or act. I truly sucked at them all." She laughs quietly, a full smile now gracing her face, making my stomach flip; a feeling I've never felt before. I don't linger too long on that realisation, unsure how to process it.

"Didn't you have karaoke on your list?" I ask curiously.

Her nose scrunches. "I do. Mostly because it feels like something everyone has to do at least once and aside from singing for my teacher in university, I've never sung in front of anyone."

I nod, understanding. "I like the list. It's a good idea," I say honestly. I move my feet under the table, tapping against hers for a moment, the contact making my body hum. What I'd do to be closer to her. Suddenly this table feels huge, and I don't like it.

"Thank you." She smiles and then pauses, hesitation crossing her face. "I think seeing Jess get her happily ever after with Liam made me realise that I am nowhere near that point in my life. And truly, that's okay. I don't want to rush, if anything, I don't know what I want for my future, but I felt like my life needed to change. I mean, it already was changing with Liam being back again, so I thought, well, I may as well make some changes that are meaningful to me." She sips the remainder of her wine. "That's not to say that my karaoke session is going to change my life, but... it lets me feel alive and I want that."

The way she waves her hands around her face when she talks, as though she'll make more of her point by gesturing all over the place, is endearing.

"Sorry, that was a bit of a ramble, wasn't it?" She flushes.

"No, I like you being honest with me. It wasn't a ramble; it was the truth." I hadn't realised how much of myself I'd not been putting out into the world too. Until right now.

Truth... my mind gets stuck on that word for a second as a memory takes over.

"You don't get to decide how much of the truth I get to hear, Mark!" my mum shouts, but only when she's really angry with my dad, like now. His face is red, and that purple vein is pulsing, the only he only gets when he and mum argue funnily enough.

"Viv, I'm not having this conversation again. Nothing happened. I was working late." He huffs, throwing his suit jacket across the room.

"I'm taking Grayson and moving us to my sister's–is that what you want? For the two of us to move to get away from your lies? All you need to do is tell me the truth."

I don't want to move. I like my friends here at school.

"Try it, Viv. Take the kid with you and see how fast I'll have him back here with me. Don't be stupid about this. He'll never want to stay with you anyway."

I don't really want to stay and listen to either of my parents, but my mum is holding my shoulders, standing behind me by the dinner table.

The dinner we made is cold because Dad was late, and Mum made us wait and now this...

"Hey, you okay?" Nora's hand on my arm breaks me from the haze of the memory. I blink a few times to get my full vision back, instead of the blurry daydream state I was in. I'm not going to divulge the childhood drama that lives in my head. If anything, that memory gave me a cold dose of reality and reminded me why I don't do relationships.

Our main meal arrives, and I place my hand over hers. "I'm fine, hungry. This looks amazing." I say as the smell of the beef fills my nose.

I'm not sure Nora buys me changing the subject, but we eat in silence for a second. That is until she moans around a mouthful of her beef, eyes rolling back into her head "Oh my god, this is incredible," she purrs, chewing and licking and swallowing whilst my mind goes straight to the gutter.

"You can't make those noises, shorty." I whisper across the table. "Like you said, this is a fancy place."

She smiles coyly, taking another bite of her beef and moaning again, but only loud enough for me to hear. The gravelly sound goes directly to my cock, that's swelling in my trousers. "Fuuuuuuck," I hiss, palming myself under the table. Her eyes spark to life, swirling caramel and chocolate.

She pulls her bottom lip between her teeth, following my hand moving under the table and I almost snap, wanting to haul her over to me so I can sink my fingers inside her hot, wet pussy and tell her to be quiet as she comes apart right here in the restaurant. But like I said, it's a fancy place and I'm not sure I'd be able to stop at that.

"Are you... hard?" she asks on a breathy moan.

I raise an eyebrow at her and cut into my beef to distract my hands that are desperate to touch either myself or her. "What do you think?"

She traces the direction of the blush on her neck with her finger and fucking hell, she's got the upper hand again. "I think I've made you hard." Her finger stops at the top of her dress, tracing the outline of the lower neckline and drawing my attention to her nipples trying to push through the material.

Fuck, what I'd do to touch her, bite her and have her again.

"I'd wager that you're soaked right now too."

She smiles and I notice her cross her legs, making me smirk. "Wouldn't you like to know?"

Fuck yes I would, but I already know that she's turned on too. We're playing with fire and flirting like this only makes me want her so much more.

We both finish our meals, our legs brushing against one another's every now and again, sending zaps of electricity up and down my thighs.

Neither of us want dessert and we've finished the wine, so I stand and offer her my hand. "Come, let's go." To my surprise, she takes it and lets me lead her to the lift again.

As the lift doors open silently, I see Nora twitch beside me. "You okay? You were shifty on the way up, too."

Her pupils are blown when she looks at me, and she's chewing her bottom lip. A total contrast with how she was minutes ago with me at the table. "Not a huge fan of small spaces, especially the type that move really bloody fast. I felt okay on the way up but now..." She fiddles with the strap of her bag as she mutters something else to herself.

She fidgets around the small space, practically vibrating, losing all her usual calm demeanour. When the lift doors close, it shudders and jolts, making Nora practically jump into my arms. "Ask me something, anything, please?" she shouts, fear lacing her voice. "I need a distraction because I'm already heating up and freaking out."

"Okay..." *Tell me all the way this can go wrong because I can name at least a hundred.* "What's your favourite colour?"

"Probably white because my favourite flower is a white sweet pea."

"Mine's black. What age did you lose your virginity?"

Her head snaps my way even in the low light of the lift I feel her scowl. "Really?"

"Really. I'm your distraction, so fess up, shorty."

"I don't know why I thought this was a good idea. God, I'm so fucking hot." She mumbles to herself, fanning her face with her hand.

"Oh, but it is. Now come on, tell me."

"Fine. I was nineteen. It wasn't good. He was a one-night stand, which was stupid on my part." She takes a deep breath but doesn't continue.

"I was seventeen."

"That's it? No, I loved her, and she broke my heart," she mocks. Truth is, I've never been with anyone that I cared about, maybe not until her anyway.

When I don't respond, I notice her breathing staccato as she grips her hand on my arm. "Grayson, I need to get out of here, seriously... I... can't... breathe."

I have zero clue about how to calm a woman down, especially one like Nora. She should be a pro at calming herself down. Don't therapists have a plethora of techniques in their back pocket?

She grips me harder.

Should I pat her back? Talk more? Talk less? I have no fucking idea and she's freaking out. So, I use my instincts. I grab her body and push her against the cool metal wall of the lift, burying my fingers in her hair as I smash our lips together.

Well damn, even I'm not sure I saw that coming.

Her lips are pillow soft and full; exactly as I remember them. Her chest rises and falls rapidly, but I know her brain hasn't processed what I've done yet because she hasn't moved her mouth. It's then I start to panic. *What have I done?* Kissed the one person who said she doesn't want to kiss me again. In my defence, she needed my help, and she smelled like fucking cupcakes and brownies, and I happen to love both of those things, so... can you blame me?

I decide to move our connected lips by edging my tongue along the seam of her lower lip, moving my mouth deeper to hers. She opens tentatively at first, allowing me one swipe of our tongues. I growl, needing more. Her hands fist against my shirt as I move mine to her arse and squeeze us together, knowing she can feel how hard I am. We taste each other for the first time in months. Memories swirl around my head, reminding me of that night – but tonight, she tastes sweet like the wine, and I need more. Our teeth clash in a frenzy of desire and lust as our tongues fight for dominance. It feels like we've been suspended in this lift for hours, but in reality, it's been seconds.

The sound of the lift doors opening ping breaks whatever spell was just cast on us. Nora shoves me backwards, her eyes blazing, and all but runs through the doors, leaving a cold draft in her absence.

Me? I'm left with a raging hard on, gawking after the woman who drives me fucking crazy, in the best way.

I cough and adjust my shirt she was just fisting, attempting to hide my erection as I walk outside. I find Nora as I hand the valet the ticket for my car before walking towards her, her arms are protectively wrapped around her body. The chill emanating from her right now tells me she's not overly happy with my choice of lift-calming techniques.

"Car is on the way."

"I've called an Uber. Go home, Grayson."

Really? Fuck.

I want to tell her that she's being petty. It was just a kiss. I was just trying to calm her down. I want to explain that I was only trying to help. But instead, I sneer, "fine, suit yourself," and instantly regret it as soon as the words leave my mouth.

And then I walk off. Boner and all.

Chapter 9

Nora

He mutters something my way as he stomps off. As though he didn't just kiss me in the lift and now, he's annoyed at me for what just happened, when he was the one who did the kissing.... mostly.

Grayson kissed me. Again.

And I liked it far too much. Yet again.

Memories of our last kisses flood my brain. I remember pretty much everything about that night because apparently, I like to torture myself, whenever I let myself think about it. How he— *No, Nora, don't do it.*

Pretty sure I stumbled into some sort of alternate universe because months ago, before we slept together, I never would've entertained him at all. So why did I kiss him back? I don't understand how I've gone from strangers to one night stand, to this weird non-friend thing to now... what? My head is spinning, a complete merry-go-round.

In my defence, I was on the brink of a panic attack. My world was foggy and confusing. Anyone could've kissed me, and I wouldn't have questioned it because hello? Panic attack?! He asked me if I was okay before we got in the lift and the truth was, I wanted to prove something to myself. It's an irrational fear that I have from when I was eight and I got stuck in a lift with my mum on a shopping trip. We were stuck for hours, I had two panic attacks. and I've not been able to kick that fear since, despite knowing all the techniques I tell my clients.

The kiss was the first thing to ever calm me down, which is something I absolutely refuse to admit to Grayson.

Last week, Grayson said that he thinks I want a kiss that would rewrite my DNA, and as much as I hate to admit it, that was some fucking kiss.

Stupid boys and their stupid lips confusing my brain.

My body sags at my internal battle and I'm so exhausted after the whole lift situation that I just want to sleep. Dragging my hand over my face, I realise that my heart is still in some perpetual state of shock because there's a metaphorical lump that I can't seem to shift from my chest.

My Uber arrives and I get in, not even trying to attempt small talk with the driver because my brain is awash with confusion, and he happily ignores me.

When I arrive back home, the house is empty, and I thank my lucky stars that I don't have to hide anything from Jess and Liam. It's near enough impossible to hide things from them both. They know me too well. I managed to sneak out tonight because they were out, but I won't be so lucky if I had to try to explain why I look so flustered and confused right now. Jess would have a field day if she found out anything had happened with Grayson, and she would demand to know if we're getting together. But that is not happening. Kissing Grayson again was a mistake. A very good... no, bad mistake.

I empty my handbag on the kitchen worktop and my phone lights up with a text.

Grayson: I'm sorry.

Two words that should mean that I start to feel better about what happened, but for some reason, I don't. I don't know if it's because I don't want his apology or that it feels like he's just saying it to placate me. I type a reply and delete it and then do it again and again until I settle on:

Nora: Are you sorry that you kissed me?

The typing bubbles pop up immediately.

Grayson: Would you be mad if I wasn't?

I feel my face blanche. Would I be mad if he wasn't sorry for kissing me? I don't know, no? Yes? Maybe?

Nora: That feels like a loaded question. One that my brain can't handle right now. Let's just forget it happened.

There. I don't want him; he doesn't want me. It was just the 'moves' from our fake date. It was just him doing whatever he does to be the playboy he is.

Grayson: I kissed you because you were freaking out, and I don't know how to handle women who freak out. I maybe panicked a little too, so I guess I'm sorry for jumping you. Can we still be friends?

Surely, he didn't just apologise to me again. I'm in the twilight zone; kisses and apologies from Grayson in one night are too much for anyone. I think about the way he asks if we can still be friends and something tugs at my heartstrings, making me realise that I don't want to push him away.

Nora: We can still be friends who don't kiss. I'm grateful for your help, but all this apologising is freaking me out. Did someone steal your phone, because I don't believe it's you.

Grayson: *sends picture* Definitely me, last I checked.

Oh. My. God. He sent a picture... a topless picture...

Okay, I'm hot, he's hot, wait what? Brain focus for a second, please.

He's topless, standing in front of his bathroom mirror, obviously fresh from the shower. Sculpted abs glistening with droplets of water. Hair wet and messy. Face looking totally kissable.

Sir, I would like to climb you like a tree... again. No, that's bad, Nora.

I take a minute to properly appreciate the tattoos decorating his chest; the lion on his chest, the script writing underneath his ribs that curls down towards the defined V on his hips. My head tilts to the side, as my bottom lip unconsciously sucks into my mouth. I never got the chance to read the writing fully and as I go to zoom in on the image, I stop myself.

Locking my phone, I close my eyes, but I can still see that picture. *Great, now he's in my brain all topless and sexy with his muscles and his tattoos and his... no, no way I'm not thinking about him. Not now or ever.*

Just a friend. Just a friend. Just a friend, I repeat to myself as I slip into bed.

Chapter 10

Grayson

Nora didn't text me back after I sent a picture last night. I don't know why I did it. She and I can't get into *this*, whatever this might be. It wouldn't work. We're opposites. More than opposites, we're completely off limits to each other. She's going to be my best friend's sister-in-law, and it's got 'bad idea' written all over it. Plus, we decided this is strictly platonic between us. Friends. I like the idea of being her friend and so, I spent all night trying to convince my cock that he wasn't hard for Nora Scott.

He's still hard this morning, so there's that.

I feel around my bed for my phone, and when it lights up, my face falls when I see there's nothing, not a single text. I'm not sure why that annoys me as much as it does, but I spend the next hour slamming and huffing around my flat like a grumpy bear. I dress in my staple black shirt and black chinos and slide on a fresh pair of white Nikes. Every day, the same.

When I stroll into work after speeding through London in my BMW i8, my mood hasn't improved. I know that if Liam catches me, he'll sense something is wrong instantly, so I sneak past his office and close the door when I get into mine, letting out the biggest breath as my back hits my door.

I close my eyes and shake my head, needing to focus on work. Liam recently closed a huge deal worth a sweet five mil, and it's my job to make sure that the finalities are in place for their office space they got from us. And that's exactly what I do. I'm his right-hand man, his work wing man. I swoop in with my own closures of properties for clients too, but mostly I work alongside Liam and settle the bigger fish now.

My calendar tells me that I have a meeting at 1pm across town and I'm grateful for the distraction. I set up some documents ready for the meeting. It's a local smaller client deal, one that Liam trusts me to do myself and I relish the freedom. We have plans to expand over the next year and split the company into two divisions. Liam's father is taking more control of the residential properties, and they are mostly outside of central London, where he lives with his wife. Whilst Liam and I will be heading up the corporate properties here.

Today's meeting shouldn't take long, though. The company is renewing their contracts with us, but they want more space, so we're going to renegotiate for them to take over the second floor of the building they're currently in, which has recently become available.

Once the documents are ready, I check over a few new contracts that are happening next week and start on the staffing rota. It's probably one of the most boring areas of the job, but I'm grateful Liam gave me his role when his dad took a step back. It means he trusts me, and

I never plan on breaking that trust, even if that includes not sleeping with Nora again.

Ready to leave for my meeting, I step out of my office just as Liam does. *Fuck.*

"Grayson, you headed over to the T&M meeting?"

I nod. "I am. I have all the documents and my winning smile in tow." I fake a smile and he frowns.

"Winning smile looks a little more like a wince if I'm honest, man. What's going on?"

"Nothing. I didn't sleep great last night. I'm going to go to the gym tonight, then crash early." I turn around to walk away, already knowing that he is going to ask me another question.

"Wait." *See.*

I turn to face him again and he continues, "where were you last night? Hooking up?" His eyebrows wiggle, and it makes me cringe all the way to my core.

"Dude, you're the least cool person I know."

I shake my head. "I was home. Had a quiet night." *I snogged Nora's face off in a lift, went home, and wanked off in the shower to thoughts of her, but yeah, totally platonic.*

"You sure you're okay?" He eyes me wearily. I know he doesn't believe me, but I have to get going.

"I'm all good," I say it with enough finality that I'm hoping he catches my tone. "But now you're making me late. Bye, bud."

I can tell Liam wasn't finished with the third degree, but I was. I was also finished thinking about Nora Scott because I can't think about how perfectly soft her lips were or how full and plump her arse was in my hands. Nope, never.

I step out of our building and take a deep breath as the rain hammers down and I pull on my coat, revelling in the chill that runs down my spine as I make my way to the underground.

As I sit on the tube, scowling at my phone, I flick through Instagram and then TikTok, mindlessly searching for something to distract me or give me a good enough reason to stop with this shitty mood. But no amount of funny dog videos do it for me today.

As the train slows for my stop, I realise that I'm never going to get on the good side of this client with this attitude, so I decide to shake it off and smile at strangers as I walk by. Unfortunately, I'm not a huge smiler and I'm pretty sure most people think I'm unwell or a total loser. Either way, I find myself chuckling at some of the looks I get.

As I walk into T&M offices, I spot the familiar reception area that precedes the small one-floor space. It is old fashioned and stuffy, just like the CEO. I am shown to the conference room at the back of the building where Tony and his daughter wait. His daughter is a tall, leggy blonde, usually my type.

"Mr King, great to see you again." Tony McDonald extends his hand and I shake it firmly and smile, glad it's not the freaky smile anymore.

"Mr McDonald, the pleasure is mine. Louisa, it's good to see you."

She blushes and her dad shoots her a look. I'm guessing she isn't here because she wants to be. Maybe daddy dearest has her learning the ropes. What I'm most surprised about though, is that I don't feel the urge to wink or flirt with her.

I turn my attention to Tony again, shrugging that thought from my brain, focussing entirely on the papers in my hands. "I've got the new contracts for you here. I thought we could go upstairs and check out the space too and make sure the offices are exactly what you need.

They are currently vacant and can be available from Monday if we sign today."

Tony nods and puts on his glasses to scan the documents that he's taken from me. Meanwhile, his dear daughter is distracted by the massive talons she calls nails; utterly terrifying if you ask me. When she clocks me watching her, mostly in fear that she'll use those nails on me, she smirks and pushes her boobs together, flicking her hair like a show pony. Now usually, I would eat that kind of attention up, but today it's not hitting the spot. Needing to put some distance between us, I clear my throat and smile whilst walking over to the water fountain, avoiding Louisa's succubus gaze.

After what feels like forever, Tony asks Louisa for a pen, which she gives him whilst popping a bubble gum bubble, classy. He signs on the dotted line and asks for me to show Louisa where her new office would be as apparently his gout is playing him up. He limps back to his office, leaving me alone with his daughter.

Excellent.

Really fucking excellent.

I stride over to the door. "Ready?"

She saunters over like I have all the time in the world, which annoys me more, and she walks past me, dragging one of her nails across my chest.

Jesus. I've never wanted someone's attention less.

I bolt to the stairs while she waits for the lift. I think I've had enough experiences in lifts lately. I shout that I'll meet her on the next floor as the doors close and she can't change course and follow me.

The offices upstairs are empty save a few discarded desks and chairs. I practically jog around the space showing Louisa, dodging each room so that we weren't ever in the same one together, refusing to get stuck in one place with her. Some might say I'm terrified, and I'll be a man and admit that I am. This woman has claws, and I don't want them anywhere near any part of me. The fact that I'm admitting that to myself for the second time today makes me think about why. Louisa is beautiful, blonde, leggy, has massive boobs, and yet... my dick hasn't twitched once.

I get distracted, wondering what is going on with me. Is it because of Nora? I know I'm massively attracted to her, and I let my mind wander far too easily when I am around her. That night we spent together is the last time I was with anyone and I'm only just realising what that means.

Fuck, over three months and I've barely looked at anyone else. Even when I wasn't actively thinking about Nora, I didn't want to go out and fuck around with anyone. I've spent more time with Liam lately and maybe it's because I know they share the same house so I might see her.

I've made decisions about my sex life, without realising I was doing it, but I'm not mad about it. I've not missed the hook up sex with random women, who I never spend more than one night with. But Nora Scott? I can't get her out of my head and my body craves her as if she's my next breath.

Maybe it's just because she's the last one my body remembers, so that's the solution to my mild Nora obsession. I just need to get back out there. Stop the drought I'm in and replace the memories of her... how she tastes, how she moans when my fingers were inside of her, how she...

Oh, fuck. I think my dick just woke up.

I subtly readjust my semi-hard erection as I walk out of the final room I was showing Louisa and swiftly say my goodbyes. As much as I want to stop my drought, I don't want to do it with her.

I manage to escape the building without a mark on me and I've secured a contract. My day is definitely looking up now.

Back in the office, Liam is sitting at my desk waiting for me.

"How did it go?" he asks.

"I nailed it." I drop the contract onto my desk dramatically, like a mic drop, and Liam stares blankly at me, waiting for me to say something. I roll my eyes. "Dude! Mic drop."

Liam doesn't catch on. "Mic drop, was there a karaoke?"

I give up.

Letting out a deflated sigh at my lame best friend, I plonk down into my desk chair. "Never mind. Mic drop means I nailed it, I did it, woohoo yay me, I'm the fucking bomb. Which I now am not because you made me explain it."

"Ohhh, sorry I didn't get that. You are the man, though." He holds his fist out for me to bump it, but I stare at him.

"Don't patronise me."

Liam laughs and takes his hand away. "Was Louisa there? I heard she's going to be an assistant to one of Tony's managers."

"She was there. She had these awful long witches' talons and I swear she could've slit my throat with them. Woman terrifies me." We both share a shudder this time.

"Well, good job anyway, man. Mind if I join you at the gym?"

Liam never joins me at the gym, he prefers running outside, plus it's not even 3pm yet. "Uh-oh trouble in paradise?"

"No," he says a little too fast to be convincing, so I glare at him, crossing my arms over my chest.

"Fine. Yes, but no. Jess is going a little crazy with the wedding planning. Her and Nora have spreadsheets and folders and magazines and Pinterest boards and it's quite possibly the scariest thing I've ever seen. I didn't even know what a Pinterest board was, but you bet your arse I do now." I scowl. I don't know what a Pinterest board is either. I'm about to ask, but I sense Liam isn't finished. "Then once she and Nora spend all evening planning and ordering things, she's too tired for sex and that is the worst bit of it all, man."

I stifle a laugh. I'm not sure I've ever seen him this stressed over Jess before. The last time was maybe when she had stuff going on last year, but he was mostly grumpy because he wasn't with her all the time. Now he's a man who needs sex and is not getting it. It's arguably worse.

"I have zero advice for you, man, except maybe make the sex more interesting than the Pinterest shit. Whatever the fuck that is."

Liam nods. "Yeah, you're right. I just need to…"

I cover my ears. "Lalala I still have to look at Jess when I see her. Please don't tell me what you're doing in the bedroom."

Liam looks at me sheepishly. "Sorry, dude."

"Get your shit. Boss is letting us off early. We're going to the gym." I slap our palms together and help him up from the chair so we can head out.

Chapter 11

Nora

It's official. I'm in hell. I'm surrounded by glitter, card, glue, scissors, every type of ribbon you could possibly imagine, and a very highly strung Jess. My planned evening of opening my new crossword book and drinking a glass of wine has been officially sabotaged.

Thankfully, I managed to persuade Jess to order her wedding invites online a few weeks ago, but she insisted that we hand make the menus, and it's actual hell.

"I'm getting you a shot," I announce as Jess continues to glare at the two pieces of card that she can't decide between. Hint: they're the same colour, but at this point, tequila is the only answer.

I return with the bottle and two glasses, smiling because I'm convinced this will be more fun with alcohol. I pass one to Jess, but she doesn't tear her gaze from the card. "Jessica, they're the same. Have a shot and maybe you'll see that too."

"Fine," she mumbles and downs it like a pro.

Four shots and twenty minutes later, things are starting to look up. Jess' mood has improved, as has mine.

"My brain hurts. I didn't know there were 700 shades of cream," I whinge.

"I know, right, and in reality, which of my guests are going to fucking judge me for choosing shade 432 over shade 890?"

"That's the spirit. No one gives a fuck, Jess. Cream is cream. Pick one."

Jess sways a little from the tequila buzz I know she's feeling right now. She squints her eyes and points to the cream on the left, which I snatch out of her hand and immediately order a hundred more before she can change her mind.

"Good job. This card will be here in five days. Considering we have less than three months until the wedding, we need to get these menus done." I pick up the glittered ribbon of gold, silver, and rose gold. "Pick one of these, too."

Jess grunts next to me and points to the gold one and I order more of that too. "I'm not usually this hung up about fucking everything. Maybe getting married so fast was a bad idea."

"I know organising a wedding is stressful, but you know what will make it worth it? The hen party. Oh, and I guess a hot as hell husband too, who you've wanted to marry for bloody years," I say, smiling at her.

Jess chuckles and I realise it's the first time today she's done that. I suddenly feel bad for hating this process. The truth is, I love spending time with her. We've always been like two halves of one whole. Although she feels like my sister, technically, my dad is her uncle. Her mum had some health issues when we were sixteen and disappeared on her. My parents took her in without hesitation and the rest is history.

When we were kids, we used to spend every spare moment together. It's only now Liam is back in her life that things are changing, and I think change is probably why she's stressing over which colour cream. Jess deserves all the happiness though, because I've seen her go through some pretty dark times. It's built a bond between us that's deeper than blood.

I put my hand on her knee, reassuring her. "The perfect shade of cream was the one you picked. You're marrying Liam freaking Taylor, Jess. It's going to be amazing," I grin and shake her leg excitedly.

"God, you're right. I'm glad you're here to bring me back when I overthink," she says, shaking her hands out to loosen up a bit. "So, tell me, how's the hen do planning? What did you and Grayson concoct?" she asks with a sparkle in her eyes that makes me double take at first, but I quickly remind myself that she has no idea about Grayson and me.

"That's for me to know and you to find out." I tap the side of my nose, remembering that there are still a few things we might need to go over. I make a mental note to ask Grayson, which includes talking to him, something I've not done since he sent that topless photo to me after our fake date. I'm avoiding him because I don't know what to say to him yet.

"I'm just glad I don't have to sort that out. I'm grateful you're doing it."

I nod. I'm glad she feels that way because this wedding might just be my demise, especially with the amount of extra time I have to spend around Grayson. I'm still spending a stupid amount of time convincing myself that I do not want to repeat of our night together. Nope, never. *How many times do I need to say it before it I really believe it?*

"So, the boys have their suits, we have our dresses, and you have yours. Your to do list is looking manageable again," I say, not letting my thoughts drift to the tall, tattooed best man whose bare chest I've stared at far too many times already this morning.

"Okay, no more. My liver will never recover." Jess hiccups and stands; I don't have the heart to tell her that she's got several pieces of glittered ribbon attached to her bum. Instead, I chuckle to myself, enjoying the moment.

Jess tipsily staggers upstairs. Liam is away for business tonight, and I know that's another reason she's feeling strange. Just as I think I should follow her, I hear Liam's voice through her phone. I'm guessing they're on a video call and I definitely want zero part of interrupting that.

I quickly pack up the wedding menu explosion and hope that Jess doesn't want to touch it again until the card arrives. I think she needs a break from it all. Hell, *I* need a break from it all. I have nightmares about the many colour palettes and decorations she asks my opinion on.

Walking up to my bedroom, I hear Jess and Liam laughing, and my heart stutters. I'm so happy they have each other, even if it makes me occasionally nauseous at how perfect they are together. I hate comparing because comparison is the thief of joy and all that, but... my love life feels like a big hot mess. I've only slept with three people, and I've barely dated because I've been busy building my career. I do not regret a single second of that, but sometimes it can be lonely. I do try, I've been on dates, but every guy I meet turns out to be an arseholes or boring as hell. Or Grayson King, who is only a *friend*.

I'll never admit this to anyone, and I hate being this person right now... but sometimes you feel better when you admit things out loud, so here goes. I feel like I'm that woman who is meant to be the bridesmaid and never the bride, or the aunt and never the mum.

I throw myself onto my bed, my head still slightly buzzing from the tequila. "No, Nora, you will not wallow in self-pity. That is not a part of the plan. We don't do pity parties. They're not conducive. At all," I mutter to myself, yawning in the process. Just as I'm about to get ready for bed, my phone pings.

> **Grayson:** Don't forget, I'm taking you for your *yes day* on Saturday. Be ready at 9.

My tummy does a stupid little dance at the sight of his name, but I quickly squash that because, no, we're friends and that's how we'll stay.

> **Me:** Did I agree to that?

> **Grayson:** If you want to get the hang of what happens on Saturday, then start right now. Say yes, because it's happening, regardless.

This is a bad idea. Yielding so much to this man is going to make me vulnerable and the last time that happened...

But apparently, my self-control has disappeared and is replaced by complete curiosity as to what the hell he's going to do with me for a whole day. A whole day where I have to say yes to him.

The thought makes me a little giddy.

Me: Fine, yes.

Chapter 12

Grayson

Knocking loudly on her door, I check my watch. It's 9am on Saturday and we're already wasting daylight. I should've told her 8am or even better, I should've dragged her arse to my gym and watched her work out first. Damn, I missed an opportunity there. I want to get as much as I can out of this 'yes day' with Nora and see how far I can push her.

Bang, bang, bang.

I call her phone again, but just as the rings sound in my ear, the click of the lock opens the door and there she is, in a crop top and leggings so tight they should be illegal. My eyes do a quick sweep of her toned body, and the way sweat is glistening over her chest finally settling on her face, which is not surprisingly set in a scowl with her brows almost touching. "What are you... Oh my God, it's Saturday." She throws her palm to her glistening forehead. Turns out, my fantasy of seeing her sweaty from working out just came true. I wonder what else I could manifest today.

"Did I interrupt something?" I swallow, ignoring the raging hormones sweeping over me.

"I was just doing a Pilates class on this app I found." Her chest heaves up and down and a droplet of sweat disappears between her cleavage. I have to look away to stop myself from wondering what she would do if I just bent down and ran my tongue over her skin. *Nope, let it go, mate.*

"Well, come on, it's 'yes day' and I'm hyped for it."

She rolls her eyes but steps aside to let me in. I try to ignore the fact that she smells good even when she's sweaty and head to the kitchen. "Go shower, because 'yes' starts now," I yell over my shoulder.

I rummage through her kitchen cupboards, hoping to find some of that granola she makes and when I spot it, happiness fills my body. "Fuck yes," I say whilst bringing out the whole tub. I'm halfway through my second bowl when I hear Nora's tiny feet padding along the hallway.

"You better not eat all of that." She points to my bowl. Her hair is now down and brushing against her collarbones when she moves. Her fresh from the shower scent has my mouth watering.

"I make no promises," I mumble through a mouthful.

"So, what do you have for me to suffer through today?" Her brown eyes assess me with sass and intrigue. My favourite combination on her.

I look her up and down, taking in her black tight jeans and cream jumper. "What you're wearing is okay."

She looks down at herself. "Um, thanks?"

"We're starting off with something here. Then we're going out. Let's make a cake."

Her forehead creases with a frown. "A cake?"

I lick the remaining yoghurt from my spoon and watch her watch me. "That's what I said. And you are meant to say…"

"…yes."

I smile widely, whilst visibly letting my body enjoy that word tumbling from her usually scowly lips. "If you feel the need to add 'sir' to that sentence, then I'd be fine with that."

She barks a laugh. "Not a chance."

"I'll wear you down."

Her lush lips twist as she tries and fails to hide a smirk. "You're not cute."

"We both know that's not true." I let my smile grow to fanboy size across my face as I stare at her own trying not to break free. When I see her bury her head into her hands, I know I've won her over. She mumbles something I don't quite catch before I say, "chocolate cake is my favourite."

Her caramel eyes roll at me when she drops her hands. "Is this yes day going to turn into 'make Nora my bitch' day?"

"Nooooo…" I smirk. "Nah, for real, I just really want cake and to get you used to saying yes. I know it's not a word you're used to saying, so we're starting small."

"I say yes!" she squeaks, her voice entirely too high for someone telling the truth. My eyebrow quirks as she huffs at me. "Fine. Cake it is."

Nora begins moving around her kitchen in defeat, her hips swaying with each movement, pulling out ingredients for my cake. Her petite frame is pretty mesmerising at the best of times, but when she's doing ordinary things like walking and bending, well, for whatever reason, that has my pulse thumping hard in my cock.

When she has the ingredients she needs, I plant my elbows on the counter, waiting for her to pile them into the huge bowl she's placed in front of us. "Crack two eggs in there for me, please."

"Sorry, you want me to what now?" I say, disbelieving. I can cook certain dishes, but baking, that's far beyond my talents and egg cracking is also not a skill of mine.

"Crack. The. Eggs." She enunciates each word.

I hold an egg in my hand, feeling the lightness of it. "And how exactly do I do that?"

Her eyes twinkle with amusement. "You've never... never mind. Like this." She takes the egg and with one hand she taps it twice on the side of the bowl opens the egg, spilling the contents into the bowl.

"What the fuck just happened?" I step forwards to survey the contents in the bowl and sure enough there's an egg. I stare at it as if I thought it'd be a fucking chicken. *It* all happened so fast, though. "You just did some sort of ninja egg cracking." I say, disbelieving how quickly and easily she did it.

She chuckles. "I just cracked an egg. Now it's your turn."

The egg in my hand suddenly feels like the most difficult Rubik's cube I've ever done in my life. How am I supposed to be as swift and calm without shattering the entire egg, shell, and all into the bowl? I lightly tap the side of the egg, not wanting to go at it too hard.

"Harder."

My eyes snap to hers, amused. "Say that again, shorty." My voice is low and gravelly.

"The egg, Grayson, tap the egg harder." The side of her mouth lifts into a smile that I know she's fighting right now. I tap the egg once more and it starts to seep out, "good, now you can use both hands to separate the shell and open it up." When the shell falls perfectly apart in my hands and the contents plop into the bowl, I feel like it's the best thing I've accomplished all year.

"I did it!" I shout. Nope, that was a very unmanly squeal and I'll own it.

Nora's light laugh sounds out through the kitchen, making me smile. "You did. Clever boy. You get the gold star today."

I narrow my eyes at her but she's not paying attention, too busy mixing the eggs into the butter. As soon as she touches the flour to add some into the bowl, I get a wicked idea, one that I know she'll hate. "Nora?"

"Hm?" she says whilst she's bending down to weigh another ingredient.

"Nora?"

Her head snaps up. "What, Grayson?" Her brown eyes are wide as I throw some flour directly at her face. It puffs out across her cheek and ear before it floats down over her jumper. "Are you fucking kidding me?" she scolds.

My shoulders vibrate with laughter. "I had to. It's the rules for baking cakes."

She dives her hand into the flour and throws some at me too, landing it in my hair. "Oh, that's it." My hands grab more flour and I round the island to get a really good hit in, smashing a handful into her hair too. She leans forwards grabbing another handful when she turns to me, her face half covered in white flour, I let out a loud laugh just as she slaps both of her hands on either side of my face and all I can see is white clouds floating in front of my eyes.

Her small, warm hands are still covering my cheeks when the flour settles. I look at her, close up, enjoying the way her nose twitches from the dust. Her lips are framed by the flour too, highlighting just how full they are, how soft I remember that they are. I exhale a breath and the cloud of powder that shoots from my lips has her stepping backwards, giggling and coughing.

Her laugh is a melody of sweet and soft sounds, filling the kitchen with an emotion that I'm betting she doesn't feel enough. The joy radiating from her right now swells something in my chest, because when she smiles, fuck, she could light up entire cities. And I'm the reason she's got that look on her face and I'll be damned if that doesn't fill me with sunshine too. I make women laugh all the time. I'm a funny guy, so why does it feel like I've just singlehandedly won the fucking rugby six nations cup?

She arches a brow. "You okay? You look weird."

Fuck I do? "I don't. You look weird."

Good one, man.

She takes two small steps closer to me, a look of pure satisfaction on her face as she reaches out to brush my nose free of more flour. "Hmm, if I wasn't mistaken, Grayson King, I'd say you're falling for me."

I laugh it off because what the fuck am I supposed to say? I have no idea what I looked like or what I felt. I was happy that she was happy, and that's probably the first time I've ever felt that way about anyone. Am I freaked? Yeah, my heart is beating a little erratically, but I'm not about to ruin this day for her and leave in a blind panic or blurt out any unnecessary declarations.

I shake my head like a dog getting out of water and watch as more powder floats around. Nora chuckles, dusting herself off. Something passes between us that ripples in the air like static electricity, both of us freezing as if we are feeling it at the same time. Nora makes quick work of going back to her mixing, and the machine she turns on makes enough noise to drown out the sudden awkward silence.

When the machine stops, Nora deftly scoops the mixture out into a tray I hadn't seen her prep and she swipes it into the oven with a clang.

"You're on clean up," she says without looking at me. I hear her footsteps trailing up the stairs as I plonk the bowl into the sink and have to think really hard about *not* following her.

Chapter 13

Nora

I'm trying really hard to keep my cool, but Grayson keeps pushing me out of my comfort zone. I'm not talking about the list either. I'm talking about the zone where we're barely friends, frenemies are probably more accurate, and we have teasing banter that leads nowhere because we both know that *we* wouldn't work. Or at least that's what I thought before his stupid self kissed me in the lift and now I'm confused. My 'keep it cool' factor completely going out the window whenever I get within a foot of him.

Did I ever have any cool factor? Debatable.

It's entirely his fault for kissing me in the first place. Grayson's default setting is sex though, so I guess I can't really blame him. Except I am, I very much am. I blame him for fogging my brain with his dick and his big soft lips that I can't stop looking at. It's his fault that my heart flip-flops in my chest when I smell his bergamot scent and I hate him a little bit more for that. Except I'm lying. I don't hate him at all. I'm actually seeing different sides to him, and I want to see more, know more about him. The connection between us is palpable but I want to feel more from him, to figure out why he doesn't want a relationship and I think he'd run a mile if he knew that.

I rake my hands through my hair, shaking out any remaining flour, hoping it doesn't stay this white all day. I splash cold water over my face, ridding my skin of that horrible dusty feeling before I search my wardrobe for another pair of jeans and jumper.

When I'm dressed, I catch my reflection in the mirror; my cheeks are flushed and my hair still has a slight white tinge to it, but I don't have time to wash it again. I quickly pop some tinted moisturiser on and a lick of mascara and make my way back downstairs just in time for the oven to beep, telling me the cake is done.

The sweet cocoa smell is filling the whole house, reminding me of my mum's chocolate cake she'd make us all the time when we were kids. The memory of Jess and me scoffing the entire cake makes me smile as I walk into the kitchen.

"Something's beeping and I can't stop it," Grayson flaps around, searching for the off button.

I press the alarm button on the oven and open it, and my nose is immediately hit with a stronger smell of chocolate, gooey goodness. I inhale deeply, letting the sweet, buttery goodness melt over me.

"Fuck, that smells good," Grayson purrs from behind me. I plunge my hands into the oven mitt and take the cake out.

"Can you pass me the toothpicks from the cupboard up there?"

He reaches up, his t-shirt riding up slightly, giving me a flash of his bronzed stomach and making my breath hitch. I tear my gaze away when he turns to me, passing me the box.

"Thank you," I say as our hands brush together and the zap of electricity that appears whenever he gets close that I've actively been ignoring jolts straight to my heart. I cough, trying to clear the buzzing feeling flooding my body before stabbing the cake probably a little too hard with a toothpick.

"Perfect," I say when the toothpick comes out clean.

"Why do you need toothpicks to tell you if a cake is perfect? I could've told you that." He cocks his head, looking like a confused puppy.

"If the toothpick comes out with batter on it, then you know the cake isn't cooked. Well, that's what my mum told me."

"I've never seen it before, but then this is the first time I had a hand in making a cake rather than just eating it."

"Have I just taken your cake making virginity, Grayson?" I taunt.

He smiles and my pitter-patter heart skips a beat. "Consider my cherry popped."

My hand flies to my chest. "I'm honoured."

"Can we eat it yet?" he asks, his face beaming with excitement.

"I have ice cream we can put with it."

"Yeah, that's exactly what this needs, Oh fuck, fuck, hot," he says as he quickly swallows and gasps through the first mouthful of cake that he's helped himself to straight from the tin.

"So impatient," I mumble as I pull out the ice cream from the freezer and stand there for a second to allow my cheeks to cool the fuck down, reminding myself that Grayson being cute and sweet is just all part of the yes day. It's not permanent.

"Only impatient for things that are delicious," he says playfully. My head snaps up from the freezer and when I look at him, he winks devilishly, leaving all sorts of implications in my head as I plate up two slices of cake.

Twenty minutes later and I'm so full of chocolate and ice cream I want to lie down for the foreseeable.

"Right, come on. We've got somewhere to be," he jumps up with far too much energy.

I groan, my stomach fully protesting at any movements. "No."

His eyebrows raise as he crosses his arms in front of his chest. I definitely do not look at the veins popping between his tattoos. Nope. "Did you just break the rule?"

I throw my head back dramatically. "Fine. Yes. Lead the way."

This *yes* business only makes me realise how much I like saying no. Or maybe I just really like having free will.

"That's my good girl." He drops his voice an octave, and it makes me shiver, but I cover it up by rushing out of the kitchen and putting my coat on.

"Ready!" I shout, mustering up the most amount of cheeriness I can, ignoring my stupidly perky nipples beneath my jumper.

He appears in the hallway with a far too cocky smirk, as he grabs his keys and coat, and we head to his car. Except when the chill of the air hits me in the face, I realise he doesn't have his car; he has a motorbike. It's not huge, but it looks expensive, black shiny, sexy, but all kinds of terrifying too. "I have to get on that?" *By 'that' I mean the bike, not the six foot four man standing next to it... clearly.*

"Are you about to say no again?"

My feet stomp with my own irritation for writing this stupid list in the first place and agreeing to have him help me. Although, *agree* maybe isn't right word. *Forced* is more accurate. "This is getting old already."

"It's so fun for me, though." He passes me a helmet and leather jacket before putting his own on. The thought of other women riding behind him on his bike, wearing these items, rushes into my brain, but I push it away before I can obsess. I slide the helmet onto my head, and his hand fastens and adjusts the strap around my chin. His touch shouldn't make me tingle, but it does. "When you're on my bike, I'm responsible for you being safe," he says matter of factly, when all I can do is swoon internally and hope he really can't see my face that well through and the visor.

He kicks up the kickstand, his hands flexing against the handles, and the effect that movement has on my body is utterly carnal. Grayson climbs onto the bike effortlessly, settling immediately and turning to face me. How did he do that so smoothly? I know I'm going to fumble like an absolute clown getting on this thing. He winks and a zap of white hot heat travels along my skin. I tell myself that my reaction is because of the bike. Definitely the charm of the bike, and not him.

"You coming, shorty?"

If only.

I move towards him tentatively, wondering how to maintain any sliver of decorum whilst mounting this shiny beast. Inhaling deeply, I decide to just go for it and fling my leg over the seat, griping his shoulders as I move. When I settle with a thud behind him, I quickly realise that I have no idea where to put my hands.

"Uhh, where do I hold on?" I yell through the helmet, removing my death grip on his shoulders.

His big hands wrap around mine, pulling me flush to his back with a thud, placing my arms around his chest. The smell of leather and petrol envelops me as I'm forced to grip him.

He's rock solid; all rippling muscle beneath my twitching fingertips. "Here. Hold on tight and don't let go." The zing that travels through me is the same as earlier. I wish he'd stop being so... so... *him.* I might be able to focus on not falling off his bike if he was just a little less Grayson.

He puts his own helmet on and fastens it, then pushes down the visor and I'm done for. That's quite enough motorbike porn from you, Mr King.

When the engine roars to life, I internally squeal and clench everywhere. The rumble carries through my body until it's deep in my bones; the vibrations making me want to clench my thighs together to ease the flood of arousal I feel threatening to soak my underwear. Grayson skilfully navigates the traffic, the wind rivalling our speed as it whips over us both. I'm grinning like a clown from within my helmet; I've never felt so alive, so free. Travelling at the speed of light through London should have been on my list because this is addicting. A little giggle escapes my mouth when Grayson zips around a corner quickly and then he stops at a red light. Tilting his head to one side, he asks, "You okay back there?"

"Better than okay," I cry, elation filling my voice. He laughs, and the motorbike roars beneath us as he takes off again when the light turns green.

A few minutes later, we arrive at a tiny little blacked out shop front. Grayson parks his bike and tells me to hop off, which I do reluctantly, and then remove my helmet. "That was... incredible," I say, not able to stop the evidence of the adrenaline beaming through my smile.

Grayson removes his helmet, too, as he grins at me. "Did I just pop your motorbike cherry?"

I nod, suddenly feeling shy. "Consider my cherry popped." I echo his words from earlier and he grabs my hand to drag me into the shop.

Inside, I'm hit with the smell of antiseptic and then something sweet assaults my nose. "Where are we?" I ask, looking around at the sketched artwork that adorns the walls.

As Grayson opens his mouth to speak, a red-haired woman appears, covered in tattoos. She's stunning. "Grayson," she purrs before pulling him in for a hug, which makes me disconnect our hands that I hadn't realised were still linked.

"Hey, Cece. How you doing?".

They break apart and I notice her bright green eyes now and how much they sparkle beneath her dark thick lashes. "I'm good," she tells him before turning her attention to me. "Hey, I'm Cece." Her hand stretches out for mine.

We shake hands. "I'm Nora."

"This your girlfriend, G-man?" Cece asks playfully, nudging him.

"No. Just a friend."

"She's way out of your league, just like I am." Cece winks.

I shouldn't be so affected by him saying that because it's the truth. We are just friends. He is just helping a friend. I take a step sideways away from him just so I can clearly draw the line for my own sanity.

"Have you had a tattoo before?" Cece asks, then I realise that she's looking at me.

My eyes bug out as I flick them between Grayson and her. "Is that why I'm here?" I ask Grayson nervously, realising that I hadn't even really taken in my surroundings. I take a quick glance around and see pictures of tattooed limbs all over the back wall. Cece

He nods, smiling. "It's on your list, shorty. Cece here is the best of the best."

I bite the inside of my cheek. It *is* on my list and now that I'm here, I regret it more than I realised. "I-I... I have no idea what to have done." And what if it hurts? I can't back out once it starts. Oh God, this was a bad idea.

"I'll leave you with our artwork books. See if anything pops out at you." She hands me four huge heavy books from beneath the counter and I take them with a polite smile. Cece goes to the back of the shop again, leaving Grayson and I alone with the books.

"I'll be right back. Don't leave, okay?" Grayson says before following Cece.

I frown, wondering if she and Grayson have been or are together, but I push the thoughts out of my head before they blossom into jealousy. I try to steady my thrashing pulse as I sit myself down on the black leather sofa at the side of the shop and start going through the book labelled '*Portraits*'. It only takes a couple of seconds to realise that isn't what I want. I pick up another book labelled '*Misc*'.

"See anything you like?" Grayson asks. I jump and make a noise that's barely human.

"God, you scared me."

"Sorry, I thought you heard me come back through," he says, plopping his big, broad body next to me.

My eyes scan the pages of butterflies, infinity signs, moons, and scripted letters. The panic of 'what if it hurts' is back again, clawing at my throat. "Maybe I haven't thought it through enough. This is going to be on my body forever."

Grayson shifts closer to me. "I know you're on the verge of saying no. If you really want to back out, then I'm not going to stop you. You're right, this is forever. But if you have an idea, then I'd really like to be there when you get it done. Even if that means it's not happening today."

My body warms to his words. "Why did you get your tattoos?"

"Some of them I had when I was younger, some are reminders."

"Of what?" I ask. He pauses and I suddenly worry I've overstepped. "Sorry, you don't have to answer that."

"No, it's not that. They're reminders of things that are important to me. The lion on my chest, he's there to remind me to be brave when I need to take risks. A reminder that they'll pay off. Then the king card on my forearm is just because of my last name and to remind me to gamble on myself sometimes. I have a date written on my ribs too. The others are just drawings that I liked, but the lion is my most important one."

"A date?" I ask, scanning over his arms with some tribal drawings, a butterfly, some roses. His skin looks beautiful.

"Yeah."

"Okay." I don't push because even though I am dying to know something more about him that he clearly doesn't share with many people, I don't want to make him uncomfortable.

His shoulders stiffen slightly as he battles with something in his head. Silence falls over us until, finally, he turns to face me. "It's the first tattoo I got after my parents divorced."

I nod, yet not fully understanding how that impacted him, but also knowing that if he wants to share more with me, he will when he's ready.

I change the subject, sensing that might be what he needs. "I want something to remind me of this... today. The feeling I just got from being on your bike for the first time, the feeling I have right now that isn't just the nerves–well, it *is* nerves—but it's also a taste of something, freedom maybe? I don't know. Do I sound certifiably insane?"

He nudges my shoulder with his, his playful side back. "No, you don't." He thinks, tapping his fingers together in front of him. "You could have the word *yes* written somewhere."

I turn my head to stare at him. His eyes are a lighter grey, dancing with the sparkling idea. "I like that, actually. It'd be a good reminder." I look over the scripted writing, but I realise that I don't want this to be just anyone's writing. "Will you write it for me?"

This time when he smiles at me softly, I see so much vulnerability on his face and it tugs at my chest. "You sure you want my writing tattooed on you forever?"

I nod. "It'll be a good reminder of today... and how much you've pissed me off already," I say, not meaning a single word about him pissing me off. In fact, I'm realising he's a bit like an onion, he has layers, or whatever non-ogre analogy that also makes sense.

His head throws back in laughter. "Okay, you got it. One tattoo coming up." He turns to call for Cece. "Wait, where will you have it?" he asks.

I look at my body, hoping for some kind of inspiration. "Maybe my left wrist."

Cece comes back into our waiting area. "You picked something, honey?"

"Yes. This clown is going to write it for me." Pointing to Grayson with my thumb.

She smiles a genuine smile. "I'll get him a pen then."

Grayson turns to me, eyes still shining brightly. "You can change your mind."

"I know, but I'm not going to."

Cece comes back, passing him the pen. Grayson writes *yes* four times and I pick my favourite one. She does some fancy transferring thing so it can be placed onto my skin, and I settle into her tattoo chair. The smell of antiseptic is so much stronger here it makes my nose wrinkle.

"You wanna hold my hand?" Grayson asks standing right next to my chair I'm in.

"Am I going to need to?" I ask, my earlier fears of it being incredibly painful suddenly flooding back to me.

"Depends on how good your pain threshold is."

"I'll be good... I think."

Cece sets up her equipment but when a buzzing sound starts, I jump. "Relax, it's just the needle." She laughs, "You ready?"

I nod my head, swallowing all my nerves like razorblades.

As soon as the needle touches my skin, my free hand digs into the leather of the seat. The sting is strange; it's pressure and tingly, and ouch, yeah, definitely hurts. My eyes are so scrunched closed. I don't want to open them in case I see something that'll make me yell stop, and having half of a tiny word on my wrist will not be ideal.

The cool wipe of a cloth soothes my hot skin. "All done," Cece says and my eyes spring open.

"That's it?" I ask, confused.

"That's it. I'm going to give you some aftercare to take away but try and keep it wrapped for at least the rest of the day."

When I look at the tiny word on my wrist, I feel something warm encase my whole body. My lips turn up into a smile as I look at the word 'yes'. "It's perfect," I say to myself. My head turns to Grayson, who I didn't notice is holding my hand, the same hand that was trying to make indents in the chair minutes ago. He exhales when he sees my smile and lifts my hand to drop a light kiss on my knuckles. A simple gesture that has me spinning.

I'm not sure if this high is because of the tattoo or the fact that I've come to the conclusion that I'm definitely not imagining this softer side to Grayson.

Chapter 14

Grayson

"Y ou ready for my next stop?" I ask Nora as she gingerly puts on her helmet. She looks so fucking cute in the riding gear when she put it on earlier that I knew no one would ever be wearing them ever again. I may have tortured myself by bringing my Yamaha, having her legs wrapped around my hips like that, her tits pressed into my back. Fuck it was impossible not to think about how badly I want her. I'm a sucker for punishment.

The glint from her cling-film wrapped tattoo catches the sun as she moves, breaking my lustful thoughts.

She lifts the visor so I can see her face. "There's more?"

I nod my head, placing my own helmet on. "It's lunchtime. I need more food."

"Of course, you do." She chuckles.

"Hey, I'm a growing boy."

She taunts a smile. "Okay, so where are you taking me?"

I swiftly pull my leg over my bike and stand it up. "Get on and you'll see."

A couple of hours later, we are filled with tacos and Nora is a margherita down, which I'm learning is the easiest way to get her to say yes. She's much more relaxed right now than she was at the tattoo place. Although I do want her to remember all this, so I need to space out her drinks.

She practically hops onto my bike once I'm on this time, and I stifle a laugh at how her mood has gone from so sour this morning to completely jolly right now.

Her tiny hands wrap around me, gripping on. "Ready," she squeals behind me. I take off in a rush, earning myself another squeal from her. Zipping around cars like a dodgem ride at the fairground. We ride around London, just us and the wind, for about an hour. It's one of my favourite things to do and it makes me happy that I get to do it with her right now.

When we arrive at the club, Nora hesitates when she sees the neon sign above the door that says, 'dance, dance'. "We're going dancing?"

I take off my helmet and hers, storing them in the seat of my bike. "You can dance for me if you want, shorty, but no. It's karaoke happy hour and you...." I poke her shoulder. "Are going to sing for me."

She snorts, and for whatever reason, I find it adorable. "Grayson, you do not want to hear me sing."

"Check your wrist."

She looks down at her freshly wrapped tattoo through the cling film and smiles to herself. "Yes."

"Atta girl."

When we get into the bar, there's a lot less light in here, except for the spotlight shining on the stage with a single microphone waiting for the karaoke chaos to start. Considering it's after lunch time, this place isn't really busy yet, which I knew could help her nerves.

I pull Nora to the bar to get another drink down because the way she shuffled in here and her eyes went wide when she saw the stage, tells me she's nervous and I know she could freeze any minute.

"A margherita and a beer please," I ask the bartender, who definitely gives Nora the once over. *Back off, man, she's mine for today.* I wrap a possessive arm around her shoulders as her eyes beadily assess what I'm doing. Honestly, I'm not entirely sure either.

When the drinks are in front of us, she shrugs me off her and I try not to act bothered by her reaction. But it makes my nerves tingle.

"You good?" I ask her.

She nods as she knocks back a gulp of her drink. "Yes."

I take her response at face value and turn around to face the room. It's filled with a dozen round tables with lamps on, each has its own booklet of karaoke songs waiting to be chosen. Some of the tables are occupied already with eager singers ready to croon their way through *Mariah Carey's* backlist to get their late afternoon karaoke fix. I spot a table to the left of the stage, and I take Nora's hand, leading her over to it.

When we're sat, the bartender comes into the bright light of the stage and announces the first song will be "It Takes Two", sung by a cute older couple that fumbles onto the stage together.

I push the booklet in front of Nora. "Pick something."

She rolls her eyes but opens the booklet, running her fingers down each selection. She slaps the book closed, gaining my attention. "I can't do this." Her voice is higher than normal.

"You can't or you won't?"

I see her pulse thrashing against the delicate skin on her neck. "Both."

My body twists to face her and I place a hand on her jittering knee. "Have I steered you wrong yet today?" She shakes her head. "Have you enjoyed what we've done so far?" Her head nods as she smiles. "Are you going to try and push against that scared feeling right now and fucking own that stage?"

She eyes me for a minute, her tongue peeking out, whispering back and forth over her bottom lip as she thinks. "Okay, but I need another drink… and a shot."

I tap her leg. "On it, boss." I stand and get her exactly what she wants. When I return, she's got the book of songs open again, and her finger taps over one song. "You've picked something?" I ask as I place her new drinks in front of her.

She nods, closing the book so I can't see her choice, then throws back the shot of tequila and doesn't wince a single bit. I'm impressed, but this side of Nora I know well; the meticulous one who takes on a challenge and who excels at said challenge. What I'm trying to do is show her that the fun side of her needs to join the party a little more. The swallow of her throat has me imagining all sorts of things I shouldn't, a spark igniting in my brain and travelling south very quickly. I force myself to focus on something else, anything else, but when she licks the salt on the rim of her margarita glass, I know the universe is testing me.

"How are you so 'up for this' all the time?" she asks, breaking the train of dirty thoughts I was falling into.

"Up for what, exactly?" I ask, my throat a little restricted.

"Up for anything—being at a karaoke bar, casually going to get a tattoo. Like you must be the most adventurous person I know."

I think for a second. "Well, when you grow up with a dad who liked to be a drill sergeant most of the time and parents who argue more than talk to each other, you learn quickly that you either conform... or rebel. I'll give you two guesses as to what I did," I say, sipping my beer, trying to be casual when all I feel is pent up anger and frustration.

"You and your parents don't get on?" she asks, concern etching over her features.

"It's not that. Well, maybe it is. They spent the last ten years of their marriage constantly arguing, and I was always caught in the middle. Used as leverage, neither of them cared how I felt. So, that's why I never wanted to get into relationships. I didn't want to make someone feel the same way, arguing all the time, making someone so unhappy they hurt others around them."

Nora's mouth gapes slightly. "I had no idea."

I shrug. "Don't feel bad for me. When my mum moved to the US and my dad moved up North, I thought I had it made. Freedom, finally, to do whatever I wanted."

"What did you want to do?" she asks.

"When I was a teenager, I had a lot of anger to work through, so I joined a seedy fighting club because I thought it would help me channel some of that anger. I stupidly got into illegal underground fights because I earned the most money that way. One fight, my last one, I was feeling weird, off my game. But I went into the ring. The guy was huge, like 250lbs of muscle and as wide as a fucking Hummer. I knew I was screwed. But I climbed into that ring anyway."

Nora's attention is rapt on me, and I like it. "What happened?"

"I lost. He broke my arm, collarbone, and almost broke my jaw. I was in hospital for a week because I had a severe concussion and surgery to fix my arm." I take a deep breath. "But my parents wouldn't come back. They said I brought it on myself." My chest twists uncomfortably at the memory of my dad hanging up on me. The only other person who knows this story is Liam. "And that's when I met Liam. I joined his rugby club because they needed coaches and I needed to get my shit together. I got the date tattooed on my ribs as a reminder that things can change. And the rest, as they say..."

"...is history." Nora smiles, but it's not her bright, happy one. It's laced with emotion this time. "I'm sorry. I don't know exactly what it's like to have parents who don't support you. But Jess, she went through a lot when we were growing up, so I have *some* experience and I know it's not easy." She takes my hand and squeezes it. My throat clamming up at her kindness. I'm never this eager to share, let alone have someone console me.

I clear the log stuck in my throat. "It's all good. I'm happy. I've built a life I'm proud of. I've learned that having fun and living is better than being bitter, so I keep everything casual in my life. It's easier that way." I trail off, realising that maybe I do want more from my life. Maybe I want to show Nora I can be more, too. If not for me, then for her. She stirs something inside me that makes me *feel*. But all of this talk feels far too heavy for a karaoke bar, so I change the subject. "What about you? I know why you're doing the list, but what's your end goal? If you have one at all."

She ponders for a minute. "I think I'm fed up with being the one who is predictable and reliable. I wanted to experience life properly, without reservations. I don't want to be married with kids and look back and think 'I wish I'd done that,' so here we are."

I shiver inwardly at her mention of marriage. "You want the whole married, 2.5 kids life?"

She nods but doesn't seem fully committed to the nod. "Eventually, I think, maybe. Do you?"

"No," I say a little too forcefully. Nora flinches, recovering quickly with an empty smile. "Like I said, I spent too long witnessing my parents' unhappy life to know that marriage, commitment, it isn't for me. I haven't been with anyone to consider kids either."

"Okay… I understand that," she says nodding her head and tucking her hands into her lap. I wonder if she's trying to use her therapist skills to assess me, but frankly, it doesn't matter. She won't change my mind.

We sit in silence, as another person absolutely destroys "Summer of '69" on the stage. When they hit a bum note, which is a lot, Nora's hand flies to her mouth and she chuckles to herself. Then a few others take on Justin Bieber, Miley Cyrus, and of course, Queen… none of them can sing but it's barely them I'm watching because Nora's hand migrates to my knee when she finds someone *really* funny to watch and she squeezes lightly.

"Don't you think it's a little weird?" she asks during a lull in our entertainment, finishing the conversation she was clearly having in her own head.

"What's weird?" I reply, watching her as she removes her hand and goes in for another lick of the salt around her second margarita. I'm doing what I can to ignore the heat pulsing through my body as she licks the crystals from her lips, but it's pretty futile honestly. *I'm never buying her a margarita again.*

"I've barely made a snarky comment at you all afternoon. It's making me twitchy."

I bellow a laugh. "I'm sure you're saving them all for another day."

"Of course I am." She winks as she stands to walk to the stage, her newfound confidence oozing from her makes me smile as I watch her walk away. She stands on that stage like it was made for her, the spotlight casting onto her dark hair making it look an even deeper shade.

She wraps her fingers around the microphone and nods to whoever is orchestrating this place like it's her own personal concert. The smile that breaks over me is all consuming, pinging joy in my chest. When the strumming of a guitar filters into the speakers, I instantly recognise the song by Sixpence None the Richer. What I don't expect is Nora's eyes to be trained onto mine when her voice sings the first line of "Kiss me". Her voice isn't perfect, it wobbles with nerves as she quietly sings.

My body leans forward as I prop my elbows onto the table. Okay, her singing is... it's awful. Truly awful. But can I look away? Not even a little bit. I watch her sway naturally to the music and sing her way through the entire song as though she's singing just for me. But I know she's doing it for her and that makes it so much sweeter.

She doesn't care that she can't sing that well, she's doing it, and owning it. Pride swells in my chest for the umpteenth time today. Nothing else exists for me outside of her in this moment. Even the imperfections in her voice have me fucking drooling over her. *Who the fuck am I and what am I doing?* One minute I'm freaking out about marriage and the next I'm falling into her orbit like a love sick fool.

The song finishes and Nora does this cute little bow that just makes her more adorable. When she stands, her shoulder length hair has flopped into her face, and as she pushes it out of her eyes, my heart somersaults. Her smile is big and beautiful, on display for everyone to see how proud she is of herself.

I'm on my feet, wolf whistling for her at the top of my lungs. As she gets closer to me, I close the gap quicker and hug her, lifting her small frame off the floor. It isn't until I hear her grumble that I put her down. "Sorry, did you say something?" I ask.

She straightens her hair and jumper, then looks up at me. "Just that you were squashing me. I'm only tiny and you're... well, you're strong," she says as she pats my biceps. A deep pink creeps into her cheeks as she talks.

"You know that was the most incredible thing I've ever heard," I say as we walk back to sit at our table.

"You're a terrible liar, Grayson."

"Not lying, I swear. Liam's singing is awful, which I tell him every time he tries to sing at work."

She chuckles, her shoulders bouncing with the movement, "Oh God, he is awful, isn't he? Cats have more tune than he does."

I nod. "But you... I like you," I reply without realising what I'm saying. My cheeks flame instantly.

"You what?" Nora gawks.

"I mean I liked *it*. Your performance. It was great," I say quickly, trying to recover my faux pas. *Should I have just left it and owned it?*

That sweet pink is colouring her cheeks again as she dips her head, pushing her hair behind her ear. "Thank you."

"So, do you have another song in you?" I ask, hoping that she doesn't pry more into my reckless words.

"I don't think so. But I like it here. Can we stay for a while?"

I nod my head and rest my arm around her chair, pulling her closer. "We can stay."

Something pings in my chest, then warms, spreading over me like a comforting blanket. I shake my head, hoping it's just the beer giving me a buzz.

Hours have passed, and it happened in the blink of an eye. The bar quietened after our karaoke session. but neither of us want to move and end up talking about everything and nothing for another few hours. I've learned that she likes crossword puzzles and board games; she broke her arm in two places when she was younger when she fell off her bike; she has insanely high standards for herself and thrives off helping others, hence her being so good at her job. She loves reading romance books because she likes to escape into fictional worlds. Honestly, I feel like I know so much more about her. She might be competitive like I thought, but it comes from a place of perfectionism, and she is far more creative than she gives herself credit for, too. But what surprised me the most is how easily she's opened up to me. It's refreshing. Earlier I thought it was the drink making her more relaxed but we've since switched to water so I'm beginning to think it's that she's comfortable with me.

Just as the happy hour evening starts to get busy, my stomach grumbles. "Wanna go grab more food?"

"God yes, I'm starving again."

We both stand and instinctively I reach for her hand. I'm not sure why I did it, but I felt like I needed to hold her hand and when she squeezes it back, I feel that zing everywhere again.

When we step outside the bar, it's dusk and I know exactly where I want to take Nora. "You like sushi?"

"I love sushi," she replies with a pep in her step.

Her mood is high and infectious, and I'm right there with her. Enjoying this day together.

When we arrive back at Nora's house, she slips off my bike, and I feel a pang of emptiness against my back. I pull off my helmet and run my hands through my hair, ruffling it up.

She removes her own helmet and holds it in her hands as her feet shift on the concrete, her gaze downcast. "I'm really grateful for everything you've done for me today." Her eyes tentatively find mine and there's that honesty again that she's been blinding me with all night. "I mean it. I never would've done any of it if it wasn't for you."

The look in her eyes makes it hard to look away. Emotion swirls in her irises and I'm mesmerised. The way she chews her bottom lip makes me want to take it between my own teeth. The way her body shifts from side to side makes me want to pull her into me and calm all her nerves. But it's more than that. There's something changing, a warmth building inside me every time I'm near her and it won't go away. It makes me wonder if my parents were ever in love and if so, did they feel like this? I get this overwhelming feeling, like I have to touch her.

But I don't. Because we're... friends.

"I had a great day," I tell her honestly, suddenly feeling nerves fluttering inside my stomach. *Well, this is new.* I'm not a nervous guy at all.

"Me too."

The fresh air around us is now heavy with whatever seems to be rippling between us. The urge to kiss her is overwhelming, but I'm frozen in place, not sure if she would want that. Based on every conversation we've had about the non-existent 'us', I'd say no.

"Well goodnight, Grayson." She smiles as she turns towards her house. When her hand touches the door handle, she spins back around, and my heart skips a beat. "Hey, what song would you have picked for karaoke?"

I smile, scuffing my shoes against the floor. "Livin' On a Prayer. Without a shadow of a doubt."

Her smile radiates off her, the gold in her eyes flickering against the streetlights making her look like she's lit from within. That smile is the fuel that runs in my veins because she doesn't give it out very easily, but it slays me whenever she offers it to me. Which has been more than a few times today. She turns back towards the door, and I realise I need to stop her.

"Hey, Nora?"

"Yeah?" Her voice is soft as she lifts her head, turning to look over her shoulder.

I take the few steps towards her, revelling in the way her sweet scent filters around me as I get closer. "I've got one more question for you," I murmur, knowing that she's technically still obliged to say yes. It's not even close to midnight, but seeing as though the last time this happened, I sprung it on her without asking, I definitely need to ask this time.

Looking down on her, I move my hand to thread into her hair at the nape of her neck tilting her head up towards me. I let time tick by, watching the way her breathing shallows and her pulse quickens against the soft skin of her exposed neck. My little pocket rocket is turned on. I can tell by the way her pupils are blown and how her palms, that have lifted to my chest, fist the material of my shirt. I wonder if she's even realised she's touching me right now.

"Would you let me kiss you?" I whisper, so close now that she can probably feel the warmth of my breath dusting against her lips. I'm probably overstepping, but I have to ask. I need to hear her answer.

Heat prickles through my body while I wait for her reply. It's heady and intoxicating and makes me want more.

"Yes." She breathes. The way my body goes from hot to boiling has me wanting to shed my layers of clothes right here with her. Right now, I don't care if she's saying yes because of the day we've had, or if she really means it. I need to kiss her. I want to possess her, claim her, and make her mine, even if it's just for the next few minutes. I clasp some hair at the base of her neck into my resting hand and lean closer to her perfect pink lips, like an addict desperate for a taste, I feel like I need her more than oxygen. My tongue dips out to wet my bottom lip and I move towards her, her breath catching in her throat.

She closes the last sliver of distance between us and presses her lips to mine. It's soft and gentle. Everything about it has me wanting more. I pull her closer to me, our bodies flush together as I cover her body with mine, completely and deepening the kiss. I lick a hot line across her bottom lip and take my time. If this is a moment of weakness with her then I'm going to savour it. Leisurely, I move our mouths together. She's warm and tastes exactly how I remember, sweet and delicious. The tips of our tongues brush against each other again and again as heat spirals around my body.

I break the kiss, rubbing my nose against hers and taking a moment to look at her. Her face relaxed, the ghost of a smile covering her lips, her eyes closed in bliss. She's breathtaking. My lips tingle, desperate to connect with hers again. So, I do. I press against her mouth again and I feel her lips tip upwards in a smile. I'm in heaven. I roll my hips towards her and push my tongue into her hot mouth, urging hers out too so I can suck on it.

Her arms loop around my neck and I groan inwardly. She's getting confident with her kiss now, diving in to take my lips the way she wants, the way I want her to. Her lips are greedy and I'm so fucking here for it. This kiss is making me lose all function and be taken over by the throbbing in my chest and my cock.

We kiss until we're both breathless and pawing at each other's clothes, out here in the street. Reality slams into me like a freight train; we could've easily been caught by Jess or Liam, and I know that's something Nora didn't want.

I place one more chaste kiss on her lips and forcibly move away from her. Everything in my body is screaming to move closer to her again, but I can't. That's it. One kiss on her yes day.

"Goodnight, Nora."

She stares at me for a beat, assessing me – trying to read me. I'm not sure I could even tell her what I'm feeling right now, because I don't even know.

"Goodnight, Grayson."

Chapter 15

Grayson

06:00am

I stare at my clock as it blinks at me, mocking me, while I wonder why time is moving so slowly this morning. I've been awake since 5am. I woke covered in sweat, vivid memories playing on my mind. My parents' arguments sometimes echo in my subconscious and cause me stress. Usually I can ignore them, but something has been bothering me the last couple of weeks, which has made them harder to ignore.

Sleep hasn't always been easy for me, my mind always racing, trying to keep itself busy. It's been two weeks since the yes day with Nora and every time I close my eyes I can see her on that stage, sitting in that tattoo chair gripping onto my hand, wrapping her arms around my chest as I speed off on my bike, looking up at me on her doorstep, lips parted, ready to kiss me again and fuck, it's messing with my head. I needed space to remind myself that we're only friends. Luckily work has been crazy busy, but we've barely spoken and it's for the best. Except I have to see her today.

I decide to stop my whirling thoughts by sweating them out in the gym.

I push my body hard, relishing in the burn. This is when I feel my best; I know my body's limits and I know how far I can push myself. It's why I liked fighting so much. Having this control over my body makes me feel like I have control in my life; even when everything is spiralling out of control like it is right now.

After a solid forty-five-minute session, I shower and dress and glance at my watch—07:30am I've got just enough time to get across town to Liam's house to collect a memory stick he needs a document from while he's away this week.

I pull up outside the house, switching off the bike's engine before hopping off, and carrying my helmet in my hand to the front door. When I knock twice, I notice that my palms are clammy and I'm suddenly very aware that I could've sent Liam's assistant, but my brain and my cock were having a battle and my brain did not win. When I texted Nora last night letting her know I'd be popping in quickly to get something for Liam, I tried to play it cool by telling her she should make me pancakes, but in reality, the last two weeks of not seeing her have been weird, so I wanted an excuse to stay for longer.

Fuck, I'm nervous.

The door opens, revealing Nora in a tight black dress. It's not low cut or short, but it hugs every single one of her curves and makes her body look like an hourglass. I swallow hard, willing my body to calm down and hoping that she doesn't notice. She's so fucking sexy, and beautiful, and... *fucking hell man, get a grip already.*

"Hi, come in." She hobbles with one shoe on and one off through the house. I'm stuck in some sort of limbo with my brain and my cock again, but thankfully my brain wins this time and I use it to make my feet move one foot in front of the other, schooling my expression as I walk into her hallway.

Nora still hops around like a Duracell bunny as my brows pull together and I wave my finger in the air, gesturing to her. "What's happening right now?"

She stops and laughs. "Oh, I um, I put these shoes on to make sure they matched my outfit. I travel in my trainers, but I always need to check my heels for when I put them on at work and now the stupid buckle is stuck." She hops again and I try to be some semblance of a gentleman here and not look at her boobs as they bounce around.

"Okay, stop." She actually listens, which is a first. "Let me help. You're making me seasick with all the jumping around."

I drop to my knees, holding her shoe in one hand when she chuckles above me. "I never thought I'd see you on your knees for me this early in the morning, Grayson."

The silence between us is thunderous, the air switching from fresh to completely charged with pure energy in an instant. An eternity passes with my hand resting on her ankle. I daren't look up and I can't even focus on unbuckling the shoe that started all of this. I'm too busy trying to understand what is going on right now after hearing that sentence and everything it implies.

All I can hear is the thumping of my heart in my ears, well, and in my crotch, because boy, has he been woken up. I shake my head and force myself to focus on the shoe. It's black and strappy and that's about as far as I get because my brain is doing everything to distract from her perfectly milky skin under my fingers.

By some miracle, my fingers work to loosen the buckle and the shoe lingers between us like some kind of barrier. If I move the shoe, I have to look at her and I can't. I know I'll find her looking down at me and seeing her with any kind of desire or want will break me. I've spent too many moments thinking about how fucking delicious she tasted that night and how badly I've wanted to be on my knees for her again. That night has been on replay for months, evidently because I still haven't been with anyone else.

Nora wiggles her toes and kicks the shoe aside, removing the barrier between us, waking me from my stupefied state. Still holding her ankle, I move it to my chest and flatten her foot against me. The whimper that escapes her mouth fills the space between us like a drug I need more of.

I let my fingertips feather touches around her ankle and calf as her foot shakes slightly against me. Memories of that night we spent together feel like they happened just seconds ago. Her taste, her smell, her pussy wrapped around my dick so perfectly; they all come barrelling back into my brain. *Fuck...* I can't stop my hand as it travels up her leg until I reach the spot of skin just behind her knee. It's like silk, so fucking soft.

A groan crawls from the core of me, fuelled by my desire. I chance a quick glance up to her face, only to find her eyes burning into me. Full of something dark and tempting. Between that look and the soft whimpering noises she's making, I'm fighting not to drown myself between her thighs right now.

"Your shoe is off," I say quietly, but I don't move from beneath her. Our eyes still locked, tension buzzing like a wayward firework about to combust. Her head dips in a slight nod as her throat swallows thickly. It would be so easy to cross a line here again. I don't know if it *should* happen and believe me, I fucking hate myself for even debating this shouldn't happen. We agreed once, and that has stuck with both of us, except for my mishap in the lift and our 'yes day'.

But the thought of having her again haunts me. We could so easily let something happen, and Nora hasn't stopped me yet.

Does she want this to go further?

I drag my palm higher over her thigh, loving the hitch in her breath that makes my hard cock pulse with need. I move all the way to the top of her creamy thigh until my hand is covered by her dress. Her whole body quivers, her knees almost buckling under my touch, but she doesn't break my gaze, her big caramel and chocolate eyes drinking me in, bowing before her.

The heat pulsing from her is like sitting in front of an open fire, one that I can't help but let myself want to be consumed by her warmth. If I moved my thumb an inch to the right, I would be touching her underwear. I could slip my finger inside her panties. *I wonder if she's wet?* The thought consumes me, so much so it must be written all over my face, because Nora says,

"Do it. I dare you." Her eyes are glossy with desire, her voice a soft, throaty whisper.

She pulls in her bottom lip between her teeth, passion shining in her eyes, daring me to take what she's offering.

I squeeze her thigh, marking her with my fingertips, and she whimpers softly. I close my eyes, revelling in her sounds, ones that are branded into my memory. As I exhale slowly, blood rushes south again, my cock weeping inside my tight trousers.

Fuck it. My rubber band of control snaps.

I grip the edge of her panties and tear them down her luscious legs in one swooping motion. Her gasp fills the room, and my cock leaps at the sound. She steps out of them, and I pick them up, shoving them in my pocket as a memento for later.

Her mouth parts, her breathing and her cheeks flush. This is it, the moment I leap across that invisible line between us, and I couldn't fucking stop myself, even if I wanted to.

I stand quickly, crowd my chest to Nora's, forcing her backwards a few steps until her back hits the hallway wall. I sink to my knees again and push her dress up, exposing her sex. Groaning when I see her bare folds that I've dreamed about touching again for months.

I can smell her arousal; sweet, musky, intoxicating, and I know I have to taste her again. I lean in closer, letting my two-day old stubble brush the inside of her thigh.

"Fuck me. I forgot that you're such a pretty girl," I say directly to her pussy. A moan escapes her as her hips roll and her thighs begin to shake, silently begging me to touch her.

I look up from between her thighs, loving how wrecked she looks already, and I've not even started yet. "Do you want me to fuck you with my tongue and fingers, Nora?" She nods, flushing everywhere I can see skin. Feeling desperate, my mouth is on her. Licking through her pink lips, finding her clit hard, waiting for my tongue. She tastes exactly how I remember, like fucking heaven. And like a drug, I need more.

Lifting her leg over my shoulder, I spread her wide, giving me better access before I grip her hip and pull her into me. Driving my tongue into her sex, I almost lose it as her sweet flavour coats me. My cock pulsing in my trousers as I eat her as greedily, starved of her. "Fuck, that's good," I pant breathlessly as I remove my tongue and replace it with two fingers.

She cries out from the intrusion, but when her hips buck against my fingers, her walls grip me like a vice tells me how much she wants this.

She's so fucking tight, my cock turns to steel, pleading to be inside her. He remembers everything about Nora Scott and he's desperate right now.

"More." She purrs and pulls my hair as I get a glimmer of déjà vu that I love. Goosebumps scatter across my neck and a guttural groan leaves my mouth as I push another finger inside her, twisting and curving them to find that sweet spot for her.

"You like that," I say pumping my fingers in and out of her once, twice, before closing my mouth over her clit, sucking hard. My fingers continue pumping inside of her as my teeth graze her clit. Her hands raking through my hair, her hips moving in time with my fingers and my tongue. It's a fucking symphony of pleasure crescendoing when she screams my name. My balls tighten and I pray that I'm not going to give it up just yet.

"Grayson, I'm going to come. Fuck, fuck, fuck." Her fist raises to her mouth, and she bites down as her pussy soaks my hand.

It is the hottest fucking thing I've ever seen. Her hips buck slowly as she rides the remaining waves of her high, leaving her rosy and panting. It's making me harder seeing how affected she is by me. I slowly remove my fingers as she lets out a quiet whimper—a sound that I quickly realise that I'm desperate for more of. Raising one finger to my mouth, I suck hard. Her gaze darkens as she watches my tongue swirl, committing her taste to memory and enjoying every fucking second of it.

I stand, humming in appreciation, moving closer to her face. "You are fucking sweet as sin, and I could eat you every day." I raise my other finger, still drenched in her arousal, and place it against her pouty lips. "Open up for me, shorty."

She doesn't hesitate, her lips open as she grips my hand and sucks so hard it has me almost barrelling over with desperation. "Fuck, Nora. That mouth. I want it. I need it." My voice doesn't sound like my own. It's raspy and fucking laced with untamed arousal for her. Unable to hold back, I remove my finger and pull her towards my lips. She dives in passionately, her tongue pushing into my mouth, frantic for a taste.

God, I've missed this. I've missed her.

My hands fist her hair, tilting her head so I can access her neck. Breaking our kiss, I lick from her collarbone all the way to her ear. When I bite her, her whole body curls around me like a snake and I whisper, "so fucking sweet."

I push my aching cock, still tenting my trousers, against her pussy, squeezing her arse removing any space between our hips. "Feel what you do to me. I'm so hard for you, Nora. I swear I've been hard for months without you." Her body ripples into mine, curving perfectly against me, as if she's telling me that she likes that I'm desperate for her. *Fuck, I like it too.*

I move my hands to her throat, and she swallows like the good girl she is. I feel every muscle contract against my palm and my dick aches with need. What I'd do for that feeling around my length again, swallowing, choking, taking all of me. "You're so fucking sexy," I rasp.

"You going to let me touch you, ponyboy?" Her voice is like treacle as her words pour over my skin.

"Take what you want, shorty." I release her and step back ever so slightly, letting her have control.

She gleams in front of me as she undoes my trousers and reaches in to stroke me, rubbing my tip before squeezing everything so tightly I can barely see straight.

"Fuck, yesssss, but carry on doing that and this'll be over very quickly." I rasp, but she just rolls her bottom lip between her teeth like a temptress. She's going to bring me to my knees, and I'm here for it.

Her hand pumps slowly up and down my shaft, her perfect touch soft against my shaft. I latch onto her neck and suck hard, not caring if I leave a mark because, fuck, I want to mark her until she's branded with me. Beads of precum leak onto her hand and she rubs them with her thumb, spreading it down my length, making me slick as she increases her movements.

"Fuuuuuuuuuuuck," I hiss. Her hand working me faster and faster, the tell tale sign of my orgasm creeping up my spine.

I think I let out a choke or a groan, but I can't be sure because Nora leans forward and purrs into my ear as she nibbles my earlobe. "I want you to come for me, thinking of me, tasting me on your tongue."

I'm fucking dead.

Call an ambulance. Call the funeral home. I'm fucking done.

Nora sinks to her knees and the sight is enough to have my balls drawing up, ready to explode. When she licks over my tip and sinks down my length, pushing me to the back of her throat, tingles explode all over my body. "Holy fuck." My eyes close, rolling back in my head, as I drown in the feeling of her contracting around me. Her hand is still holding the base of me as she slowly and tortuously drags her lips to my tip and then sucks me harder, hollowing her cheeks. I open my eyes to watch her. She looks so beautiful on her knees whilst her eyes water, struggling to take all of me.

Jesus, I'm barely holding on.

My jaw goes slack as a tingle begins to build in my balls. "Fuck, keep doing that," I force out as she twirls around my tip and then licks up my length, pushing me to the edge. She moves her hands to grab my arse and deep throats me again and a white hot heat zaps through me. My body clenches and I grip her hair as I empty myself down her throat with a roar.

"Fuuuuuck, Nora. Jesus," I pant, barely able to keep myself upright.

Fuck me. Two pump chump. I blame the vixen staring at me, pupils blown to shit, licking her lips that are smeared with my cum.

I pull her up into me, desperate to taste her again. My tongue dives into her mouth roughly, devouring her, tasting my release on her tongue. Our kiss is frantic, teeth clashing, tongues swiping for dominance, chests heaving together. I could go again because this woman makes me crazy for her, but I slow the kiss down to soft brushes of our lips and pull back slightly.

"No pancakes then?" I smirk against her mouth.

"You're unbelievable," she scowls playfully at me, pushing me away.

"Never thought I'd hear you admit that." I wink, before I look down at the dishevelled state of us. "Shower with me?"

Her smile falters as she looks away, awkwardness blanketing her. "Oh, I'm going to be late for work. I have to get going. I'll wash up in the other bathroom down here and leave the key for you to lock up. Just put it in the lock box outside when you leave."

I shift, suddenly feeling a jolt of cool air. "Right. Yeah. Okay. I'll head up." I pad up the stairs and turn to watch her from a distance.

Unaware I'm watching, she twists her hair in her fingers, hesitating, unsure of what to do next, the total opposite of how she was only minutes ago with me.

I have no idea what's next; I hadn't expected any of this to happen between us, but I know that Nora is not going to get away from me after that. Nothing is going to stop me going after Nora Scott now.

Chapter 16

Nora

*R*ight foot, left foot, right foot, left foot, right foot... I pace around the kitchen, checking I've not forgotten how to walk because Grayson King just straight up made me weak in the knees.

It all happened so fast. One minute my shoe was on my foot, and the next, I was daring him to touch me, and he was buried between my legs using his, oh God, his tongue. Yep, I definitely have goosebumps right now. In fact, I have goo-Grayson-umps because he owns every single shiver that exploded on my skin. The fact that I'm making up words tells me I've lost my mind. I must have. I mean, why else would I play with Grayson King?

I don't know what came over me. This has happened twice now and now I need to have the awkward talk where he tells me that he doesn't want to date, but I do and so this'll never work... blah blah blah.

Whenever I'm with him, I feel this sense of bravado, or maybe it's just me not wanting to back down to his banter. But when he looked at me, on his knees, silently questioning if he should move his hand higher, my body craved him. I dared him because I needed it. I *needed* to be touched. By him. God, it was so much easier when we were staying out of each other's way. No list, no sex, no sexy hallway encounters. I don't know what's going on or if I should feel this giddy about it. I've lost all that confidence I had in the hall and I'm pacing, flapping around like a headless chicken. No post high haze over here, just panic and confusion.

"I thought you'd be gone already; you left the key, so I assumed." I startle at his sudden presence. *God, how long have I been pacing?*

But I instantly warm at his voice. It's so deep and gravely and makes my lower belly tremble. When I spin to face him, his black shirt is undone, showing me those perfectly carved abs and his tattoos again. Seriously, I didn't think I'd have a thing for a guy with tattoos, mainly because most guys I've dated haven't had any. But Grayson's tattoos and muscles and hair. He screams *bad idea,* but looks like he'd make sure you had a smile on your face whilst doing said *bad ideas.*

Not knowing exactly what to say, or how to say what I planned, I flatten my hands over my dress. "Oh yeah, I um, needed to check something." *I checked nothing.* My wild brown eyes meet his cool, icy ones. God, songs could be written about the ice in his eyes. "You look great. Are you great? I'm great... great." *Nora, shut up. .*

Grayson chuckles, crowding into my space. He bends his head to reach my mouth but doesn't move closer, even though my body is once again betraying me and desperate for the enemy. "You're fucking smoking when you come, but you're adorable when you're nervous," he whispers, and the words pulse over my skin. He runs his nose against mine just centimetres from my lips, making my knees wobble for the second time today.

I place my hands on his chest and push him back, closing my eyes and taking in a deep breath. "You're confusing me. I know you're just trying to get me hot and bothered again."

"Is it that obvious?" he muses.

Before I can think, move, or breathe. Grayson has grabbed me and is kissing me like he's never going to kiss me again. It's short, but Jesus, it's winded me enough to make me pant like a dog in heat. And at this point, I think I might be.

"I wanted to kiss you again, so I just did it. See how that works? Impulse, action," he says so calmly, like this is all very normal, and the world isn't turned upside down right now.

I'm still panting.

"What are we... did we... should we? Christ, I think I've forgotten every word in the English language." I've got a way with words when I'm flustered. It doesn't happen often, but when it does, I tend to spectacularly lose the ability to speak.

He grins at me proudly. "I make you speechless? Aw shorty, you flatter me."

"Oh, God. Stop talking," I moan and bury my head into his chest, basking for a second in his scent, which has changed because now he smells like me – he must have used my shower gel. The combination of his usual masculine scent and my sweet cupcake shower gel – yes, I'm obsessed with smelling like cupcakes at nearly 27 – is sending me over the edge. I'm a little hot and ragey inside because that stuff is expensive but then smelling it on him is a whole new sensory experience. One that makes my brain think he's mine because he smells like me. *God, I need to stop reading that paranormal romance book, fated mates and imprinting is for fiction, Nora. Get a grip.*

"Hmm, I like it when you moan like that." He bends to kiss my neck and as his cool lips make contact with my hot skin, the earlier annoyance dissipates in mere seconds.

Those insane goo-Grayson-umps are back and tempting me to be weak again. Yeah, I've lost my mind.

"Was that better than okay this time?" Grayson asks with a smirk, but I can hear a little vulnerability in his voice. He damn well knows it was better than okay. I open my mouth to respond when he interrupts me, placing his finger over my lips. "Will you leave me an expert review on Google? Riveting tongue action. Excellent length and girth? Made me come harder than I ever have? 15/10, would recommend."

He removes his fingers and I roll my lips over my teeth, stifling a chuckle. "Riveting tongue action?"

"Don't tell me you didn't enjoy that." He buries his head into my hair again, something I'm realising he likes to do, and caresses my neck with his mouth, reminding me what he did minutes before with that tongue.

"Okay, okay, review is pending but now, I have to go to work, and you need to be elsewhere, not making me feel flutters in my vagina anymore. Key is here." I back away from his embrace and slam the key onto the table, not able to look at him again. "Bye, Grayson."

I hear him call out after I left the room. "You forgot your knickers." My eyes squeeze shut. My fucking knickers, the ones he took off and stuffed into his pocket.

I'm a little mortified, and a lot turned on. "Okay, no worries," I yell as I stomp out of my kitchen. *Fucking okay, no worries?* Like he was just telling me he'll be home late, and not that he's holding my underwear hostage.

I bolt like I've never bolted before. Olympic athletes got nothing on me, especially since I look down and realise I'm wearing my heels. I *know* that my feet are going to be on fire later... just like my vagina is right now.

I text the only person who might understand my brand of crazy right now.

Me: SOS I've lost my mind.

Zoey: Tell me everything. This is about a guy, right? Wait, I need to see your face. Meet me for lunch at the café across the street from your office.

Me: Oh God, it's so bad, Zo. So bad.

Zoey: Stop teasing me! Tell me later. xo

I casually walk into my office and pretend that I can't feel my heart beating in my feet. My stubbornness has cost me today because I flat out refused to go back into my house to get my trainers and my knickers. Yep, that's right, I'm commando, in heels – at work. Fuck my life.

"Miss Scott, I just had a call from Ella's mother, and she is going to be five or ten minutes late to the session today." Jo, the receptionist for our side of the office, tells me. She's a lovely lady and I'm trying to not snap at her because my feet are not her problem, and neither is a client being late.

"Thanks, Jo." I stumble into my office and immediately take off my shoes. Breathe in, breathe out.

That's better.

My working morning flies by relatively quickly. Ella was late and only ended up scowling at me for twenty minutes instead of her usual forty, but that's fine with me.

I'm on my way to meet Zoey because I need to talk to someone about what happened this morning. As I walk into the café, I'm immediately hit with the fresh smell of coffee and freshly baked cakes. I see Zoey sitting by the window, her almost white hair blanching in the sunshine.

"Nora! Sit, sit. I ordered us both the chicken salad and a flat white because I don't want to waste any time. Tell me everything."

I sit opposite her, my salad already waiting for me on the table, briefly checking around the coffee shop in case there's anyone I know. It's quiet though; a few elderly people mumbling together on the other side of the shop.

"Okay, so I did something. Something bad... with Grayson."

"Wait, Liam's friend Grayson? The one who was at the picnic last year. The really hot, tattooed guy?"

I nod sheepishly.

"Oooh, when you say *bad*, how bad are we talking?"

"I maybe let him, um..." My mouth dries at the thought of admitting what happened. "Well actually, if I'm going to tell you..."

"Spit it out. I'm ageing here," she pushes.

I hold my breath and blurt out, "He came over this morning to grab something for Liam, but my shoe was stuck, and he got on his knees to help me, and I blurted something rude out, and the next thing I know, his tongue was between my legs."

And breathe.

Zoey's mouth falls open. Wide open. And she doesn't say a word. I don't think I've ever seen her shocked or speechless. This is the girl who talks her way into any nightclub. The girl who picks up men with a look. And I've broken her.

I twirl my fingers in my lap, but it doesn't help with my nerves, so I just continue, "that's not all."

"It's not?" She's yelling now. The elderly couple sitting across from us glare, and I feel my cheeks turn a fetching shade of magenta.

"No... I might have also made him, I mean he definitely, we, umm..."

"Jesus, Nora, if it's this hard to talk about it, how did you actually do it?"

I huff, burying my head in my hands, dropping my voice to a whisper; something Zoey is incapable of doing. "I also gave him a happy ending too... in my hallway." *Seriously though, what the hell is wrong with me?*

"With your mouth or your hand?"

"Um, both?"

"Fuck me, Nora. Happy early Valentine's Day to you!"

I nod, then wince before picking up my fork and aggressively stabbing my chicken salad. "Also..."

Zoey waits on bated breath for me to continue.

"This isn't the first time this has happened. We... may have slept together at the end of last year, too."

"You fucked him already?!" Zoey shrieks to a level only dogs can hear, turning all the attention to me. *Great.*

"Zoey, Sshhhhh," I hiss as I glance around. Lowering my voice, I begin, "Now I don't know what the hell to do. I mean, we'll see each other because of Jess and Liam, but now it's weird because we have no rules or boundaries." I take a breath. "And apparently, I cannot control myself around him, and that is *not* a good thing." I shove some chicken and tomatoes into my mouth, stress eating at its finest.

"Bet you didn't think it was bad this morning," she sniggers.

I playfully swat at her. "Stop. Please. I'm mortified." The waitress appears at the perfect time with our coffee, distracting Zoey from asking more questions for at least three seconds.

Zoey blows on her coffee as her brows meet. "Wait, you said you blurted something rude out. What was it?"

I'd hoped she wouldn't ask. I close one eye with a cringe because, if I look at her whilst I admit what I said, I might spontaneously combust from embarrassment. "Something about me being surprised he is on his knees for me."

Zoey's cackle attracts even more unwanted attention. "I'm sorry, but that is genius. Girl, you're a dark horse." Zoey is practically shouting whilst still laughing and I sit across from her, wishing the ground would swallow me up. "But I don't see what the problem is," she adds.

"The problem is that Grayson is Liam's best friend. He is not someone I *should* be interested in. He told me himself he doesn't do relationships, and great, good for him, but I want one. Plus, if we did get together, and it doesn't work out, it will make everything awkward because he'll still work for Liam and be his best friend. Oh and, if Jess and Liam find out, they'll be planning our wedding before we can even figure out *what* we are. God, we aren't anything. I don't even know why I'm entertaining this." I fan my face, suddenly feeling incredibly flustered.

"Nora, sweetie. I think you deserve to put yourself first right now and not think about how it might affect other people. Have some fun with him, fuck around, and damn the consequences. Isn't that the point of the list?" She bites into her salad. I can't do the same because I've lost my appetite. How can I fuck around with him? I don't know how to fuck around for one and two. It's Grayson. He won't be the one crying when it ends. It'll be me.

Zoey's attitude to everything in life is 'do now, ask questions later' and whilst that might work for her, I've never been able to do that even though I've been trying. But can I also be around Grayson and not want to touch him again? And not get jealous when he has other girls in his bed? Do I even like him like that? I'm not sure. I've seen there is more to him, he cares more than he lets on, but also I'm confused between lust and like. I like his tongue and his ability to make me come, but is that it? Despite not seeing him for two weeks before this morning, I had been thinking about him. A lot.

"You're thinking really loudly. Talk," Zoey demands as she sips her coffee. I've known Zoey since we were in school, so this really shouldn't be so difficult to talk about. The thing is, I rarely talk about sex and boys to my friends because I'm so inexperienced. Jess gets the brunt of most of it, and that's because we've lived together forever.

"I don't even know what this is or could be," I admit. "It's weird for me to be even thinking about any of this with him. Before that one night, I could categorically say we didn't like each other; we've spent the last, what, eight months actively taunting each other and being in a state of dislike and banter. I don't understand how any of it happened."

"Babe, there is such a fine line between love and hate, and there's an even finer line between lust and hate. Turns out that line was your G-string this morning." Her tongue pokes out to tease me and I try to not push her face into her salad in retaliation.

"Maybe I should go over tonight to talk to him."

"He asked you over to his house tonight?" Her eyebrows raise.

I shake my head. "No, but maybe it's a good idea to talk."

"So, the whole relationship thing, is he dead set on it? Because I'm willing to bet he would overlook that for you. And then he can fuck you as often as he wants. It's a win-win and the guy clearly wants you." A scoff sounds out from the couple behind me, and I cringe.

"Stop. Please. I'm dying right now."

"Grayson and Nora sitting in a tree F-U-C-K-I-N-G," she sings songs, and I am seconds away from darting out of the café door, away from my incredibly annoying friend.

"That's the x-rated version and you know it."

She shrugs and smiles, then checks her phone. "Shoot, I've got to run. Text me later. If I don't hear from you, I'll assume you're getting railed—See you tomorrow night for the parties too, babe." *The hen party—which I'll see him. Wonderful.*

Chapter 17

Nora

The music pumps through the packed nightclub. We've come to The Point near London's Southbank to meet the boys for the hen/stag party. The whole left side of the club is windows that overlook London city life and the river, near the black sparkling dancefloor. It's probably the most boujee place we've been to in London. And right now, we are being led to the 'private' section of the club.

We've spent the day lazing in the spa at the hotel Jess works at, enjoying massages and naps. We started drinking around lunchtime and haven't stopped since.

After a pit stop at the salon to have our hair done, we came back to the house to get ready. My hair bounces in a blowout and I love it.

The boys from Liam's stag party are trailing behind as a hostess, wearing a black jumpsuit, takes us down a winding staircase to the back of the club. My nerves are heightened knowing Grayson is near me, but I'm actively trying to ignore those feelings right now. Laughter echoes off the walls as we descend. Everyone is happy, and that is all that matters tonight.

The hostess stops us in front of a huge metal door where she swipes a key card. My jaw drops as the door opens, giving us a view of the women performing on the stage; leggy, gorgeous, and half naked. I knew I'd see plenty of flesh tonight, but I guess I hadn't given it *that* much thought.

I cast my eyes over the room. There are dim corners that look empty, but they definitely aren't, I'm guessing from the brief glimpses of skin that peek out from the shadows, it's clients getting private dances. It's weird to be so exposed to this sort of thing. It's like you shouldn't be watching, but you can't stop.

"You fancy giving me one of those, shorty?" Grayson whispers, his voice deep and seductive as he pulls me flush against his chest from behind. "I'd kill to see you grinding on my lap, you know." I suck in as much air as I can because I need to keep my cool around him tonight. Too many assessing eyes.

Somehow, I manage to stop the shallow breathing before it starts, which feels like a lot of effort because his hand is wrapped around my waist, burning a hole through my short, dark green, silky dress. I turn my head slightly so I can see the profile of his face. "Not in a million years, ponyboy," I taunt, then stride away from him but Zoey stops me with a shit-eating smile. She looks straight behind me to where I know Grayson still stands.

"Hey pretty boy, have you seen the new paint job in Nora's hallway?" *Oh god, kill me now. No, second thoughts, kill Zoey.* I tug her arm trying to encourage her away from him, but she won't budge. I *can't* turn around. I *won't* turn around to see his face.

"Can't say I was looking at the paint last time I was in her hallway," he says smugly. Now I want God to kill him too.

"Oh really? Such a shame, I guess that means you'll have to go back and check it out another time."

"Zoey!" I hiss harshly, unable to stop myself.

He steps behind me, his chest grazing my back as he dips his head to my ear. I'm hot all over, like a fever has just struck me. "Let me know if you need help... redecorating any other rooms. I happen to be really good with my hands." *And your tongue and your dick. No, bad girl.*

Zoey laughs maniacally, snapping my eyes to her again. I grab her hand and forcefully yank her away from Grayson this time, ignoring his offer and my rapid heart beating everywhere.

"Girl, he has it bad for you." Zoey says linking our arms.

"He does not," I protest weakly. "Also, what the fuck was that back there?"

"Fun is what it was. You're living in denial if you think you won't go home with that sex God tonight," she giggles as we arrive at the bar, and she orders us all a round of shots.

I can't go home with him tonight. My logical brain won't let me. I'm going home with Jess and Liam to our house. Not Grayson's flat. No way. It was definitely a fling that has flung, and we do not need to fling anything anymore. I just need to tell him that it won't happen again. It doesn't matter how much I might want it to.

Zoey passes me a shot and I down it along with everyone else just before we're shown to a private section with a large booth where several bottles of champagne sit in ice buckets on the low table in the middle.

"The dancers will be out in around ten minutes. If you need anything in particular just flag me down and I'll get it for you," the stunning hostess says before she leaves us. We settle into the sofa. Jess' colleague Kylie and her girlfriend have joined me, Zoey, and Jess. Whilst Liam and Grayson are joined by Zoey's twin brothers, Max and Owen, apparently another guy friend of theirs is coming later too.

As we pour the drinks, we all chat loudly, trying to be heard above the music blaring out, two men without shirts approach the table. One of them, who looks like Channing Tatum, veers off to another table; the second one looks like a sexy Viking. Zoey instantly grips my hand and squeals, "I want them both. At the same time, please and thank you, sir."

I giggle at her confession. They're both gorgeous and ripped, but neither are really doing anything for me. "Hey beautiful, are you the bride?" The Viking comes up to me and immediately traps me against the sofa with his huge arms on either side of my head. I swallow hard, my eyes flicking everywhere but at his naked, oiled chest. When I catch sight of Grayson sitting on the opposite sofa, his jaw is clenched and ticking as he watches our exchange, making me wonder what is going through his head exactly.

"She's the bride," I tell the Viking, pointing to Jess next to me.

"I'll be back for you later then," he murmurs against my ear before moving over towards Jess. I watch Liam's eyes bug out as a scantily clad woman straddles him and Jess is lumbered with the Viking, and I have to stifle a chuckle. They're both in hell and it's very amusing to watch.

More women appear and one of them immediately recognises Grayson. She saunters over to him in her red, barely-there bikini and perfectly curled blonde hair, leans over him, and whispers into his ear. My skin feels hot and itchy, like I want to crawl out of it, as I watch her hand rise up his leg and graze his crotch. He smiles as she talks to him, standing right next to him, practically trying to straddle him, and that's far too close for anyone who needs to have a conversation with someone.

My feet push me to stand before my brain can compute and I'm striding towards the bar, wondering why I was having such a reaction to someone touching my *friend* like that.

Why could I hulk out and drag that girl off him? I can't sit and watch someone else touch him. But why? How have I got myself here? I've gone from a normal, slightly straight edged woman who was determined to keep things platonic between Grayson and me, to possessive and feral, desperate to claim someone who was never mine in the first place.

I flag down the bartender and order a shot of tequila, and that's when I feel *him* behind me. His hot, firm body presses into me deliciously, and his warm scent encases me, trapping me between him and the bar. I'm exhausted by the way my body seems to constantly scream for him. And by exhausted, I really mean keen, desperate, and needy, of course.

His hands rest on either side of me, griping the bar as he lowers his head to my ear and nibbles ever so slightly. My head lolls to the side lazily, giving him more access to my neck. He burrows his nose into my hair and inhales, sending fireworks erupting all over my too-hot skin.

"Jealousy looks good on you, shorty," he hums.

"I'm not jealous," I lie, my voice sounding far too croaky.

"You looked it." He runs his nose up my neck, causing my skin to burn like a bonfire in the wake of his touch.

"Oh yeah? How did it make you feel when that hot guy was all over me?" I have no idea what I'm doing, but I want to see if he was as affected as I was by someone else touching him.

He stiffens slightly, and I know I'm right; we were both jealous. Which is ridiculous, as we've agreed to be 'just friends'. He growls low into my hair, finding my earlobe again and nipping it between his teeth. My knees wobble and I have to grip the edge of the bar to stay upright.

"Grayson..." God, why do I have to be so breathless around him? I'm not exactly sure why I'm saying his name at all. What am I going to say next? We're in public, for goodness' sake. Just as I realise that fact, the fog of him clears in an instant and I slip myself free from his cage. My body is pretty mad at me, but my brain is pretty happy that it won this time.

Wide eyed, Grayson stares at me as he licks his lips, which sends a direct pulse of arousal to my clit. Needy little thing when he's around, it's becoming a problem.

"You can't just say my name like a prayer like you just did and then ignore me all night," he says, finally breaking the spell between us. I straighten, ignore the feelings flooding my body, and finally grab my shot from the bar.

"Watch me," I say, throwing back the tequila before walking away, swaying my hips just a little more than usual because I know... no, I secretly hope he's watching my every step.

When I get back to the VIP area, more dancers are on stage, while Zoey's brothers get their own private show. Zoey pulls me into the seat next to her and laughs.

"Thirty seconds – that's all it took for Liam to push the stripper off his lap and move Jess onto him instead," Zoey says, rolling with laughter. "The poor man looked ailed."

I look over to the other side of the small area, where Jess is still on Liam's lap. It's adorable. She gives me a finger wave and points to Liam, who has a vice grip around her waist, and rolls her eyes playfully. Seriously, this guy shouldn't exist. He ticks all kinds of boxes for a perfect book boyfriend and Jess gets to keep him forever.

"Who is that guy with Grayson?" Zoey says, with a deep growl in her throat. Jess comes to join us on our side as I spin to look at the man she's spotted and Zoey groans. "Real subtle Nor, your head spun faster than the Exorcist."

I look at Zoey and give her a weak smile, silently apologising to her, then look back at the guy she's talking about. "Oh, he's here. I think that's Harrison. He runs an I.T company and I'm pretty sure Grayson brought him in to update all of Liam's office tech," Jess says.

"Well, he is all kinds of delicious. I mean, look at that... ruggedness. I'd climb him like a tree," Zoey practically growls, tipping back the last of her champagne.

"I heard he has a girlfriend," Jess says, glancing over at Harrison too.

"Of course he does. Look at him. Ugh, lucky bitch. Whoever she is."

I look at Harrison again. Grayson is talking animatedly with him at the bar a few feet away. Sure, he's hot, but Grayson is the one who keeps my attention and that annoys me and turns me on too – I'm a mess. I've never had such a reaction to someone before. Maybe it's just physical. The stars have aligned for us to share an insane physical connection, that's all it is.

But what if... my brain clearly wants to play devil's advocate tonight. But what if it isn't?

An hour or so later, I glance over to the dancefloor, and I can just about spot Zoey. She is absolutely trashed. She's debatably had the best time tonight, sweet talking every single hot-blooded male and flirting with bartenders. It's amusing to watch as she sways to the music that is in her head and not the sounds blaring through the speakers right now.

Jess nudges my arm, her sleepy eyes finding mine. "When is my lover boy coming back?" she slurs then hiccups. Jess has had a lot of tequila and a tequila drunk Jess gets soppy and wants snuggles and Liam.

"Soon, sweetheart. He's just in the bathroom." I pat her head as she buries it into my shoulder.

The rest of the party has gone, leaving me Zoey, Grayson, Jess and Liam, and given that it's 1am right now, I don't blame them. Even with my tequila high, I'm sleepy. I honestly don't know where Zoey gets her energy from.

Liam comes back around the corner with a lovesick look in his eyes when he spots Jess. "Oh, my girl," he coos. He bends down to whisper in her ear, and she immediately perks up and throws herself at him.

I hadn't realised that Grayson had sat next to me until he speaks, "It's sickening how perfect they are for one another, right?"

My head turns to find him close... too close. His voice echoes in my bones, vibrating through every nerve I have. He smells so fucking good. Although I was a little weak when I could smell my cupcake soap on him, I can't lie. But his masculine scent is bergamot, with a hint of warmth, and it fills my already dizzy head. His presence is feeding my desperation for him, which is something I'm not proud to admit.

The top two buttons of his black shirt are undone, and I can't help but look at the skin showing. I can see his ink peeking out, begging for me to touch it. But I can't, not here. My skin sizzles with need. I feel like a raging inferno and he's the one who lit the match.

"Yeah, they're adorable." I look back at Jess and Liam, and Jess has her head buried into Liam's neck and he looks happier than a pig in shit. Meanwhile, I swipe away the bead of sweat that is threatening to form on my upper lip from his proximity.

Grayson stretches out his arm, resting on the booth behind me, and scoots closer. Every cell in my body is in a battle with my brain right now. I want him to touch me and I'm pretty sure he knows it, but he's only touching me ever so slightly with his thigh. Teasing me seems to be his speciality.

"How's the ignoring me going?" he asks casually. His finger lazily traces over the thin strap of my dress on my shoulder and down to the skin on my exposed back, and my body is possessed with a shiver so fierce that it forced a noise from my throat instead of letting me form any kind of coherent answer to his question. I glance at Grayson as he stares at me, smirking at exactly the same time as Liam looks over to us, his brows furrowing in a silent question. I jump to my feet, suddenly feeling like I'm fielding a thousand fire ants marching merrily along my skin.

I can't have Grayson touching me right now. I need to get away from him, so I bolt to somewhere I know he can't follow. "I'm going to the bathroom," I shriek, gaining far too much attention than I need to.

After I wash up, I stare at my reflection, psyching myself up for another encounter. *You've got this. You are in charge, not your vagina,* I mutter to myself, running my hands down the front of my dress. As

I walk out of the bathroom, determined to not sit next to Grayson again, I feel an arm tug me into the darkness of the hallway.

The light is dim in here, but enough that I can make him out, more than that though, but I know it's him. I'm immediately hit by his scent. In the darkness, it spreads over my body like smoke, drifting around me, choking me into submission. "Take off your underwear, Nora." His voice is deep, and purrs at me like a fucking tiger, dead set on eating me alive.

I pause, my body stiffening in defiance as I refuse to obey his request, hoping I don't get trapped in this spell he seems to cast over me every bloody time I'm near him.

"Did I stutter? I said take... them... off. Now." His hand squeezes around my wrist, reminding me he's still holding me; the sensation heats my blood to boiling.

Good fucking God. What the fuck am I *supposed* to do? I know I'm *supposed* to push him away. Last year's Nora would've done that, pre-hallway sex Nora had more self-control, but today's Nora can't seem to comply. Today's Nora battles with her vagina and her brain. *And talks to herself in third person, apparently.*

Here in the darkness with Grayson, it feels too easy to sneak a taste of him again, to dip my hand into the snack cupboard and I'm not sure I can stop myself... or if I want to.

"If you don't take them off, I'm going to do it for you, and I won't be gentle. Give me your underwear, Nora. I want them." His words scatter like goosebumps all over my skin and I shiver as I decide if I actually want him to tear them off me. Eventually I obey his request. I lift my dress enough to slip my hand to my hip. My flesh exposed, my eyes flutter closed at the thrill of being caught mixed with the cool air brushing over my exposed skin is intoxicating.

His breath catches on his next intake as if he can smell me, making my eyes fly open to see him. Pushing him to the edge of his control, I pull down my underwear and shimmy it down my thighs, letting it hit my feet. I step sideways, my body grieving the loss of Grayson's heat, but right now, I want nothing more than to tease him.

I hold his eye contact, arching my back so my breasts almost touch his shirt. "You're used to being on your knees for me, right? Pick them up if you want them." I command, biting my lower lip as his eyes dart to where my discarded underwear lies on the floor. His grey eyes flare with arousal and victory sings in my chest.

And I walk off, with a fire in between my legs and a thumping in my chest. Silently questioning who I'm teasing more.

I focus on my feet, carrying me back to my friends, deciding that if I do give in to Grayson, I need a pros and cons list. I like how my resolve has gone from *absolutely not* to *if*.

Jesus, I'm weak.

Okay, so, reasons this is *really* bad idea:

He's Liam's best friend and if we don't work out that could make things awkward.

He's not one for romance; no chocolates and flowers in my future with him (but he'd sure as hell fuck me until I forgot all about romance)

I'm not looking for a quick fuck.

He's insanely hot.

I'm incredibly horny.

He has muscles for days...

Wait, I'm not sure what this list was meant to be anymore. Am I convincing myself or deterring myself? Fuck, I've forgotten.

I decide to find Zoey as I need a distraction. And when I do, she's still absolutely dancing to her own music, and I join her on the dance floor. It doesn't take long for my mind to wander back to Grayson. Realistically, this *is* a bad idea. A very bad one. He's going to break my heart, and that's what puts a stop to all these lusty, naughty thoughts. It won't work. It can't happen. I just need to convince my body, and maybe my brain too. *But remember, you wanted more adventure and to make your life less vanilla.*

I roll my eyes, remembering my list and how much he's helped me already. I run my fingers over the tattoo, thinking about how he's so much more than I thought he was and how much that scares me. The playboy version, I can handle but the sweet, kind version–he leaves me feeling things I don't know what to do with.

I push the thoughts away for now as I move my hips, rolling them to the thumping beat, my body heating with the knowledge that Grayson is the only person who knows I have no knickers on right now.

Zoey and I dance for a few songs until I feel a heavy presence behind my back. Zoey has turned her attention to a guy next to her, ignoring my silent pleas to save me from the mistake I know I'm about to make.

Grayson's fingers dig into my skin deliciously hard as I involuntarily, or maybe very voluntarily, grind my hips backwards into his pelvis. When he groans into my ear and his grip tightens to the point of pain, I know I'm done for. My entire body responds immediately, open and raw like nerves without skin. My nipples ache, my mouth parts in a silent moan, and my insides clench in anticipation of his proximity.

"Fuck Nora. Do you even realise how naughty you are? Teasing me like that will only earn you a punishment." He tuts into my ear and excitement pulses in my veins. I never really had a kink, but he just might be the one to bring it out of me.

"What kind of punishment?" I look around to see if anyone can see us. As if he reads my mind, he walks backwards moving us to the shadows of the dancefloor. He smirks, knowing I'm intrigued, and while his smile tells me he likes it, his hard cock pressed between us tells me he wants it.

"That's for me to know, and you to enjoy when it happens." He squeezes my arse and I have to stop my eyes from rolling in pleasure. His hands are one of the things I've never hated about him; big, manly, tattooed, corded with thick veins that lead up his forearms. I'd like to completely give into him right now. Feel him cupping my breasts as he fucks me from behind, wrapping those perfectly massive hands around my neck and making me see stars.

Instantly I feel wetness pooling between my thighs, that I desperately try to ignore.

"We should get back to the table. I think Jess needs to go home." My voice cracks on the last word because the last thing I want to do is go home alone.

He huffs, and a hot shot of his breath assaults my skin, "Always thinking about others and never yourself. Tell me shorty, when are you going to take something for you?" With that he steps away from me and disappears back to the table, leaving me panting and needy. For fuck's sake, resisting Grayson is quickly becoming a full time job. One I don't have time for.

Maybe you shouldn't resist then.

Entering into an agreement with the devil is everything I swore to myself I wouldn't do but, he's far too tempting. That's the problem with Gods of the underworld, corrupt characters in books and even

Satan himself, isn't it? They lure you in with their irresistible charm and fake promises only to watch you burn when it's all ripped away again.

So why can't I convince myself that this is a bad idea? Why am I falling for his tricks and waiting for his next instruction like a good fucking girl?

Chapter 18

Nora

We all walk, well some of us – Zoey - stumble, out of the club, to head home, but when I see a huge, black stretch limo waiting on the edge of the pavement, with a grinning Grayson standing next to it, I freeze, making Zoey bump into the back of me. He's staring directly at me, as if he's silently reminding me that *have sex in a limo* was on my list. There's no way he got this limo for me.

"Everything okay?" He nods his chin towards me, smiling far too smugly.

I compose myself and pick my jaw up off the floor. "Fine, just fine. Did you organise this?"

Everyone brushes past me, excited to get in our ride home, whilst Grayson steps towards me and I realise I'm losing air quicker than I can gain it back.

"Don't worry, shorty, I won't fuck you in the limo... not unless you're a really bad girl for me." He smirks, dropping his voice to a seductive purr. My body responds in kind, pulsing, throbbing, and wanting to throw itself at him. But I don't, I can't because everyone is waiting for us inside the limo... the one that I'm not going to have sex in.

"Did you get this for me because of the list?" I ask.

"Of course I did. One more thing ticked off. Although I am disappointed, we're probably going to stick to your PG version of the limo ride."

I wonder if he remembers that if you play with fire, you're going to get burned, so I decide to fan the flames a little. "You know I don't think you've fully thought this through... how crazy will it drive you knowing that I'm in a limo... and my underwear is in your pocket?" I whisper into the night air, just loud enough that he can hear me.

The wave of lust that vibrates from him can be felt streets away. He moves to the open door, holding his hand out for me to take. When I step forwards his hand brushes the small of my back and I tremble, inwardly cursing myself. Inside, the only space left means we're forced to sit next to each other and right now that feels like torture.

As I get seated, readjusting my dress, I find Zoey staring at me with a look that I choose to ignore. I hear a curse and a grunt from outside Zoey notices too and gives me a suggestively raised eyebrow. Seriously she's going to make things obvious if she carries on. Two seconds later, Grayson eases himself in next to me. Our thighs are pressed against one another, and he moves his arm behind my shoulders to rest on the back of the seat. I look at the ceiling, which is decorated with tiny little star lights, and start counting them to distract from everything that's *him*. I've sat next to him before. This is just like any other time.

Having said that, I can't look at him. I know he'll have the very same look on his face that got me into bed with him months ago, and my resolve is hanging on by a thread after tonight.

The limo makes its way into the London traffic and Jess, with her head firmly resting on Liam's chest, starts full on snoring, making everyone chuckle.

"She's a keeper, you know," Zoey says to him.

"Yeah, she is," Liam says quietly, before he kisses her head as she snores louder and my heart squeezes for them.

As we drive past Oxford Street, the local shop windows are littered with Easter displays, even though we've just had Valentine's Day last week. That's the thing about living in a city; everything moves a million miles an hour, even the shop displays. I love living in London, but sometimes I wonder what it would be like to live in a tiny village in the Cotswolds, where everyone knows everyone and there are still Christmas lights up in March.

Maybe I'll do that, add that to my list, because my current ability to do things that are *new to me* are limited to letting Grayson put his head between my legs and brand me with his handwriting. Going to the Cotswolds is surely a safer option than doing that again.

When the limo jolts to a halt outside Grayson's flat, he jumps out so fast it pushes me against Zoey. He pokes his head back in to say goodbye but doesn't look at me. Just like that, he's gone.

This is why we can't get involved. I'll get attached and he will be aloof all the time, leaving my heart in shreds when he leaves me because he will leave. It's definitely better this way.

We drop Zoey home and then arrive at our house. The three of us stumble out of the limo and somehow Liam persuades Jess to walk to the front door. "Jesus, she's like Bambi. How much did we drink?" Liam asks, amused, watching Jess zigzag up the path to the front door.

"I honestly lost count, but she's happy. You make her really happy."

I see a flicker of gratitude cross his face as he smiles at me and then back at his future wife. "She makes me really fucking happy, too."

Inside, I'm immediately hit with warmth and comfort of being home. Liam leads Jess to bed, and I flick the kettle on. *A night out isn't complete without a cup of tea.* As the kettle boils behind me, my phone lights up on the counter as Grayson's name flashes across the screen. I hesitate, unsure if answering is the best idea. Well, that's what the rational part of my brain is saying. The other part has grabbed the phone already, and accepts his call like it's a siren only meant for me.

"Grayson, you, okay?" My voice is trembling, not knowing how to keep it even anymore. I breathe out a long silent exhale, willing my pulse to slow.

"Yeah," is all he says.

"Wait, tell me what's wrong."

He pauses, and if it wasn't for his ragged breathing, I would think he's hung up. "Nora, I want you. I shouldn't. I know it's a bad idea, but I can't stop this feeling and it's driving me fucking wild. You drive me wild. You have since last year and I can't get you out of my head."

Oh. *Oh.*

I clear my throat, but he doesn't let me talk.

"Don't say anything. We can't. You were right before, it won't work. It's fucked up, but since I tasted you in your hallway, it's all I can think about. I want to fuck you so hard that you'll feel me for days. I want to hear you whisper my name and beg me to fuck you harder... Fuck Nora, I haven't wanted anyone like this in my entire life."

Yep, that'll do it again. I'm speechless. My mouth is dry, and my heart is pounding like a drum. Don't even get me started on the throbbing I feel elsewhere.

"I... I don't know... what do you want me to say?"

"You feel it too, right?" he asks, his voice deep and delicious.

I swallow hard. "Feel what exactly?"

He takes a purposeful breath in, and for some reason it gives me goosebumps. "Whatever this energy is between us. It hasn't gone away. If anything, it's burning me alive and making me feel like I'll die if I don't touch you." His breath is heavy against the speaker of the phone and my body echoes his words, feeling hot and needy.

He sighs loudly when I don't respond, and frustration laces his words. "I know I'm no good for you. But fuck, I want to be good for you."

We sit in silence for a few minutes because he's not wrong, he doesn't want a relationship and I would. He wants to fuck me and I... well, I want that too, but it comes with feelings for me. He can't handle that. "If we sleep together again, I know I'll want more, and you don't. Let alone the fact that we have two very important people in common, it could end up ruining your friendship. I don't want that for you."

Silence.

I'm right, and he knows it. What else is there to say? As much as my body wants to jump him, I know I'll get hurt.

"How can you know I won't want more, if I don't even know that?" he sighs sombrely.

"I don't want to be your trial run, the one who you test out a relationship with. I deserve more than that," I say honestly.

"Nora, I know I'm not perfect and I'll probably mess up a few times, but I want to see where this goes because I hate staying away from you."

My heart leaps. Him giving me honesty is more than I thought would happen. I don't need him to be perfect, but I need him to be careful with my heart if I give it to him.

"Can I think about it?" I ask, needing a minute to process everything that's happened and could happen between us.

He sighs loudly. "Okay, I'll keep my distance until you tell me what you want."

"Thank you. I promise I'm not trying to be difficult. I'm...I'm—"

"Scared? Me too, shorty."

Chapter 19

Grayson

I know we talked the other night. I know I said I'd stay away. I've thought about her every night since the hen and stag party. It's now Wednesday and my reasons for staying away from her have eroded a little more each night.

Every night, as I fuck my hand, my resolve to stay away from her weakens. The thing I've come to learn about Nora is that I don't want to *just* fuck her again. I mean, I do, but that's not all. I want to be around her. The day we spent together ticking things off her list has been on replay in my head. The way she moves, laughs, gets this cute little crinkle on the bridge of her nose when she finds me really funny, or really annoying. I want to see more of it, of her.

I'm not this guy, relationships and even double tapping, makes me break out into a sweat. But with Nora, the only kind of sweat I get is caused by a huge swarm of butterflies that rage in my stomach when I see her. She makes me want to try for her. She makes me want to feed her grapes and fan her with a fucking palm tree leaf – what the fuck is up with that? My life was always uncomplicated until her. Nora Scott is an enigma, one I want to spend time figuring out.

I'm seeing her tonight because Liam invited me over for dinner. I could've come up with an excuse and bailed, but like I said, my resolve is fraying. That and apparently, I'm a glutton for punishment. Rules are meant to be broken though, right?

I pull up outside their house in my black i8, letting the engine rumble for a minute, trying to regain my composure. I can't control what my body might do at the sight of Nora again when a memory pops into my head.

I sit with my hands over my ears. Not wanting to hear my parents argue anymore. I hate this. Every night, every weekend, my parents have changed. They're these angry versions of themselves that continually tell me relationships are full of shit. They don't have time for me and that makes my heart hurt. I'm not going to pretend I haven't thought of running away, even at fourteen, but I can't leave them. They're my parents and all I want is for them to be happy and us to be together... happy.

I turn off the engine and take a deep breath, shaking the memory from my brain. That memory, like so many others, has stopped me from finding someone like Nora and I want to break the cycle... for her. So we can give this a chance.

I've thought about what I'll say to Nora tonight, and I figure I'm just going to be myself. I lock my car and walk to their front door. When she opens it, her scent invades my senses, sweet brownies and cupcakes, which I realised last week is her shower gel. My mouth waters and my body trembles internally, but I steel my expression, not wanting her to see the inner battle I'm having with myself just yet.

When a nervous smile graces her face and she tucks her hair behind her ear, all I want to do is pull her to me for a hug, and being there for someone else is new to me too.

I manage to keep things brief. "Hi, shorty." I bend and plant a chaste kiss on her cheek, desperately trying not to react to the little gasp that leaves her mouth.

"Hi, ponyboy," she breathes. I move away from her before I really do something inappropriate. Like groping her round arse, or kissing her slender neck, or sucking her nipples, or going down on her again in this hallway. *Yeah, fuck, I need to stop.*

Making my way into the kitchen, I find Liam standing behind Jess as she stirs whatever is on the stove, groping her boobs. "Fuck's sake, guys, keep it PG." I cover my eyes. If I don't get to grope anyone, then they shouldn't either.

"Mum and Dad are up to no good again?" Nora appears beside me, amusement all over her face. Her smile makes me smile, a warm feeling spreading across my body again.

"It's a good job we've found a place just for ourselves then, hey?" Liam sings into Jess' ear.

"You're moving?" Shit, does that mean Nora is moving too? I glance at her, trying not to give away the urgency of my question.

"We are. We found somewhere two streets over, so we won't be far." Jess eyes Nora, pinning her in place.

"Not that I need to have babysitters or anything. In all honesty, it'll be nice to have the peace and quiet after months of you two." Her tone is playful but honestly, I'm just grateful she isn't moving.

"Need a roommate, shorty?" I wink at her and for a second her face pales, but she recovers with a coy smirk and a slap to my chest.

"A roommate like you? You'd never pass my background checks, bad boy." She blows me a kiss and I blush... I actually blush, my cheeks tingling from that one little gesture.

I turn my attention to Jess as a distraction. "Dinner smells good Jess. What we having?" I plant myself onto a barstool, my back to Nora.

"I've made creamy chorizo and chicken pasta with green beans on the side. Family recipe and I've been dying to try to make it."

"Mum is the queen of cooking. I'm surprised she let you have one of her secret recipes." Nora beams proudly.

"Do your parents live in the city, Grayson?" Jess asks innocently. Liam shoots me a look and his wide eyes tell me he hasn't told Jess anything about my family.

"Uhh, nah. My mum lives in America and my dad is up north. They divorced years ago—it was messy." I don't fancy elaborating.

"You don't have any family here in London?" Jess asks, concern lacing her words.

I shake my head. "Liam is it." I pass my fist over the counter for him to bump it and he does with a smile.

"Well, it goes without saying but you're always welcome here with us." Jess offers me a smile which I return because I'm grateful to have these people in my life. "Can you grab the plates from the cupboard in front of your knees, Grayson?" Jess asks, changing the subject. I hop down and grab four large pasta bowls, giving them to Jess. As the food is plated up, my mouth waters at the spicy, creamy scent. *Fuck, I'm hungry.*

We all devour Jess' delicious dinner in a matter of minutes. Everyone humming noises of appreciation. Including Nora, who sat next to me.

I offer to clean up after dinner, forcing the other three into the lounge. It's probably best that I do this alone to curb my temptation. Or so I thought...

Nora

I walk into the kitchen where he's washing up the dishes, wearing yellow marigold gloves, and I have to stem my laughter. His head whips around to me, my reaction obviously not as stifled as I'd hoped, his stare pinning me in place across the kitchen island.

Grayson has the most captivating eyes; grey and stormy but also clear and bright. I could easily get lost in them but the heat he's throwing my way now could set the world on fire. It's addicting having someone look at you like that. Maybe that's why I keep coming back for more.

"Need some help drying the plates?" I offer. A poor excuse for being here considering he ushered us all out of here five minutes ago stating he could manage. He nods, his expression firm. I tentatively walk towards the sink, picking up the tea towel, and drying the plates in silence.

The truth of it is, after the hen party I feel like I'm the reason he's miserable and I want to check he's really okay with what's happened between us but also, I think we should probably set boundaries to make things less awkward. Him stealing my underwear in dark corners doesn't really qualify as friend behaviour and now knowing he wants more has made me want it too.

He frowns down at the pan he continues scrubbing viciously. I don't have the heart to tell him that the pan has a burn mark that probably won't ever come off. He stays quiet until all the plates are washed and dried and ready to be put away.

Our elbows brush together and something between us snaps. He edges me against the counter, his strong arms caging me in. I take a sharp inhale, enjoying the crackle forming between us. His head dips close to my lips as his eyes close with a vibration from his throat. He's battling with temptation, I can feel it. It's flying off him in waves. The problem is that I'm the thing he could destroy if we give in to the temptation. But I can't keep doing this back and forth with him.

The room fills with a pulsing that's entirely stemming from him. He is electricity and I am the vessel he wants to channel it through. A live untameable wire, hellbent on burning us both.

He grips the counter, his arms vibrating slightly, making his tattoos ripple and the veins in his arms pop to the surface of his skin. God, it's the hottest thing to see him battle with his control like this, knowing that I can bring him so close to the edge. I let my fingers trail along his arm, edging over his King of Hearts card, watching his body tremble, sending heat directly to my core.

I desperately want him to touch me, to kiss me, to do it without hesitation. I know this is a terrible idea, but for the life of me, I can't remember why when he is so close to me, so close I can almost taste him. My very being is singing for him.

"Tell me you want me, Nora," he whispers, his voice husky and hissing onto my skin like the embers of a fire. The playful hatred we once shared has dissipated into something much more tangible and real, something filled with passion and hunger.

I suck in as much air as my body will allow, placing my palm flat to his chest, I look up at him. "I want you to kiss me."

He doesn't hesitate taking my mouth with such a fever it knocks the wind from my chest. His kiss is bruising, claiming. It's everything I love about the way he kisses me.. His tongue dances with mine, and he groans, deepening our kiss further. My hands drift to the back of his neck urging him closer, demanding he take more. His hands slide down to my waist, as he gently bites my lip just as footsteps alert us to someone coming into the kitchen.

We break apart like two magnets being repelled from one another as Liam rounds the corner of the kitchen, shouting back at Jess about a cup of tea. In a desperate attempt to act casual, I grab the tea towel and dry an already dry plate in the hope that Liam didn't notice anything. Grayson is hunched over the sink, staring at the bubbles, his chest heaving. My heart thrums in my ears so loud that I can barely hear a thing. The thrill surging through my body is indescribable.

Liam doesn't give anything away. In fact, he barely looks at us, completely oblivious that he almost caught us kissing. He walks over to the kettle, flicks it on, grabs two teacups, and asks us if we want one too, then asks me to make them before he leaves us alone again. Usually, I'd have a smart-arse comeback for him, but I'm still struggling to breathe.

"Nora." Grayson says my name with such desperation that my stomach flips and I can't tell if it's a good flip or a bad one. I'd planned on coming in here to set things straight, but it seems neither of us can stay away.

Focusing on the plates in front of me, I pick them up and put them away, only to be caged in once more by Grayson. My body responds immediately, searching for more of him as his stubble grazes my ear and neck, making me shiver with desire. I lean back from him, my brows furrowed.

"God, you're hot when you scowl at me," he mutters playfully.

"I can't help it. I feel like you disarm me," I whisper.

"Oh, yeah?" He leans in, licking a flame right from his devil tongue across my collarbone, weakening my resolve and my ability to stop him and my body responds with delight.

Morals? Gone.

Self-control? Vaporised with one lick from him.

My will to stop him? Non-existent.

When Grayson touches me anywhere, he leaves a scorching trail that makes me desperate for more. He makes me want to be reckless, and I'm not used to that feeling.

"I don't want to fight this anymore. Come on Nora, be bad with me. You know you want to," he purrs into my neck.

This man has the match. He lit it and now I'm on fire for him.

Chapter 20

Grayson

Trying to escape Jess and Liam turned out to be relatively easy. They're so wrapped up in each other, I think they were grateful I was leaving. I told Nora to make excuses, and I'd wait for her in my car.

Something seriously snapped in my head when she came into the kitchen. When I realised that she wasn't trying to avoid me at all, but wanted to be around me, fuck, that was it. I couldn't stop myself lunging for her any more than I could stop myself breathing.

Twenty minutes pass by, my fingers impatiently tap my leather steering wheel, the sound of my chunky silver ring on the leather. I worry my bottom lip, thinking she's changed her mind; that she doesn't want me like I think she does. *Fuck, I've read it all wrong.*

Lost in my thoughts, I hadn't noticed her step out of her front door, but when I do, I let out a sigh of relief. She's still wearing leggings and now a black hoodie. I'm not sure how she looks so fucking good all the time, but she does, especially when she's relaxed like this.

My car door opens, and she tentatively climbs into the passenger seat. Her breathing is erratic, like she's terrified she's going to get caught any second. I lean over, grab her face and smash our lips together, taking another searing kiss from her pillowy lips. We break apart, both filling our lungs deeply.

"How did you get away?" I ask when I finally catch my breath.

"They were getting handsy, so I sent them up to bed. No one needs to see them desperate for each other. Teenagers, I swear." She laughs lightly.

"They won't notice you're gone?" I already know the answer. There is no stopping those two once they're together.

She scoffs and pins me with a look that says *really?*

"Let's go." I rest my hand on her thigh. It feels natural to touch her like this. She's in my space, so I don't hesitate. I just do it. I've come to the conclusion that I'm done resisting Nora Scott. I want all of her and she wants me too.

I drive the short distance to my place. We're both quiet, apprehensive even about obliterating the line we're going to cross again. I want her to understand how much I want her and that I don't want to hurt her, but that I can't make her any promises because I'm not sure what the future holds for us. Is that considered progress from a playboy? Likely not, I have no fucking idea and no point for reference here.

Parking my car in the underground carpark at my building, we walk to the lift, and I feel Nora hesitate in her steps. I glance at her as she fidgets with her hair. *Shit, she hates lifts. How could I forget?* I grab her hand and kiss her soft skin below her knuckles. "We can take the stairs if you want. I'm fifteen floors up. I'm game if you are."

The lift doors open, and Nora audibly lets out a breath. "No, let's do it. If you're here, I'll be fine."

Her words slice something in my chest, cracking open any charade I usually find so easy to hold up. Nora just admitted she trusts me, and the thought of her actually believing that blindsided me. I pull her into my chest and kiss her softly, walking backwards into the small space she despises, flinging my hand out to press the button to my floor. I don't think I've ever kissed a woman so gently. I let my hands roam over her clothes, wishing I was touching her soft skin. I love that where I'm hard, she's soft. I kiss every inch of her face as I hold her to me and revel in her chuckles as they vibrate in my chest.

"My distraction techniques are a little rusty."

She hums and laughs again as I gently tickle her ribs and the lift doors open, making her yelp. Her dark eyes find my light ones. "It worked, no freak out, see?" she says. I walk us over to my door and open it. Nora walks in ahead of me, taking in the space. My apartment is a good size. Liam's company owns it, and he leases it to me. I can't complain, its high ceilings, large windows, and open spaces give it an industrial feel.

"Wow, this is beautiful," she coos as she walks around the living room.

"Yeah, it's decent," I reply.

She spots my crossword puzzle book on the table that I picked up because I remembered she liked them. She flicks through the pages, smiling as though she likes it.

"It's really big."

I snigger, "N'awww thanks, shorty." Hauling her into my chest again, I press our lips together. I'm desperate to claim her, now she's here in my flat. Nora deepens the kiss, and the feel of her hands in my hair makes me shudder. I peel off her hoodie up over her head slowly. When she's finally free, her big brown eyes beam up at me, full of anticipation and expectation of what happens next.

Next, I strip off her oversized Foo Fighters t-shirt, leaving her in her bra. I stare at the t-shirt in my hands and stifle a giggle.

"What's funny?"

"Nothing. I never pegged you as a Foo's fan."

She frowns. "There's a lot you don't know about me, Grayson."

Fuck, I hope she lets me find out for myself.

"I saw the Foo's when I was twenty and it changed my life. Their passion, their talent, it was incredible," she says with a huge smile. Honestly, when I thought she couldn't go up in ranking she just did.

"Favourite song?" I kiss her neck as she thinks about it. She lets out the sweetest little moans as I lick and nip at her skin.

"Everlong."

I pause. I thought she would be a "Learn to Fly" fan or maybe "Times Like These." "Everlong" is my favourite too, but I don't tell her that. Her hands grip harder around my neck, and I watch tiny goosebumps sprinkle across her skin. *Fuck, she's beautiful.*

Her eyes glitter with emotion while anticipation burns a hole in my chest.

This time it's her that leans in. She kisses me slowly and softly, using her tongue to sweep over my lips and into my mouth. Letting her control the pace has my body relaxing into hers with need. I grip the backs of her thighs and tap them to let her know I'm picking her up; she jumps slightly, wrapping her legs around my waist. As I walk to my bedroom, I tease her nipple through her sports bra and the noises she makes echo and bounce around my head like an aphrodisiac.

My bedroom isn't spacious. It's compact with enough room for my king size bed and a wardrobe in the corner near the window. The curtains are open, letting in the glow from the city lights reflect warmly.

I lay her on my bed, her dark hair contrasting with my white bed sheets. Her legs instantly fall open for me. *Good fucking girl.* Her eyes gleam with desire as she looks up at me, giving me all the power to have her.

"I need to taste you again, Nora. All I do is think about you and how fucking good you taste. Are you going to be a good girl and take everything I give you whilst I fuck you with my tongue?" Her breath hitches, her head bobs in agreement, dark pupils swallowing the sweet caramel of her eyes. I watch as her tongue darts out to wet her lips. "You like behaving for me?"

"Yes," she groans in reply as her eyes roll back into her head and her body writhes on my bed, searching for touch.

"Too bad. I'm dying to bring out that bad girl I know is inside of you."

I peel her out of her leggings, muttering under my breath about how fucking sexy she looks in them. "Do you realise how fucking hard I was when you were setting the table tonight? It took everything I had not to bend you over the kitchen table and fuck you right there."

Nora whimpers, her body throbbing for me. I see it in the flush of her cheeks, the lick of her lips, but mostly, in the way her pulse is thumping against the delicate skin of neck. I hook my index fingers into her black lace thong and lightly drag them back and forth across her skin, loving the way her back arches off the bed from my touch.

"Look at you, your body is begging for me. So fucking perfect for me, aren't you, shorty?" I praise.

I pull the flimsy material away from her pelvis and let it go with a snap against her skin. Her head snaps up, showing me the desire pooling in her eyes still. Fuck, she's beautiful.

"Grayson, I need..." she whines but can't continue because I cut her off by covering her mouth with my hand and use my other to cup her pussy. She groans against my palm, the noise so feral and needy that I almost put her out of her misery and thrust my fingers inside her, but I'm enjoying this far too much.

"I know what you need, but I get to control your body tonight and I want to make your pussy so desperate she's practically purring for my cock."

I move off her, taking her underwear down her legs, licking a wet trail from her navel, over her hip bone, down the front of her thigh, purposefully avoiding her sex until I get to her ankle where I stop and throw her thong to one side.

Nora

Send me to hell. All of my feminism just exited my body with a salute.

Grayson King's mouth is dirty. No, it's more than dirty, it's a mortal sin. I swear if he calls me a *good girl* again, I'll go up in flames. I've never known anyone be so open with their sexual desires as he is, and I like it.

At least I'm going to hell with a smile permanently etched onto my face.

He's hell bent on teasing me tonight and I'm dizzy with desire. His head reappears from where he removed my thong and quickly disappears between my legs and as he parts my lips, a hiss leaves his mouth when he sees how wet I am... how wet he makes me. He slides a finger inside me as his breath tickles my sensitive skin, and fuck if it doesn't make my body roar for him. I hum from the feeling of his thick fingers inside me.

His voice is raspy and low as he speaks. "You're drenched, Nora. Is all of this for me?"

I nod frantically. "Yes, I want you inside me," I say biting my lip, wondering where my own sexual tones are coming from.

He inserts another finger, curling them as he works them in and out of me slowly. The way he skilfully finds my G-spot should be illegal. Plenty of men wouldn't be able to find it with a map and a compass, but Grayson fucking King found it in a second. *Damn him.*

"You like that, hmm?" he rumbles, as I whisper 'yes'. He moves upwards, licking and kissing along my stomach and the sound of me saying yes becomes much more garbled. He breathes a chuckle against the skin under my breast and I angle my head to watch him climb me. Fingers still stroking me inside, he takes a nipple into his mouth, lightly nipping as he moves. The cool bedroom air against the wetness he leaves on me makes my skin tingle. He peppers more kisses along my collarbone, my jaw, and along my neck leaving a hot, wet trail in his wake.

I fucking love it. I want to scream that I've never been touched the way he's touching me right now and that he should never stop. He inserts another finger—three fucking fingers, and my insides are molten. My hips jolt as he slowly creeps down my body again, teasing my skin with his tongue, his lips, and every nip from his teeth has me reeling. My core quivers as he licks over my bundle of nerves, giving me the friction I so desperately need. A moan falls from my mouth when he licks once more and then stops.

His eyes look up to lock with mine and the sides of his mouth tip upwards in that smile that I hate to love. He knows I'm dying for more.

"Grayson, please..." I thump my fists against his sheets and pull at the cotton beneath me.

"What is it, Nora?" he replies smugly.

"I need more. I need you inside me. You're being a tease."

"I am, huh?" he muses as I tighten my grip on his sheets and groan loudly. "I love feeling your body beg for me. The way you're sucking my fingers inside of you... fuck, yes... just like that. Mmmm. You don't even know how sexy you are. You drive me wild."

"*I* drive *you* wild? That's fucking ironic. I'm so turned on I think a cool breeze could set me off," I huff angrily.

My body is being lulled into a haze of lust, an ache that's too good to ignore. "You don't get my cock until you've come all over my hand and my tongue," he demands into my sex, darting his tongue out to lick and moving his mouth closer to suck my clit hard.

Being in his bed, I'm surrounded by his scent and it's making my head spin. I mutter the word "more" and he doesn't disappoint, driving his fingers in harder and faster, swirling them inside me, whilst his tongue devours me.

A warm sensation starts coursing through my body as he touches me like he's been doing it for a lifetime. It's all consuming. I want him to occupy every inch of me and brand me so I can never belong to anyone else ever again.

"Come for me, Nora, let me have all of you. Gimme that orgasm I'm working so hard for," he growls breathlessly into my apex.

His words echo in my head. I want him to have all of me and I want all of him too. The realisation pushes me over the edge. A sweat breaks out across my body, and a supernova bursts to life in my belly, twisting, writhing, demanding to explode. His free hand drifts upwards towards my breast and I arch into his palm as he squeezes me, making my walls flutter around his fingers. When he pinches my nipple, I detonate.

"Oh my... Grayson!" I shout as my orgasm rips through me, my pleasure stealing the colour from the world until all I see is black.

When I just about float back down to earth, I feel him hum against my sensitive clit. I drag him up to meet my mouth and kiss him softly, tasting my release on his lips. His hands immediately thread into my hair and his tongue passes through my lips gently.

My thrashing pulse evens out a little more and with our bodies flush, I relish the feeling of his weight on top of me and his thick, hard cock against me. "You and that fucking tongue, Grayson. I swear to God, it's going to kill me," I mumble into his mouth.

"You love my tongue," he says, grinding himself into my sex again, my wetness coating us both. "And I love your pussy." His voice gravelly and needy.

"I want you inside me, now," I beg, desperation lacing my words. He thrusts between my folds a few more times, the friction of his boxers rough on my sensitive skin, yet my body meets his every move. He eventually stands to go to his bedside drawers, shedding his trousers and boxers, my body instantly missing his heat. When he opens his bedside drawer, I see a foiled wrapper that he holds up. "Condom," he mumbles before he opens the packet in the sluttiest way a man can... ripping it open with his teeth and spitting out the wrapper.

Holy shit.

I know I've seen him naked before and I know I've touched him and done a whole lot more. But I can't stop my mouth as it gapes at the man in front of me. His naked skin is smooth, slightly tanned, and totally lickable. The rippling movement over his taut abs make me clench. His tattoos scatter across his chest and arms, the lion growling proudly on his chest. The date scribed on his ribs that makes my heart clench because I know what it means now. The ink on his body isn't there for anyone else but him, the way he wears it so well. The contrast of the shading and dark ink against his tanned skin is beautiful.

And his cock. It's a goddamn masterpiece. Thick, long, with a vein running down its length, pulsing visibly, and the glistening tip has my mouth watering as he pumps the head twice before smoothing the condom over himself.

"You look like you're starved," he muses.

My brain is definitely melting.

"I am," I admit. "Don't you want to feed me? Fill me up?" I pop an eyebrow and he groans at my forwardness.

"Fuck, yes, I do."

He lowers himself to loom over me again, turning my body into liquid. I push my chin towards him as he trails a fingertip over my hard nipple, down my stomach, over my pelvis and into my sex once more.

"Fuuuuuck, I love how wet you are. You sure you want this?" His words are filled with an emotion that he rarely shows: honesty. The more time I spend with Grayson King, the more I'm starting to believe that he might have a heart underneath that playboy exterior, but it's almost too much to process, so I push it all to the back of my mind, opting to play with the bad boy instead.

I nod my head and pull him to me for a quick kiss. "Grayson. Fuck me. I need you inside of me."

He hesitates for a second and I don't know if I've said the wrong thing until I feel him lining the head of his cock against my entrance, moving in shallow movements against me, never giving me what I crave. "For the love of—" I'm cut off by him thrusting deeply and unapologetically inside me.

My mouth is open in an O shape, whilst his face is pure smug satisfaction on top of me. "God?" he asks, amused, finishing my earlier sentence. "I prefer Grayson on days when I'm balls deep inside you. Let's not give him all the credit, hm? You can scream *my* name as much as you want, shorty."

When he pulls back and bottoms out once more, he curses under his breath, looking down at where our bodies are connected.

Another thrust has me burying my head into the crook of his neck with a silent scream from the burn of him stretching me, filling me so deliciously. I'd forgotten how fucking good this felt.

"You, okay?" he grinds out between licking and kissing along my collarbone, stilling his hips for a moment. I feel full, but I feel... good, the pain morphing into pleasure.

"Move, Grayson," I plead, because I might die if he doesn't.

He growls and thrusts in again slowly, as though he has all the time in the world, letting me feel every hard inch of him. He rocks his hips, hitting my clit as he moves towards me, sending sparks of pleasure through me. "Fuck, I forgot how good you feel. I've been craving you, your pussy choking me, Nora. Fuuuuuuck me, you're so fucking tight." His stormy eyes find mine as he dips down to my lips, tracing his tongue over my lower lip. "Breathe... relax for me, yeah?"

Before I can respond, he's kissing me again, taking all the air I had in my lungs and owning it like it was his all along. My body instantly relaxes from his caress I grip him close to me, never wanting to leave this bubble we're creating.

He pulls out and breaks the kiss just before he pushes gently back into me. The burn has turned into a desperate tingle as our skin caresses together, sparking flames everywhere as he moves deeply inside of me. His pace is delicious torture. He's taking his time with me, and I appreciate that. I need that. His hard body feels so good under my fingers as I run them down his back, sometimes using my nails, earning a groan from him every now and again. My hands fall to his arse, and I try to push him in deeper. I watch his eyes darken when I do, and he smirks at me.

"What do you want, Nora?" His voice is dark and deep, igniting my need for him to give me more.

"Harder. I want it harder," I breathe out, watching the passion spark over his face, that bad boy coming out to play with me.

He pulls out slowly, before driving so hard into me that I almost hit the headboard. My hands fly upwards, pinning me in place as he does it again and again.

He stops suddenly, sitting up and reaching for my ankle to hook it over his shoulder before driving himself deeper than he's ever been. I cry out, unable to contain the noise.

"Fuck, yes, right there, huh? That's good?" he asks, throatily.

"Right. Fucking. There," I pant, between each thrust.

Each roll of his hips hits me in exactly the spot that I'm now begging for. Our bodies meet at each of his merciless pushes. My body omits white hot heat, and my building climax feels like it's going to be one that tears me in half.

He sits upright, letting my leg drop to his hip again as he leans back on his knees to look down at where our bodies are connected. "Nora, fuck, you're such a fucking good girl, taking every inch of me. You were made for me."

I move my hazy gaze down, propping myself up onto my elbows to see what he sees. His pace slows, his jaw is slack and the groan that leaves his throat as his eyes roll back into his head is pure desire. Knowing that I'm having that effect on him has me in a tailspin.

Feeling confident, I look up at him determined to do something I didn't get a chance do to last time.

"I want to ride you. Sit in the middle of the bed, back against the headboard," I command, and he does, hooded eyes, licking his top lip, his thick cock glistening, covered in my arousal. I straddle him as his hands move to my hips, and I guide him into my sex. Lowering myself slowly, I hold my breath until he fills me completely again.

His eyes close and I grab his chin, forcing him to look at me. "Keep those pretty eyes on me," I say through a shudder of him pulsing inside me.

"You're going to ruin me."

I bend to kiss him and bite his bottom lip as he gropes my bare breasts. "So let me."

I move in slow strokes up and down to begin with as he mutters my name, his hands roaming my naked body before he settles his attention on my nipples.

He leans forwards changing the angle he hits, and I pull his hair back so I can lock eyes with him. I need to know that he feels what I feel. His eyes are so full of want that I might explode just looking at them.

My core heats, my body sizzling against his equally hot one. He drives into me, moving his hands to my arse to control the speed of my movements. Somehow, I lost control of being on top and I'm barely mad about it because the intensity of my orgasm climbing up my body is stealing my thoughts, coiling tightly into my stomach and making my body tingle.

"Fuck, gonna come, you need to come… now," he shouts, bringing his thumb to press against my clit, bucking harder, grazing against my G-spot. My body shakes, trembles and collapses into him as I give myself over to the high that's delivering me the most intense orgasm of my life. I feel him throb and fill the condom inside me, cursing and whispering my name, like I mean everything to him, even when I know I don't.

As my heart rate settles and his fingers dance lazily up and down my spine, I know I'm screwed. Because that was so much more than *just a fuck*. That felt like the start of an addiction.

Chapter 21

Grayson

I 've never had an orgasm that intense in my life, and I'm willing to bet she hasn't either. Not even the first time we had sex was that good. I mean, it was still amazing, but we topped ourselves tonight.

I quickly remove the condom and tie it, tossing it on the floor for now. My head turns to her next to me, where she collapsed into a heap. "That's another one ticked off your list."

Her mane of dark hair flies upwards as she moves. "What?"

"You just had mind blowing sex. With me, again. Wasn't that top of the list?"

The bark of laughter coming from her pistons directly into my ego. "Bold of you to assume that." *This woman, honestly.*

I roll onto my side so I can see her face better. "You can't tell me that wasn't incredible."

Her eyes assess me, scanning over my face. "Are *you* telling *me* I'm the best you've ever had?"

My hands instantly gravitate towards the exposed skin on her back, needing to touch her. "Fuck yes."

I watch her face transform with tiny wrinkles lining her mouth as she smiles, and my usually quiet heart beats loudly in my chest. "You don't need to fluff my ego."

"I'm not." I hold my hands up. "Total honesty. You, Nora Scott, just obliterated all sex with other women." My head hits the mattress again with the memory of her riding me. "Fuck, I'm getting hard again thinking about it."

She hauls herself over my body again, a wicked smile in place as my hands wrap around her hips. "Think I can top myself?" She grinds her core into my now hard-again cock, her wetness dripping onto me, and I groan, pulling myself upwards to take her rosy nipples between my teeth.

"I want to find out," I say, popping her out of my mouth.

She lines herself up and slowly sinks down onto my eager cock again. Every perfect inch of her grips onto me for dear life. Our moans fill the room as I lift up and down my shaft. *Fuck, she's goddamn perfect. I'm never going to last with her feeling this good.*

Her wide eyes find mine as she freezes. "Condom."

"Fuck." I say, "That's why this feels so fucking good. I've never had anyone bare before."

"I'm on the pill and I'm clean," she says. I push up into her again, watching her jaw slacken at my movement.

"I am too. I got tested right around New Year."

"But what about the women in between now and then?" she questions.

"There, uh, I haven't been with anyone else since you." I feel my face heat at my admission, but it's the truth. I haven't wanted anyone else since her, so I've been practicing self-love instead. Nora's eyes simultaneously widen and soften. She opens her perfect mouth to speak, but nothing comes out. Her hand moves up my chest, then she buries it into the hair on the nape of my neck as she leans down and takes my mouth possessively.

God, her mouth should be illegal. "Grayson..." she hums against my lips, her voice soft and gentle as her deep caramel brown eyes hold mine, telling me things I think we're both beginning to feel but can't figure out how to say yet.

I roll her hips as I match her rhythm, desperate to chase a high that only she seems to be able to give me. "I need you, baby," I tell her because it's the truth and I think I like needing her.

Three orgasms later and she's lightly snoring, nestled between my shoulder and my body. I've never had a woman in this bed before. But I want her here. I find myself staring at this gorgeous creature occupying far too much of my bed, considering her size, and listening to her little mewls and puffs of breath that keep tickling my chest. Fucking sappy behaviour on my part. We've only slept together twice and I'm already listening to her breathe, and cooing over her. *Who even am I?*

Just as I find my body relaxing into sleep, she fidgets in my arms, and I know she's awake. Her body is not soft and cradled into mine anymore. It's stiff and full of unknown emotion. Palpable, the universe, and me, are waiting for her to freak the fuck out with the waves coming off her right now.

I let one eye peek open and catch her wide Bambi eyes staring at me. I smile and tug her closer to me. "Don't."

She relaxes a little and lets me hug her. "Don't what?"

"Don't freak out."

She hesitates for a second and begins twirling her finger over my tattoos, specifically the lion on my chest.

"I was thinking I should go. We haven't decided anything for whatever this was..."

Nah, fuck that.

"So, let's talk about it. Don't run, Nora." Am I above begging? Apparently not with her. I surprise myself when I whisper the word, "please."

She stills, her fingers stop moving, and her head tips up towards me again as when she smiles when my heart trips over itself a little. "You start. My brain can't handle the fact that you're begging me to stay right now."

We shift so we are laying on our sides, facing one another. Despite the evening we just spent wrapped in each other's bodies, staring at someone pillow side, when you're both naked, feels like the most intimate thing ever.

"Okay, I really enjoyed last night, and I want to do it again."

She smiles but keeps her gaze locked on my chest. "I really enjoyed it too. How... how would it work with us doing it again?"

"Well, it would start with kissing and touching and..." I move in closer to her, slaps my chest playfully, something I'm learning she likes to do.

"No, smarty-pants, I mean, do you want to do it again only once? Is this a thing? A frenemies with benefits thing? A... relationship? God, there is so much going through my brain." My mind boggles at the word relationship because I've never had one and I don't think I'd be very good at it. Instead of lingering on that thought, I pull out my old faithful trick—for the second or third time tonight, I kiss her until her equilibrium comes back, ignoring my own worries. She hums into our kiss.

"Better?"

A frown appears between her eyebrows. "Yes."

"Really? Your face tells me otherwise." I brush her frown with my fingertip, and it softens.

"I mean no, but yes."

I'm not sure what that means, and I don't think she does either. "You have this innate way of calming me down. You did it in the lift up here. You make me feel... different. You can see when my brain is moving a mile a minute and you swoop in with your soft lips and I'm instantly at ease. That scares the shit out of me because we can barely have a conversation to figure out what tonight was, let alone actually stand to be friends or whatever this is." I smile as I pull her into me and she mumbles, "you're doing it again."

"I know." I want to add that I'm okay with it too because I'm not sure what to do, but I don't put pressure on myself like she does. She sighs, as though she's giving me a little bit more of her vulnerable side with that sound. Whatever it is, I'll take it.

I don't want to let her go or confuse us both with what this is because I have no idea. Most girls see me as a good time, but with Nora, I know it's different already. We're both inexperienced and a little scared, so I'm hoping we can navigate whatever this is together.

"Stay tonight, please," I mumble sleepily and the next thing I know, it's morning, the light is shining in through my slightly open curtains and I'm in bed alone.

Chapter 22

Nora

I stare at the message I've been trying to send Grayson for the last thirty minutes. I've spent most of the time overthinking everything, writing it, only to delete it again. It's a nightmare. *I'm* a nightmare. For a therapist with a plethora of tools at my disposal, this man makes me forget everything I've spent my whole career learning and I become a teenager who has zero clue about anything. How are you supposed to text your current-frenemies-with-benefits man? I don't even know what to call him, let alone what to say.

When I woke up about 5am he barely stirred, which made for an easier escape. I called an Uber and thankfully it was quick to arrive. Jess and Liam had zero clue that I'd gone out and I snuck upstairs before they were awake, showered, and came back down to make coffee before they'd even woken up. I felt like some sort of double agent sneaking around. It was thrilling.

I hate myself a little for admitting this, but last night I got it. The animalistic attraction that women have towards Grayson. This idea that maybe I'd be the one to tame his wildness. That the bad boy image he covets so much could be smashed to pieces by me. To let the beast devour you but come out riding him with a muzzle. I totally get it now. The power he gave me last night was like nothing I'd ever felt in my life. It was raw and exhilarating, and it terrified my poor, romantic heart, but I'd be lying if I said it didn't wake something deep inside of me.

Liam comes around the corner just as I'm still frowning into my phone. He's in his usual work suit and looks very dapper for an early morning. "Morning, Nor." He yawns and reaches for my coffee cup, which I snatch out of the way just in time.

"Nope, not today, cowboy." I sip it with a smirk.

"Ugh, fine, I'm running late anyway, I've got a meeting with Grayson in Richmond today and we need to get on the road five minutes ago." He glances at his watch, patting his pockets to check for things he needs. My ears perk up at the mention of the man I've been trying to text, and there is a knock at the door.

Liam casually walks off, and two seconds later I hear muttering between them both in the hallway and then someone goes upstairs. Too scared to poke my head around the corner of the kitchen door, I decide to stay still... stoic, one might say. Another might say hiding, but that wouldn't be true, or at least not completely true.

Just as I think I might get away scot-free from this situation, Grayson comes into the room. He doesn't hesitate, grabbing me roughly around the waist, and pulling me into a kiss that knocks the wind out of me, along with any words I might've been able to form.

Anyone would think he didn't get his fill of me last night. He moves his mouth against mine, skilfully licking, tasting, biting my lips, leaving me completely breathless.

When we break apart, he slaps my behind sharply and I yelp far too loudly for a quiet house. He doesn't let me pull away from him and the glare he's giving me tells me he might not be too happy with my escape this morning.

"You left," he says in a tone that is completely contradictory to his steely glare. Have I hurt him? Oh God, I hadn't thought he'd be upset with me leaving.

"I had to get back before the lovebirds woke up. I didn't want the third degree. I'm sorry, I didn't mean to just leave. I just wasn't sure what to do, and you looked so peaceful." That's only a half-truth because I still wasn't sure of the rules of our arrangement, plus it all happened pretty fast that I didn't plan, I just did it.

He softens slightly, giving my bum another squeeze, pushing me into him once more, and giving my lips another chaste kiss that has me wanting more.

"Come over again tonight and bring clothes for tomorrow," he says calmly and firmly, as though he didn't just make a rule in our arrangement. A sleeping-over rule that feels like it might enter another kind of relationship territory, one that I'm terrified of but also desperate for him to offer. *God, what kind of fucked up am I?*

"Nora, if you overthink every single thing I say, you're going to get kissed a fuck ton more than you were counting on because it's the only way I've learned to calm you down. Stop. I can practically see your brain whirling. We can talk tonight and then you can make it up to me for leaving this morning." His hand connects with my bum again and I squeal, partially in excitement and definitely in anticipation of whatever he might do to me later.

"I still don't like you, you know." I throw an empty insult his way.

He sniggers at my scowl, which only deepens it, then gives me that smile that I am trying really hard not to like every time I see it. "You don't have to like me to fuck me, shorty."

But he's wrong, I'm wrong, it's all wrong. My stupid brain *is* starting to like Grayson King. Even his snarky attitude and holier-than-thou arrogance and it pisses me off that all it took to admit how I felt were a few measly orgasms (lies - they were incredible and there was nothing measly about them).

He's still got that annoying but fucking adorable smile on his face and I can't stop the next thing out of my mouth even if I wanted to. "You know, something about your face makes me want to sit on it. Maybe it's because I want you to shut up."

His mouth opens and stares at me for a second. To be honest, I don't know where these quips come from sometimes, but the man makes me want to argue with him something fierce and the annoying thing is, I like it. I hear Liam shout out to Grayson and he shoots me a look with a devastatingly charming wink. "Promises, promises, shorty." He kisses me quickly and turns to leave.

Chapter 23

Grayson

I'm waiting outside my building for Nora. She said she's two minutes away and, even though I'm freezing my balls off out here waiting for her, I can't bring myself to leave her to navigate the lift alone.

My phone buzzes in my pocket, but I ignore it because a black cab stops at my feet. When the door opens, I'm met with two big caramel eyes staring at me. "Grayson, it's freezing. You should've waited inside."

I roll my eyes and grab her hand, hauling her soft body into mine. I'm suddenly surrounded by her heady sweet scent, something inexplicably Nora.

"If I didn't know any better, I'd say you're becoming obsessed with cuddling me," she mumbles into my chest.

She's not wrong. I've never been much of a cuddler. "I told you, you're ruining me." Which feels like a lot of the truth, I haven't been able to stop thinking about her, all the time, except when I'm working and even then, any spare moment I have, I play the last forty-eight hours on repeat like a goddamn homemade movie.

She chuckles and drags me inside, muttering about how freezing it is, even with my arms wrapped around her, so we head inside. The journey upwards is uneventful because I pretty much snog the face off her the whole way. I'm getting good at distracting her in lifts, I'd say, plus it means she can tick conquering a fear off her list.

In my kitchen, she moves around opening cupboards and sussing everything out. I'm staring, I know I am, but what hits me most is how a woman in my space would usually have terrified me, but with Nora, I want her here. I want her to be comfortable here with me. If that means she needs to see inside all my kitchen cupboards, then so be it.

Plus, she's hot and I like watching her. My body responds to the way she reaches upwards and opens a top cupboard, showing me perfect slivers of her milky, soft skin. The fact that I can sink my teeth into that flesh without having to stop myself only makes me more feral for her. I flex my fists by my sides, trying to let her explore instead of throwing myself at her.

"Are you hungry?" she asks, peering into a cupboard and then turning to look at me.

I thought she'd never ask.

I stalk behind her, spinning her around quickly and landing my mouth on hers whilst hooking my thumbs around the back of her tight, black pencil skirt to undo the zip, unable to control my need anymore. "Fucking starving." I want to devour the knockout dark-haired beauty in my kitchen. She returns my kisses and lets me strip her naked from her waist down. I grab her and haul her onto my kitchen counter, readying my feast.

Her anticipation fills the small kitchen space, radiating off her. I manage to devour her exactly how I wanted to and get her to scream my name several times over, plumping my ego enough to warrant plunging into her and fucking her on my kitchen counter and enjoy every single second of it before we make it to dinner. Which I ordered before she even stepped foot in my apartment anyway. I know she likes Chinese food. I can't remember how I know that, but I do, so I may have ordered most of the menu to learn what she likes.

With a just fucked flush on her face, she sucks up a noodle into her mouth with a grin. "I'm the least sexy when I eat, you know." Her mouth is full of food and my cock twitches in my boxers. But really, is there anything she can do that would not wake him up? Probably not. Even the sight of her in my jogging bottoms and sweatshirt–which she stole post sex–is unnervingly hot.

"I beg to differ." The memory of her on her knees in her hallway, with her mouth hollowing out around my cock, flashes across my mind.

When we've finished our food, Nora turns her attention to me. "So, I was thinking about the list." I nod my head to let her know I'm listening. "I think I'm good to do the rest myself."

I pause my noodles before they reach my mouth to stare at her. "You don't want me to help you anymore?" I pinch my brows together, trying to figure out where this is coming from suddenly.

She blushes. "It's not that."

"Then what is it?"

"I don't want you to feel like you *have* to help me. This, whatever this is between us, has changed things and the first thing on the list was sex, so..."

"Hold on." I cock a seriously irritated eyebrow at what she's saying, "you think I'm only fucking you because of the list?"

Her dainty fingers twist a piece of hair behind her ear. "I assumed..."

My hand flies up to stop her. "No." I take a breath to calm some of the anger building inside me. "I'm not fucking you because of a list, Nora. Do you really think I'd do that?" She shrugs and my blood thrums inside my head. I'm not having that. I put our plates on the coffee table and pull her onto my lap, gripping her face between my palms. "I'm not fucking you for any other reason than I like you."

Her eyes widen slightly as her lips part on a gasp. "You like me?"

I nod, brushing my nose against hers, relaxing my body against her. "I like you. Yeah, sure. I also like fucking you, but I want to keep ticking things off your list. I promised you I'd help." What I don't say is that I do it because I like seeing her happy and even though that makes me happy, it also scares me because I think I'm feeling more for her, but is it more than lust or desire? I don't know.

The steady thrumming of her pulse flickers beneath my fingers. "I-I... you..."

"It's not often you're speechless, shorty, but I'll take it." I kiss her lips feverishly, needing to feel her against me again. "Oh, and we are going to keep fucking, too. That's non-negotiable." She pulls back to smile at me, and my heart somersaults in my chest. Her cute little button nose wrinkling. "You're a knockout, you know that?"

She warms from my compliment, and I like it. "Thank you... you're not so bad either," she grins.

We finish our food between us, and I try and ignore the hungry eyes she's been throwing my way since I fucked her in the kitchen, but my self-control is zero around her.

She picks up my crossword book and pen from the coffee table behind us. Watching her bite her bottom lip as she deciphers the words she needs is hot as fuck. Not because of the biting thing, but because the girl uses her brain so much and that sexy.

I move closer to her, resting my chin on her shoulder, as I take in the crossword. "I'm stuck," she admits, pointing to a five down.

I read over the hint, *long legged bird*.

"It's not Heron or Stork. I can't think of another, and it's annoying me."

I think for a second. "Try Crane," I offer, watching her write the word in and turning to face me.

"Are you a secret crossword do-er?"

"Mayyyyyybe?" I wink, nuzzling back into her neck. God, she smells so good all the time.

"You can help me with the rest," she announces. And I do, because it makes her smile.

An hour or so later, the TV is on, but I'm not watching it at all. My need completely renewed for the gorgeous woman next to me. I lean towards her, placing soft kisses to her cheek, neck and collarbone. With each peck she hums, sending desire flooding through me.

Sitting back, my finger rubs over my bottom lip as I think of all the things I want to do to her... with her. I don't want her to think I'm only with her for a list. I mean, it's served us a lot of fun so far, especially that 'more mind-blowing sex' one that we need to practice more. She licks her lips where I just touched her and I stifle a groan, feeling my need growing for her again. I want to see her, all of her.

"Need something over there? You're like a baby grizzly bear, growling at me."

I smile. "I do need something. I need you. If I asked you to strip for me, would you do it?"

I'm fully expecting her to say no, but to my surprise, she stands and starts taking off the hoodie she borrowed from me, leaving her in her black lace bra. Fuck, I want to worship every curve of her body.

"What do you want from me?" she asks whilst her fingertips lightly dust across her chest and collarbone, drawing my eyes to her full breasts spilling out of the lace. My pulse speeds up, sending heat signals all over my body.

There's a lot I want to do right now. I want to rip her bra off and suck her nipples until she screams. I want to dive headfirst into her pussy and eat her for every meal, but there's one thing I want more.

"Touch yourself. I want to see you play," I say, palming my hardening cock over my joggers.

I expect her to shy away, to blush that sweet shade of pink that I love to see, but once again she proves me wrong and slides the joggers down her legs along with her lace thong, then she sits on the edge of my coffee table with her legs spread. I can see all of her, perfect, pink and goddamn. It takes every ounce of self-control not to touch her right now.

I lick my lips, imagining her taste as I watch as her hand move from her neck, over her nipples where she takes a detour and unhooks her bra, dropping it to the floor and returning to graze over her breasts. She lets out a sharp inhale as she pinches one pebbled nipple between her fingers and her hips roll forwards letting me know she's desperate to be touched. Her hand trails down her stomach, eyes on me the whole time, looking at me through thick eyelashes, until she reaches her apex.

Her hand slides effortlessly between her lips, touching the bundle of nerves I know will be dying for attention. Her knees spread further, and I let my eyes hungrily search all over her, seeing how her breathing shallows to a pant, watching goosebumps erupt over her skin.

She's a fucking goddess. One that I want to worship.

"Are you wet, Nora?" I ask, and she nods her head hazily as she bites her bottom lip.

"So wet," she hums.

Just as I'm about to tell Nora to put a finger inside herself, but she pushes her hand down lower and does it herself, then brings it back up to her mouth, glistening with her arousal, and sucks... hard.

"Hmmm, I can taste you inside me still."

Holy fuckballs.

A guttural groan rips from my body, stemming from pure desire at the sight before me and the knowledge that I'm dripping from her still. I palm my cock again to relieve some of the strain, but I know already that the only thing that can satisfy my hunger is the vixen in front of me. But I can wait. I need to watch her fall apart first.

She pushes her finger back inside herself, pumping it in and out slowly, the sound of her arousal punctuating the silence around us. Tilting her hips and widening her legs, she presses the heel of her palm to her clit and begins to fuck herself faster and I wonder if I could blow right here without even touching my cock.

"Fuck baby, you're a dirty girl. Do you like showing me my pussy? Do you get off on being a slut for me?" She whimpers as I watch her body beg for release. When I see her legs shaking and her nipples pebbling, I place a hand on her thigh, gaining her attention again, "You don't come until I say so. Understand?"

Her breathless moans are frantic, and I know she's close, so close that I can't help but move my hand from her thigh and roll one of her nipples between my fingers and watch her perfect body bend into my touch. "Grayson, I need to come," she begs.

My lip lifts into a smirk as I watch her. "Beg for it."

Her hazy eyes snap open to find mine, the gold flecks in her eyes brightly burning. "W-what?" she rasps, her body still squirming.

"Beg for that orgasm. I want you right on the edge, ready to fall off into my arms, but more than that, I want to see the desperation in your eyes when you say please."

Her chest heaves as she works her clit harder and harder. The flicker of defiance in her eyes makes my cock even harder for her. I remove my hand from her nipple and take out my cock, watching her track my movement, trailing her tongue over her bottom lip. Her legs shake against the wooden table beneath her. She lets her head drop backwards on a moan when she sees the bead of precum leak from my slit.

When our eyes connect again, her pupils are blown wide and I see her jaw tick before she pleads, "Please, can I come?"

Euphoria fills my veins at her obeying my command. I move to the edge of the sofa, gripping my cock in my tight fist. I watch as Nora holds on desperately to her orgasm, edging herself to perfection. "Yes, you can come for me, Nora."

She shakes with such force that the coffee table rattles. "Ohhh... my... yessss... Grayson." She squirms, reaching her peak, coming hard with my name tumbling from her lips.

Now I'll have a new home movie playing on repeat in my head because that was fucking hot.

Chapter 24

Nora

I round the corner to the kitchen cautiously, to find Grayson cooking and dancing to the music coming from his speaker system. His dark, messy hair flops around on the top of his head, his broad, bare, muscular shoulders occupying the space in his industrial-style kitchen, giving me a chance to just watch him. Bloody hell, he's mesmerising. He hasn't noticed me yet, totally captured in the moment.

After we came back to his house on Friday night, we pretty much haven't left. An entire dirty weekend which hasn't been interrupted once.

But seeing him being so domesticated. I'm swooning. Which is dangerous. Swooning leads to feelings. Feelings I shouldn't be having for something this casual. Because this is all we can ever be. Casual.

His head swings around, when he realises it's me, the tips of his mouth turn upwards, and he looks at me with *that* look that tells me we are definitely in over our heads.

"Hey, shorty," he beams whilst pressing pause just as another Foo's song starts blaring.

There are a bunch of white sweet peas on his kitchen table that definitely were not there this afternoon when I left to grab my laptop from the office so I could pick up my schedule for next week.

This is starting to feel far too much like a relationship. The worst part? I like it. Too much. I wonder how he feels about this, about us. We've stayed over more than a few times a week and he's not freaking out. He's really trying for me, for us. God, that gets me. I feel a pang of something in my chest and will it down for now.

"You know, a girl might get used to someone cooking them dinner and buying them flowers," I say, gesturing around the room.

"Oh yeah? Someone or me?" He leans over the counter in front of me, urging me to move towards him and like a magnet I do.

"Hmm, as long as he cooks and gives mind blowing orgasms, I don't think I'd be that picky." I'm close enough to kiss him but I don't.

"Mind blowing, huh?" His breath tickles my lips as he speaks.

"Mmhmm."

I won't give in and kiss him first. We're both stubborn at the core and if he knows anything about me, it's that I like to win. "Well, I guess then if it could be anyone, I'll just pack my things and go," he sighs.

Fine, let's play. My pulse hammers in my chest, but I force every emotion to stay below the surface again.

"Okay, bye," I say, smiling sweetly, knowing he definitely won't leave his own flat.

"Nora," he warns.

I bat my eyelashes at him innocently. "Yes, ponyboy?"

His breathing changes, it quickens to a speed that tells me he's begging his body to practise some restraint still and it sends heat to my core. I live for that hot tingle that starts low in my belly, creeping up through my nipples, snaking around my neck and finally diving straight down to my sex.

"Fuck," he says, his voice deep and throaty as he stalks over to me. His lips land on mine passionately as his hand pulls me, almost lifting me onto the kitchen worktop, bristling when the cool surface seeps through my leggings. His tongue pushes into my mouth and he groans when he tastes the mint I just finished. When he pulls away his eyes are like the sky before a storm hits, grey and black swirl together, drawing me into him.

I grin triumphantly. Something flashes across his face, and it hits directly between my breastbones. I rub the area that aches. "So, you're cooking?"

"You're a regular Sherlock, aren't you?" he retorts, playfully.

"Right, of course you're cooking. I knew, I mean I know that. I didn't realise you *could* cook. You've only ever made me toasties and freaked out over cracking eggs," I say as his eyebrows raise in amusement at me.

"For the record, this pasta is the only thing I'm actually good at cooking from scratch and I'm sorry I'm not an egg cracking ninja like you."

I'm practically shimmering with happiness, feeling all sorts of feelings tonight, and I need to get a handle on them. Fuck, how am I here? And what exactly am I feeling right now? I decide not to think about it right this second and just enjoy the moment.

"I got you something today," he says, not looking up at me.

"You did?"

"Over there on the kitchen table." He nods towards the corner where I see an envelope with my name on it. As I pick it up, running my fingers over the seam that's not fully sealed, I pause.

"Wait, is this some sort of trick present? An empty envelope? Or maybe you've filled it with those annoying sequins that'll pop out when I open it?"

Grayson chuckles as he stops stirring the food and turns to face me with a heart-stopping look on his handsome face. His arms cross over his body, alerting me to the fact that his veins are obviously feeling slutty today as they pop against his tattooed skin. "Just open it, shorty."

The mixture of lust and that nickname, that I'm ashamed to admit has grown on me a lot, makes my eyes roll as I lift the seam and pull out two tickets.

I scan over them and my mind reels. "You got me tickets to a festival?" Looking in more detail, my eyes widen. "You got me tickets to Glastonbury?" I shriek, catapulting myself towards him. Thankfully, he catches me under my thighs and keeps me steady against him as I litter his face with kisses and whispered thank you's.

When I pull back after showering him with affection, the look on his face makes me feel all warm inside. "Thank you, Grayson," I say once more.

"You're welcome. I got you two tickets, but you don't have to take me. You can take Zoey. Pretty sure Jess and Liam are on their honeymoon so, I didn't get them tickets."

I wiggle in his hold, signalling for him to let me down. He does reluctantly, but when my feet hit the floor, I move my hands to his face to make sure he hears me. "I want to go with you," I say, meaning every word.

A hint of a blush ghosts across his cheek and he side eyes me bashfully. It's so adorable and it boggles my mind how I've managed to make this confident, adventurous man feel something like this.

"I'd like that," he replies.

Something shifts in the air between us. Being open and vulnerable isn't usually what we do together, but the tone of his voice was soft and unlike his usual banter that he voices so easily, that I can't help thinking if there's something more happening here. Is he feeling things like I am tonight? And that leads me to another thought: will it scare him to realise that maybe there is more to us than just a casual fling?

Pushing those thoughts away for now, I ask him, "how long until dinner? I'm just going to wash up." I hike my thumb over my shoulder and my body does a weird awkward backwards wobble that I know I'll hate myself for later.

Grayson just chuckles. "Thirty minutes."

"Perfect." I stop and whirl around to face him once more. "How did you know sweet peas were my favourite flowers? Did you ask Jess?" Another reason why my heart is galloping in my chest over him; he's the first man to every buy me flowers.

"I remembered your favourite colour is white and the night in the lift you said specifically white, like sweet peas. I honestly had no idea what they were, but the florist did so yeah..." He looks down at the food, frowning as though he isn't sure he should be admitting all of this to me. "... it's no big deal." He says that a lot, that things aren't a big deal when they are, the smallest things he does always have me spinning and he doesn't even realise.

Gratitude and something else that I can't name flutters in my chest. "Thank you... they're beautiful," I say before heading to the back ensuite bathroom to try and calm these new emotions flickering inside me.

I shower quickly, head back into his bedroom in a towel when I notice Grayson, still topless, lying out flat on his bed.

"Uhh, what are you doing?" He looks at me expectantly, kicking up my temperature a few degrees.

"Making you a seat, you can choose my face or my cock. But right now, I really hope you choose my face, because it's all I've been able to think about since you walked in."

Oh. Jesus. Wept.

My legs almost give way, my mouth gapes, and my brain is somewhere melted in the corner of the room. This man is going to ruin me if he hasn't already.

He crooks his fingers summoning me, and as if by some magical pull that I have zero control over, my body floats towards him.

Stopping in front of him, he gestures to my towel. "Drop the towel, shorty," he purrs. I do exactly that and am rewarded with an appreciative groan from him. "Fuck, yes."

I crawl up his body until I straddle his hips and his fingers dig deliciously into the skin on my hips.

He quirks an eyebrow when I pause my movements at his chest. "Come. Sit," he demands. "Well, actually I'd rather you sit first, then come." I hesitate, shuffling higher, hovering over him. "I'm offering you a chance to ride my face and shut me up. I thought you'd jump at the opportunity. You've got ten minutes until dinner." He taps the face of his watch and winks.

I will my body to move upwards towards his face and he moans as I approach. His body shuffles further down the bed until he is perfectly underneath me. His eyes crinkle into a smile as he takes me in. "Fuck, you're pretty when you're wet." I stifle a laugh and he shoots me a devious look. "I'm not talking to you. I'm talking to her, and she knows exactly what she wants. So come the fuck on, shorty. Sit. Now."

So, I do. I ride his face until I come so hard, I see stars and he is completely satisfied that I'll never use the word 'okay' again when talking about our sex life.

Chapter 25

Nora

I've learned that when Grayson King sets his mind to something, he's determined and absolutely unrelenting. The man has given me more orgasms in the last week than I've had in my lifetime. I've been constantly satisfied by him. He's insatiable. But I find myself searching for hidden parts of him that'll let me connect with him on a deeper level. The Grayson I've got to know isn't just a playboy. I'm beginning to see a softer side to him, and I want more.

Focussing on the task in front of me, I pick up a box from Jess' room that says, 'stuff I'm stealing from Nora'. Of course it does—typical Jess. Ever since we were kids, we've shared everything, so not telling her about me and Grayson makes me feel like I might break out in hives at any moment.

"Oh, you weren't meant to see that box." She blushes and takes it from me.

"You think I don't know you're stealing from me? I knew you and your sticky fingers would take something of mine." I bump her hip and her blush fades into a smile, showing me her dimple.

Jess and I have lived together since we were kids. When her mum disappeared, she was officially moved in with us and we all relocated to Kent. Then, after university, Jess and I moved back to London together. There's a funny tight feeling in my chest that is telling me this next stage of our lives might be the first thing we've not actually done together. My eyes sting as tears threaten to fall. I think about the fact that she's holding a box that is full of my crap and I'm not even mad. I want her to have it because from today onwards, stealing my things is going to become a lot harder. Not impossible. I mean, she's only moving a couple of streets away, but still, there's change afoot, and that's a little scary.

"Hey, hey, don't you dare cry. You'll set me off." But it's too late. We are both pushing out our bottom lips, our eyes full of unshed tears. I can barely see her through the blurry haze. We both let out a sob at the same time, which actually helps because in the next breath we're laughing just as Liam comes around the corner into their old bedroom.

"Oh..." He freezes. He's always been the worst with crying women. He gets all flustered. Which is what is happening right now. He twirls around looking for God knows what, and the look on his face is pure fear and panic. A bubble of laughter erupts from my chest, watching him lose his mind.

"Liam, it's fine, we're fine. Just sad."

He deflates in front of me, dragging his hands over his face, the fear disappearing, and he grabs us both into one of his famous bear hugs. "I hate seeing my girls cry." He rubs our shoulders and then squeezes us. My eyes burn once more as more thoughts of being alone in this house flood my mind. The fact that they won't be here if I need a cuddle might sting the most.

I pull back, fighting the rising lump in my throat to smile at Liam. "Let's get you two in your new house, shall we?"

Seven hours can really feel like seven days when you're moving house. Or moving someone else's house to be more accurate. If I could sleep standing up I would. My feet feel like lead, my arms are jelly, and my back is in bits. I need a long, hot soak in my tub and a glass of wine.

I close the door to my house. My house, wow that feels weird. The stairs are long, far away and feel like Mount Everest right now but that bath is calling my name. The thing I adore most about this house is the huge roll top bath in the main bathroom. It could easily fit two people in. I know this because I've walked in on Jess and Liam before which I quickly erased from my memory bank.

My heavy weighted feet pad one step at a time and stopping halfway to lean against the cool wooden banister before I force myself to trudge up the few remaining steps. When I finally reach the bathroom, I flick on the taps, empty some bath salts and my favourite cupcake scented bubble bath and I sit and watch them multiply into soft fluffy peaks on top of the water. I don't have the energy to go back downstairs and get the wine, no matter how much I want it. My body needs this bath much more.

I begin to strip when I hear the front door unlock. Fuck's sake. Turning the taps off, I wrap a towel around my body and shout out to who I assume is Jess or Liam. "What did you forget? If you need me to lift anymore boxes, I'm done for the day. Find someone else."

Just as I'm rounding the landing to the top of the stairs, I bump into a wall of muscle. My body doesn't seem to be that scared that it could be an intruder, or even Liam. The jolt of bumping into this person has made me lose my towel and my arms scramble to collect it and hold it against my body so I don't flash whoever is standing in front of me.

Still too consumed by my delirious tiredness, I still haven't looked up at them.

Two arms wrap around the tops of my shoulders to steady me.

"Woah, it's me Nora," our eyes lock and I realise it's Grayson. "I had to swing by Jess and Liam's house after my meeting. He asked me to make sure you weren't crying into a bottle of something." He bends and kisses my cheek. My body deflates, I adjust my towel again sleepily. I'm dead on my feet and I might even wobble a little again because Grayson's grip tightens on me and his eyes narrow. "You, okay?"

"Yeah, I'm just so tired. I was about to get in the bath when you came in." I gesture a thumb over my shoulder towards the bathroom.

"Go." He kisses my forehead. "Get in. I'll bring you up a glass of wine."

"Mmm, my hero," I hum as I plod over to the bathroom again, drop my towel and drag my aching body over the side, letting it sink beneath the warm welcoming bubbles.

"Here you go." Grayson appears with a chilled glass of white wine, and I pop open one of my eyes and take it from him, letting the sweet, cool nectar trickle down my throat as I hum in appreciation.

"Thank you."

He takes the wine and places it on the side of the vanity. Perches on the edge of the tub. "Give me your foot," he insists. I lift my foot out and let him guide it to where he wants it, which happens to be his thigh. I flinch, lifting my foot slightly, not wanting to get his trousers wet.

"Relax, shorty," he insists, pulling my foot back down. So, I listen and relax as he begins the most wonderful foot massage I've ever had in my life. His hands are big and slightly rough as he wraps his warm hands around my heel, dragging his thumbs through the arch of my foot. It feels good. So good that I can't stop the moan that spills from my mouth. I'm practically purring from his touch.

"Oh, my God, that feels..." I can't even finish my sentence.

Grayson's eyes darken. "I love the noises you make. If I could only hear one thing for the rest of my life, it would be you, moaning my name and whimpering when I touch you."

The rest of his life? My mind gets stuck on those words, but I'm too chicken to ask what it means for him. Did he mean he wants me for the rest of his life?

His large palms flatten, and he pushes them around my calf muscle, needing my skin as I become putty in his hands and forget any and every thought that was just taunting my tired mind a minute ago.

He releases my foot and gestures for the other, repeating the process again. I watch the muscles in his arms flex and his tattoos on his hands dance with the movement. We don't speak, but I know he feels the intimacy of the moment as it swirls around us.

"You know, you're making it harder to hate you, Grayson King," I admit, playfully narrowing my eyes.

He snuffles. "Yeah? What if that's my plan?" I have to look away and break the tension with a hollow laugh because it's too much; the weight of his words combined with the intensity of his stare is confusing, but isn't this everything I want? So why do I feel like I'm waiting for the other shoe to drop?

Chapter 26

Grayson

An hour after her bath and she's fidgeting again. The hard work I did relaxing her has dissipated pretty quickly. The way she twitches and mumbles incoherently every now and again. She is chewing her bottom lip and her eyes are shifty as hell. I've come to learn that this is what Nora does when she wants to ask me something. She weighs the outcomes and options in her head before she asks me whatever is playing on her mind. We've been sitting in her living room for around half hour and most of that time she's been internally freaking.

"Ask me, shorty. Give that poor lip a rest, yeah? You've been biting it for ten minutes." I lean over and release her bottom lip from the torture of her teeth, running my thumb back and forth a few times.

Her eyes narrow, as if she's wondering how I knew she wanted to ask me something. Taking a deep breath, she exhales and says, "are you taking a date to the wedding?"

I scratch the back of my neck, suddenly needing to move my arms somewhere. That's what she's been thinking about? "I hadn't thought about it." I really hadn't, the thought of bringing someone else or her... "Wait, do you have a date?" I rush out, suddenly panicking that I'll have to deal with watching her with another man all night, which would not be my idea of a good time.

"No." Her nose scrunches up. "I hadn't thought about it either, but then Jess brought it up the other day and since then it's all I've been able to think about. I'm fine if you want to bring someone." I perk up knowing she won't be bringing anyone but also feel a pang of irritation that she is fine with me bringing someone.

I narrow my eyes. "You'd be fine with me dancing and touching another woman all day and all evening?" She shrugs, acting nonchalant, but as I lean in closer to her, letting my lips almost touch the skin on her neck, I can see her pulse flutter like a hummingbird. "Because honestly, I'd want to rip the arms off any man who touches you, let alone gets to call you his date."

When I look up at her, those beautiful caramel eyes drink me in and she smiles the biggest smile I think I've ever seen from her, which steals the breath from my lungs. "I think I'd want to bitch slap anyone who came near you." *There she is.* I like that she's jealous. Excitement zips around my body with the knowledge that I might have as much of an effect on her as she does me.

As we stare at each other, the humour fades from the room, the air stifles between us again, and there are unsaid words and unconfessed feelings floating around the atmosphere. Neither of us ready to give in and admit we are in deeper than we planned. It makes me feel jittery, like I need to move. My chest tightens with each breath in, and I know I can feel a line of sweat forming down my spine.

I stand before I become breathless, leaving her alone on her sofa. "I'm gonna go make us some cheese toasties."

Nora hums, side eyeing me, assessing my sudden need for food. "You okay?"

"All good. Hungry," I reply like a caveman who hasn't discovered sentences yet. But I feel the panic rising in my chest when I turn the corner to the kitchen and as a memory washes over me.

My face presses against my bedroom door as I listen to the fourth argument this week, and it's only Tuesday.

"Maybe I don't want to be married to you anymore Viv, have you ever thought of that? Maybe you make things more difficult for me and Grayson than it's worth."

"How fucking dare you. Grayson loves me. He barely sees you; how can he love someone who isn't around for him? How can you think you're the better parent here?" Mum shouts back to Dad.

"Oh, fuck off. You day drink. You forget to pick him up from school."

A loud slapping sound echoes through the door. "Fuck you, Mark. Maybe I wouldn't need to drink if you started giving a shit about your wife and son."

"Don't pull that shit with me, Viv. I have to work, and I work fucking hard."

I open my door. I've had enough of this. Twenty minutes of shouting is my limit for today. Both sets of my parents' eyes widen when they see me step into the hallway.

"I need you both to get a divorce. You hate each other and you're making me hate you both, too."

I watch her breathe. I watch her perfectly pink lips part as air puffs out between them. I watch her chest rise and fall with a steady rhythm matching my own. I watch her creamy, silky soft skin as it pebbles under my touch. My hand runs aimlessly up and down her arm, exactly how she likes it. Nora loves being tickled softly. So much so that she's fallen asleep this time. Usually, she ends up snuggling into my side and falling asleep, but tonight I've got a front row seat to watch her just be. She's so fucking beautiful it hurts.

Her dark, almost black hair falls around her face, contrasting with her creamy skin. She's like day and night all in one picture-perfect package.

Watching her sleeping reminds me that she's the only woman who I've ever done this with. Other hook-ups haven't lasted an entire night, yet here I am, breaking all my rules and doing *something more* with her. Now, I don't like the thought of her not being with me.

I'm in way deeper than I ever thought I would be. I can't seem to get this little beauty out of my head. And I'm scared. I want to be good for her, but I keep getting this overwhelming feeling that I'm not. My memory of my parents' love is so filled with mistrust, arguments, heartache that I feel as though I don't fully understand what love should feel like and that isn't fair on her. I'd be dragging her into something I have no control over, and I don't know what to do about that.

But earlier, when she was talking about the wedding and dates, I was honest. I don't want her to go with anyone else. The thought makes me sick. I'm a mess and I only have myself to blame. I've been allowing myself to fall into this, whatever this is, with her, and I've never done any of these things before. I don't date; I don't sleepover; I don't double tap; I don't act like a total melt; But for her, I have been. And despite her not asking for anything, I've somehow landed in unchartered waters.

Her eyes flutter open before they focus on me.

"Are you that creep who watches women sleep?" Her voice is croaky from sleep, but she still manages to make my pulse speed up.

"Only one woman," I say as I continue stroking her arm, trying to stop the tightening feeling in my throat that I can't explain.

She moves her hands underneath her head, tucking them in like she's getting comfortable, studying me for a second before one of my favourite smiles blazes across her face. It's the type I dream about; honest, raw, sweet and fucking with my head in a big way.

I tangle our tongues, tasting her enough to leave her breathless. When I'm with her, I can't see past wanting to touch her and it blinds me, leaving me more confused than I've ever been. I've never known how to show affection outside of sex and a cuddle, because I've barely been this intimate with anyone and I'm beginning to feel things that I don't know how to manage.

"Nora?" I say, breaking our kiss.

"Hmm?" She shifts, resting her head against my bare chest.

My heart is beating out a gruelling rhythm with things I want to say. I'm being choked by my own head and heart, battling against one another while they decide on what I say next. Because what I say to her will change everything, and I don't know if *I'm* ready for it. I don't know if I ever will be.

I want her more than anything, but my parent's arguments ring in my head like a constant reminder of what can go wrong. *What if we end up like that? What if we're wrong for one another a way down the road? What if we end up living in unhappiness? Fuck, I could never do that to her.*

I exhale roughly, encasing her in my arms as I dip my head to her ear. "I want you." It comes out in a breath, fuelled by the desperation of all the things I can't vocalise.

The one thing that only I know for sure is that I want her more than I've ever wanted anyone. Her head turns to meet my lips, her small body twisting as she places her soft hands to cradle my face, keeping me anchored to her. I push her back and lay my body over her naked body.

Her breath catches as I nuzzle into her neck while I free my cock from my boxers because right now, I have to feel her. To pour everything into her that I'm too fucking chicken to admit. Her legs fall open as I nudge her entrance, her moans drifting against the skin on my neck. She feels like velvet as I slide into her slowly, gently. Her arms wrap around me, pulling me closer, her legs lock around my waist, urging me deeper. Her whimpers tell me that she wants me... needs me, as much as I do her.

Pulling back to see her face, our eyes lock and I wonder if she can see everything I feel for her. Because in her eyes, I can see the whole fucking galaxy. I want to dive in and explore everything I didn't know existed for me, but I'm scared of falling. Of being the only one who feels this way. Of hurting the only person who's ever looked at me like this.

"Give me everything, Grayson. I need it. I need you," she says, touching my face with a softness that I've never felt before.

I let myself get lost in her, slowly moving in and back out again, leaving her pieces of me each time I retreat. Being with Nora has always been electric. I've never been able to get enough of her, but tonight, right now, I never want to leave. I want her to stay with me and be mine. But I also haven't ever felt this way about anyone, and I don't know what the fuck to do about these feelings. *What if I'm not good enough for her? What if she hates me in a few months' time? I won't want to let her go. Fuck, my mind is on a carousel.*

A groan leaves my chest, fear slipping into my mind as I roll my hips into hers, pushing myself deeper into her, trying to drown myself in her body and not my own thoughts. Arching underneath me, Nora's hands drift all over my upper body and around the back of my neck, searching for more from me. She licks her full lips, gasping out that she's close, and it's all the permission I need. Burying my face in the curve of her neck, letting her have all that I can offer right now, I come hard. Spilling inside her at the same time her orgasm chases her to her highest peak, her walls spasming around me, making me come harder and longer than I've ever done before.

We lay entwined together, both panting. My heart echoes loudly in my chest, my throat, fucking everywhere in slow motion as time stands still. Nora's hands stroke my back as she sighs tenderly in my ear. I'm no expert, because I've never actually done it, but that felt a whole lot like making love, not just fucking. And fuck... my head's even more of a mess. I feel like I'm torn in two. I want so badly to tell her how I feel, but I can't bring myself to say the words to her.

What the fuck is wrong with me? She deserves so much more. I'll never be able to give her it all.

I push myself up slightly, my now semi-hard cock still inside her. Her eyes are hooded with a look of bliss and her lips are swollen from my kisses. Her hand cups my face, her thumb rolls over my bottom lip and I catch sight of her tattoo, the one that *I* wrote for her. I lower my head and kiss her wrist, right over the word yes. An unfamiliar emotion floods my body, I feel like I'm drowning on dry land, all the air has been stolen from my lungs. *What the fuck is going on?* The weight of my feelings crushes me as I slip out from inside her, turn onto my back and stare at the ceiling. Immediately, she snuggles into me humming with satisfaction, placing her head on my chest. Even though we've cuddled a thousand times, my body suddenly feels weighted and stiff. My vision blurs as I force a swallow, managing to take a few slow breaths.

After a while Nora's breathing becomes rhythmic against my chest. I try to fall asleep too, but sleep evades me. My whirling thoughts keeping me wide awake. Eventually, with my eyes burning from no sleep I decide to slip out from underneath her. When she grumbles and moves to her side, I stroke her hair and look at my dark haired beauty with my heart in my throat.

She deserves someone who can give her the world and I don't know if I'm that person for her.

So, before the sun comes up, I leave.

Chapter 27

Nora

Thank God I have Zoey. She knows about Grayson and is the only person I can talk to about him. I think I would've driven myself mad by this point if I didn't talk to someone. I want to tell Jess, but we really haven't seen each other since she's moved out and I don't want to do it over the phone.

"So, tell me all the juicy, saucy, delicious gossip with you and your man."

"He's not *my* man," I say emptily, ignoring that little possessive voice that seems to be getting louder lately. "But we've spent almost every night together the last few weeks. I swear he knows every single pleasure point in my body, and he memorises them so he can go back later and explore them again and again." I sigh, resigning myself to the fact that I'm ruined for any other man now.

"If I didn't know any better, I'd say you're catching feelings for him." She bites into her sandwich and acts like she didn't just tell me I liked Grayson more than I'll admit.

"No, we agreed—no feelings. It's casual, we're casual. That's all there is to it. He's helping me with the list and I'm helping him... with orgasms," I say, questioning what he's actually getting out of this besides sex. I'm not convincing anyone of the truth of the matter here, which is I am definitely catching feelings.

"You'd be really bad at poker, you know." She waves her coffee in my direction.

I roll my eyes. "I don't have feelings." Saying that out loud feels wrong though.

"Uh-huh, keep telling yourself that, princess," she muses.

I shift my eyes around the busy coffee shop. The same people come here often, just like Zoey and me. Sometimes Jess joins us too, but weddings and events at the hotel she works at often take up a lot of her time during working hours and Liam takes up the rest.

"Maybe I do care about him. There is something between us, but I think it's just because of the sex. It's intimate, and he's sweet and kind..." I trail off, not really sure where I was going with this. "We know exactly what we're doing." *Even though I don't think we do.*

"Intimacy is a good foundation for love, babe. I hate to tell you, but you are already in deep with feelings even if you won't admit it," she says around a bite of her sandwich.

She's possibly right, but I'm living in denial, eating denial for all my meals and sipping on it every day. I know I'm not kidding anyone, though. I have feelings for Grayson King. I just need to figure them out before I blurt out something embarrassing.

"Does Jess know?"

I shake my head as my throat grows thick. "I haven't told her yet, but it's because I haven't seen her."

Zoey nods. "It wouldn't have anything to do with the fact you're scared to admit it?"

My eyes narrow as I take a big bite of my own sandwich, loving the burst of tomatoes on my tongue. I wipe away any crumbs with a napkin before I speak again. "I thought I was meant to be the therapist."

My mind wanders as I chew on my sandwich. I think about the last few weeks with Grayson.

"Did you know I'm afraid of lifts?"

Zoey shakes her head. "I don't think I've ever been in a lift with you."

"It's silly, but when I was younger, probably around eight, my mum and I got stuck in a lift. We were there for about an hour, but it felt longer. I had my first panic attacks whilst we were waiting. I still hate them now."

"Oh babe, how did I not know that?"

"It's not important, I guess. But the thing is... Grayson knew that was a fear of mine and so every time we go to his place, I have to get in a lift." I pause because the reality of what I'm about to say feels like a big deal. "He's helped me rationalise that fear. He started off by distracting me, kissing me, but now I can do it almost completely by myself and..." I feel myself getting emotional, but I swallow it down. "It's probably nothing but, it feels like something."

"Well, isn't he just the dark horse—bad boy on the outside, cutie pie on the inside?"

Yeah, don't I know it? What I can't seem to tell Zoey is that the sex we had last night was different; there was definitely something deeper going on. Something that made me feel that this was so much more than a casual thing. But then this morning, he was gone before I woke up. And I've not heard from him all day.

We finish our lunch, and I head back to the office for the afternoon.

I keep my head down at work, writing up notes and organising future appointments with clients. When I glance at the clock, I realise it's past 6pm and I pack up my office to head home.

Unlocking my door, I walk into the house, immediately noticing a key on the floor, like it was posted through the letterbox. I pick it up, frowning, wondering where it came from. And then it hits me. Grayson. This must be the spare key, from when Liam asked him to check on me and he's given it back to me.

I pull out my phone and try to dial his number, but it goes straight to voicemail. There's a strange staccato rhythm beating in my heart that tells me something isn't quite right. My phone rings and I don't check the caller, but I answer it straight away, with far too much hope in my voice.

"Hello?"

"Oh my God, babe. I know I saw you at lunch, but I need to go for a drink somewhere. My afternoon was intense, and I need to vent... my parents are actually insane. Call Jess. Tell her it's not optional. Meet me at Bar 69 in an hour," Zoey demands breathlessly.

I deflate. I hadn't planned on going out tonight and now finding this key just makes me want to try and figure out what the hell happened between last night and now. "I don't know Zo—"

"I said it's not optional. Come on, girl. I'll call Jess. One hour, Nora!" she hollers before hanging up on me.

I stare at my phone, feeling the weight of the key still in my other hand. My thumb hovers over the call button again, but I decide to leave it and listen to Zoey instead. Taking myself upstairs, I change into black jeans and a black sheer blouse. Easy, simple, and nothing too much. I top up my makeup, seeing as though I hadn't put much on this morning for work it doesn't take me long. The swipe of a lipstick and a little bronzer and I'm looking slightly more perky.

I call an Uber and whilst I'm waiting, Zoey texts me a picture of her and Jess waiting at the bar. They must've already been in the city because I've only been home for half an hour.

Twenty minutes later, I arrive at Bar 69, a tiny little hole in the wall place that we all love to come to after work. It's not far from Jess' hotel and Liam's offices, so we've been here plenty of times. The familiar smell of fruity cocktails fills my nose as I walk towards my friends.

"Hey," I say as I plonk myself into the booth with them. Zoey has a drink poured from the cocktail pitcher for me before my bum hits the leather. "Oh, thank you," I say, taking a sip. "Ughh, that's so sweet." I shudder slightly as the vodka and orange juice mix slides down my throat.

"What's wrong?" Jess eyes me curiously. I can't get away with feeling anything without her picking up on it.

"Nothing. I'm fine," I reply, my voice taking on a strange high pitched quality it doesn't normally do, but then I don't normally lie so easily to my sister. Zoey shifts in her seat, sipping her drink to keep her mouth shut. I feel on edge, but I'm not about to admit why to Jess. I can't. Not yet.

"You're such a bad liar, Nora," Jess says flatly. "Fine, don't tell me." Something catches her eye over my shoulder, and she laughs sardonically. "Oh, look, it's Grayson on the prowl for his next victim. Should we go and embarrass him?"

Her words turn my blood to ice. My breath is laced with blades on each staggered inhale. I don't want to turn around and see. Zoey's hand reaches under the table and squeezes my knee, whilst I try to unfreeze my whole body.

"She's definitely his type, too. Blonde, busty. Fake everything," Jess continues, her words causing tiny cuts on my heart without her even realising. I know that turning around is going to slice me open and I'll bleed out all over the table, but I can't help myself. As I turn, I see a blonde. A beautiful blonde, in a low-cut red dress, her hair perfectly styled in a curled ponytail, swept over one shoulder. Her nails lipstick co-ordinate perfectly. Nails that are currently touching a chest I know all too well. Trailing them down an arm that was wrapped around me only this morning.

Bile rises to the back of my throat, and I force it down. The noise of the bar echoes in my head so much louder than it seemed a second ago. The clink of the glass as the barman empties the dishwasher, the shrill laugh of the woman canoodling with Grayson, the conversations of happy people enjoying their evening all makes me feel like I'm being suffocated. *I need to get out of here.*

When he touches the woman's hand, I physically recoil. *How could I have been so stupid? How could I have thought that this man wanted a relationship with me?* He told me from day one that he didn't do relationships and here is proving himself right. Zoey and Jess begin talking behind me, but I can't hear what they're saying. Instead, I watch as another woman joins Grayson. Red hair, long legs, massive boobs again. His eyes trawl over her body, looking at everything I'll never be for him.

"I'm going to use the bathroom," I say, managing to propel myself upright.

"I'll come too," Zoey says. "Jess, can you order us more drinks?"

Zoey grips my hand tightly as I walk along behind our booth towards the bathroom. As soon as the door closes, Zoey has me wrapped in an embrace so tight it stops me breathing. The sting from holding back tears prickles the back of my throat as I heave in as deep a breath as I can manage.

"I know, baby. It's okay," she soothes me, but I'm not crying. I'm vibrating with anger, frustration, rage, and hurt. When she finally releases me, one tear rolls down my cheek.

"I'm stupid, so stupid. I went and caught feelings for the guy who was definitely going to break my heart." I fall apart on the last word, my voice cracking because I feel like a fool.

"Want me to go out there and make out he has diseases?" Zoey offers.

I shake my head. Then nod. Then shake it again. And then another tear falls.

Chapter 28

Grayson

The two women standing in front of me are as fake as they come. Their lips, their boobs, their hair. Nothing about them is real. How do I know this? Because I've spent more time with a real woman lately and now the fake ones stand out a mile.

When I was with Nora last night, I freaked myself out. I panicked, plain and simple. I felt something I've never felt before and as soon as she fell asleep, I left. I went back, like a coward, when I knew she would be at work and posted her key through her letterbox. I didn't trust myself not to use it and be in her house making her dinner, torturing myself with how perfect she is, reminding me how badly I want her, but how I don't deserve her.

The fear that I've gone and fallen for a girl I was never meant to fall for plays on my mind, along with my fear of relationships, and that I'm never going to be enough for her. My fear drove me away from probably the best thing to ever happen to me.

I'd walked here like a zombie after work, managing to avoid Liam all day by some kind of miracle. I hadn't intended to pick anyone up, but standing at the bar, drowning my sorrows, I accidentally attracted the attention of the women beside me.

The blonde leans in closer to me, her sweet sickly perfume makes my stomach roll. "So, gorgeous, what do you do?" Her talons run up the side of my arm, making me shiver. I've got a thing against really long nails – gives me the heebie-jeebies. I shudder at the memory of Louisa's nails from the office visit not long ago. The woman in front of me doesn't notice, though. I assess her, trying to figure out why I feel nothing. She's attractive, it's just all fake. Her blonde hair is wrong, the red lipstick she has on is wrong. Everything is wrong.

"Uhh, I'm in corporate real estate," I reply, not overly paying attention to her. I lift my cool beer to my lips to calm the ongoing storm inside me, but it does nothing.

"Oooh, that sounds interesting," the blonde purrs. I can bet my arse she has no idea what corporate real estate even is, if she's even listening to me at all. The way her eyes eat up every inch of me tells me she probably can't even remember my name.

Is this what I used to be like? Is this how I was with women? Non-committal, not actually listening to them. Fuck, I hate myself if it was.

I look at the blonde and the redhead again, willing my body to react to either one of them. But nothing, nada, zip, zilch. Not even a twitch from my dick.

"Fuck," I curse, running my hand down my face.

"Oh, honey, are you sad? Want us to cheer you up?" The blonde leans in closer, too close. My adrenaline kicks in just in time as she tries to plant a kiss on me. I duck and weave out of the way, causing her to stumble slightly. As I step to the side, I catch sight of Jess sitting alone at a table. My head cocks to the left, confused. Then my body breaks out in an immediate sweat as I see Nora and Zoey exit the toilet.

Zoey leads Nora over to the table in a flurry of quick movements. Her head is down but I can see her cheeks are flushed – Fuck, has she been crying? When she lifts her head, giving me a look of utter disgust. I want to run to Nora and talk to her, touch her and tell her how I feel so I can be with her. I don't want anything to do with the two women behind me. Nora's sad eyes lock with mine as the two women lean in close, whispering things in my ear that I'm not listening to.

Fuck. Fuck. Fuck. This is bad. What, the ever-loving-fuck, am I doing? My hands are suddenly incredibly sweaty, and my heart feels like it's free-falling down a thousand flights of stairs. I'm a goddamn moron even entertaining these women, when the one I want is right fucking there.

Nora pales and grabs her bag, quickly hugging Jess before she rushes towards the exit, hurrying to the cool London air. And I feel like my whole heart is fracturing from the look of pure hurt in her eyes as she gives me a fleeting look on the way past.

Before I can form a thought, my feet follow her, rushing through the exit with so force that the door to the street flies open and slams against the side of the building. I whip around, searching for my dark haired beauty that I stupidly, stupidly let go.

When I spot her practically running away from the bar, I shout her name, but she doesn't turn around. Instead, she speeds up. I run to catch up with her and when I do, my hand lands on her shoulder, but I'm not prepared for what I see when she turns to face me.

Tears, a lot of them. Falling freely down her flushed cheeks. Guilt slams into me, hitting me square in the middle of my chest. *She's crying because of me.* I lift my arms to pull her towards me, but her hands fly out, stopping me. "Fuck, baby, I'm—"

"Don't Grayson," she scolds harshly.

"I'm sorry... I don't know what the fuck I was doing." Which is true. When I think back to the moment, I freaked out last night and then to right now, being with her again, I feel like a different person. She makes me feel like things are good and right, and that scares the shit out of me because any encounter I've had with relationships has been met with pure chaos. My parents, my one night stands, even friends growing up... they all ended badly. I run my hands through my hair, tugging on the strands, giving absolutely no relief to the pain lancing through me.

"I don't need to hear it. You can go back to those women. You clearly had an agenda because your key was in my house this evening. Was that a not-so-gentle hint that you were done with me? Have I been so fucking blind to all this?" Her words burn me, her tears gut me, the truth of my actions slapping me hard in the face.

I never meant to hurt her. I just felt blinded by something I couldn't put into words, but I see it now. I see how fucking wrong I was to run. How fucking childish it was. And how badly I've messed things up.

I take her hand and place it on my chest, and even though she glares at me like she wants to murder me, she doesn't move her hand. "Nora, I'm so fucking sorry. I panicked. Last night was... it was a lot. I don't know what I'm doing. I don't know what I'm feeling, and I lost it. I thought I needed to give you space. I thought you deserved more. I didn't... fuck, I don't know. I never meant to hurt you." Emotion lodges itself into my throat, stopping me from continuing. I need her to understand that there is no one else, but the words get stuck. "Look at me, please."

She breaks into loud sobs as she stares at her hand on my chest, then our eyes connect. Hurt and betrayal replace the once warm caramel in her eyes with darkness, and I hate that I'm the reason for that. "How could you think this wouldn't hurt me?" She swipes at the tears on her face with her free hand.

"I don't know what I was thinking. I got too in my own head. My dad's voice kept echoing in there, like a fucking broken record. But now I realise I was fucking wrong."

She stiffens and assesses me now with fury. "Okay, first of all, your parents' situation isn't your situation. Second, we aren't married, Grayson. We aren't even officially a couple. We're glorified fuck buddies, at best. So don't stand there and feed me bullshit and hide behind excuses. We both went into this scared, but you said you wanted to be good for me."

"Fuck!" I shout into the smoggy city air. "I was scared, okay? I *am* scared. These..." I try to take a breath, but it's stuck in my chest. I rub her hand over the area, and it eases slightly. "These feelings I have for you, I've never..." Fuck, what is going on? I feel like I can't breathe. "I've never felt them before."

Nora softens briefly as she swipes another tear away. She drops her hand from my chest, leaving me feeling empty. She takes measured steps away from me, away from the person who just destroyed everything we had. "Please, Nora, I'm sorry," I say, silently pleading with her to not leave me.

"I need more than an apology right now. I need space. I've spent the last couple of months trying to convince myself that this was casual, and I wasn't catching feelings for you, but guess what? I did and now my feelings are hurt." Her eyes, filled with unshed tears, stare coldly. My shoulders slump forwards, the urge to ground myself becomes too much to ignore as I take in her confession. She has feelings for me? Maybe on some level I knew, I hoped, but I still didn't let myself go there. My mouth parts, heart pounds, ready to explode any minute. Her eyes fill with tears again and it fucking kills me because all I want to do is wipe them away from her beautiful face and tell her that I feel the same. "You need to grow the fuck up and figure out what you want. And I don't just mean with me. If this issue you have is deeper than me, then you need to plan out how you can move on from it. One thing I will say is that I can't live with these blurred lines we've created."

She spins around, frustration emanating from her. "I'm so sorry, Nora, please just wait..."

My body lurches with fear, I need to stop her but how the fuck do I do that? "We haven't completed your list," I say feebly, grasping at anything.

Fury builds on her face as she glances back over her shoulder. "Fuck the stupid list, it means nothing." She heaves air into her lungs. "I can't do this," she sobs.

"Please don't go. I don't know how I can make this better. I don't want to lose you."

Her watery eyes meet mine, looking like blackened infinity pools, and the way her lip trembles breaks something inside of me. "What's that saying? You can't lose something you never had."

Before I can stop her, she's walking away from me again and I can't fucking blame her. I fucked up, and I was careless with the one person who means the most to me. But what she doesn't understand is that she's taking my whole heart with her. It doesn't belong to me anymore; I gave it to her, and I didn't even realise.

Chapter 29

Nora

A lead weight thuds into the pit of my stomach as I walk away from Grayson.

The puff of air that escapes me involuntarily leaves my mouth forcefully, my chest caving inwards, as I stumble completely out of view of the restaurant and down towards the tube. The happiness I felt this week is snuffed out by a heavy feeling of foolishness.

The cool breeze from the approaching train grounds me. The voice over the tannoy in the station feels like they're inside my chest. The rumble of the trains begins from my toes and travels to the tips of my ears. The air that I crave suddenly feels toxic in my lungs.

I shake the feeling, trying to weasel its way into my subconscious, the same one I felt months ago before I wrote my list. When I felt... empty. Like something was missing. Then Grayson had to go and help me – if I look back, I never stood a chance at resisting him. I knew on some level that I'd fall in love with him because I knew there was more to him than he lets on. Confusion builds in my mind, along with the prickle of irritation at myself for letting my feelings get in the way.

I clench my jaw tightly and squeeze my eyes closed as I take a deep inhale of the smoggy underground air. My movements are robotic and uncoordinated as I step onto the tube, the jolting motions of other passengers barely registering as my mind drifts to him.

I don't know why I thought I could be the one to tame Grayson and his playboy ways. I shouldn't be upset, I shouldn't be angry, I should've prepared better for this. But I let my guard down. I started to trust him and let him in. Whatever that was between us a few nights ago was real. I didn't imagine it; I know I didn't. I can't figure out his motives with me. One minute he tells me he wants me and the next he's at a bar picking up women. I understand his parents' marriage fell apart, and that was hard for him. In fact, I get it more than most people because I see it in patients at work.

What I can't figure out is how can he be that way with me, so kind and show me a side to him that I know he doesn't show many, but then pick up women at a bar? It feels like I'm being tossed aside. He said he's never felt these feelings that he has for me before, but I had no idea he was feeling them because he left before I woke up. I want him to feel them and tell me and he's obviously not ready to do that yet.

This list we've been doing was meant to be fun, and it has been for the most part. But now that I'm left with a heart that feels like it's broken it feels a lot less fun.

I swipe the tears I didn't realise were falling again from my cheek, ignoring the unwanted hurt lancing through my chest, where my stupid naïve heart still beats for him. When the train gets to my stop, I hastily speed past slow movers to the exit and when the fresh air hits me I inhale deeply.

Inhale. Exhale. Inhale. Exhale.

Grayson and I never made many promises to one another, but I can't stop feeling hurt. I power-walk the four streets to my house, each step echoing in my ears.

My heart stumbles, my breath suddenly stuck in my throat and as soon as I open my front door, hot angry sobs are drowning out any silence in my hallway. My heart feels like delicate crystal in my chest, and any more damage and it might shatter. I curse because the truth is, I was in deeper than I even realised. Seeing him with those women confirmed that. It's changed everything.

I clear my throat, dry my face and pull out my phone and text Jess and Zoey to let them know I'm fine. I ran out of there, faking illness and I couldn't hang around because Jess would know I was lying.

Nora: I'm home, and okay. Going to bed x

I toss my phone onto the counter and drag myself upstairs. Relieving myself of my clothes that feel heavier somehow, I turn my shower on and crank up the heat filling the room with steam. When I step under the water, the steady thrumming of the jets soothes an ache inside me, and I lean into the release.

When I close my eyes, his face appears in my mind, taunting me with how his dark hair falls in effortless waves. Or how his grey eyes burned into my soul and reach depths no one else has ever dared to look. How my heart thumps just at the thought of him. My heart has never done that for anyone.

After what feels like hours, I turn off the shower and wrap myself in the fluffiest towel I can find as I hear a knock at my door. I quickly throw on some comfy clothes and head down to answer it.

Zoey and Jess burst through the door like a grade five hurricane, snacks and all. "Are you okay?" Zoey asks as she sets her bag down and pulls me into a hug, and those tears I tried so hard to keep back are right there again filling my eyes.

"I'm okay." I sniff.

Jess looks at me over Zoey's shoulder, her face full of questions. She has no idea why I'm crying or what the hell is going on. A jolt of guilt runs through me for keeping this from my sister.

When Zoey releases me, Jess takes my hand and guides us all to the living room.

I sigh as I plonk myself onto the sofa.

"Nora? What's going on? I'm definitely missing something. Are you still sick?" Jess says, the unconditional love in her eyes is mixed with confusion.

"I'm not sick... I've been sleeping with Grayson," I admit, although 'sleeping with' him doesn't feel accurate for what we were doing, but there it is. Jess looks like she's frozen, mouth open and eyes flicking around in confusion. "I'm sorry I didn't tell you. I didn't want it to become a thing. It wasn't supposed to become something but now... I don't even know what's going on." I rub my temples to relieve the tension headache slowly creeping into my head.

Jess comes to sit next to me on the sofa and takes my hand from my head, squeezing it gently. "And those women at the bar?"

"I don't even know what they were but, it's safe to say, we're not sleeping together anymore."

"Fucking dickhead," Zoey mumbles, sitting opposite us on the low coffee table.

"I really wish you'd told me. I would've at least given him a warning that if he hurt you, I'd kill him," her eyes soften. "But I know you,

Nor. What's going on in your head?" Jess asks, placing her hand on my knee that has started jittering.

It's futile ignoring Jess. She knows me better than anyone, which is probably why I never actually told her about Grayson in the first place. It's out of character for me and now I know why.

"I think I'm falling in love with him. Or *was* falling, or am. God, I don't know," I say, dropping my head into my hands with a groan.

I'm terrified that I'm too far gone for him. I've fallen headfirst into something that wasn't meant to last. *I'm afraid.*

"Why are you afraid?" Jess asks. *Shit, I must've said that out loud.*

I let my honest feelings free, admitting them to myself for the first time as I say them out loud to Jess and Zoey. "Well, let's see. I'm terrified of what I feel for him. Like hiding from a mega storm scared. He doesn't seem to want to do the relationship thing. In fact, he told me that several times but clearly my brain and body didn't get the memo. Plus, in reality, I haven't had a relationship that wasn't a disaster."

We're quiet for a second before Zoey leans in towards us both. "Let me tell you a secret. No one is good at relationships. Everyone is trying to make things work, day in, day out. There's no manual for this shit, you have to take the risk sometimes... if you think he's worth it."

"For someone who doesn't want a relationship, you're pretty invested in how they work," I laugh emptily, wondering when Zoey became such a relationship guru.

She shrugs. "Meh, I don't need to want one to know how they work., I guess we're all hardwired to want someone to share our life with. My hardwiring just got fucked up along the way, with my shitty parents with more money than morals, but that doesn't mean I'm unhappy. I have lots of people I care about and who care about me. Don't psychoanalyse me for saying that either." She points an accusatory finger at me. I mime locking my lips and throwing away the key.

Focussing back on the feeling in my chest, I admit, "I'm hurting. What if he slept with those women? What if he's doing that right now?"

"He didn't come back into the bar after he left to find you," Zoey states.

"Outside the bar, he said he had feelings for me, but it's made me more confused," I admit, emotion lacing my voice.

"Do you want to talk to him?" Jess asks.

"I do, but I don't. I'm upset that he told me he liked me *after* I saw him with two women. It may have been nothing but if the roles were reversed, I'm sure he'd feel the same as me and right now, I just want a bit of space. God, my brain is a mess."

"I'm so sorry, Nor. I hate seeing you sad. How can we help?" Jess leans her head against my shoulders, and I take a deep, cleansing breath.

"I'm not sure. You both being here is helping. Do me favour though?" I ask and Jess nods. "Don't say anything to Liam yet. I need a few days to process. I never wanted to put a strain on their friendship. It means a lot to Grayson."

Jess lifts her head to look at me. "Promise."

Zoey claps her hands and stands up. "Right, we're going to do something, no more crying. Wanna watch a movie where the good girl meets a bad boy?" Her eyebrows quirk playfully.

"Do you think she'll be as stupid as I am and fall head over heels for him?" I scoff.

"I'd be disappointed if she didn't," Jess replies.

Chapter 30

Grayson

We're standing in the rugby club waiting for the kids' practice to begin this week. Liam and I have been coaching this under 11s team for a few years now every Sunday. It's fucking freezing today. The shiver of a thought runs through me that we have to go outside into colder conditions makes me want to run back to my bed. But then I don't want that either because for the first time in a while, my bed was empty last night, and I hate it.

The kids are hyped today, running around the changing room like lunatics. "Boys, five minutes and you need to head outside!" I bellow, giving them a time limit to get changed. They all scramble to the door and Liam follows us all out to the pitch. When the cold hits us both, we shudder and zip up our jackets.

"Dude, I need advice," I mumble to Liam. I've been debating whether or not to ask him for help because he doesn't know anything about Nora and me yet. And I'm sure he'll have a lot to say with his fists if he finds out I've been messing around with her behind his back. Although, it's more than messing around and I know that now. I spent the last two nights thinking about her after she walked away from me. I'm an action kind of guy so storming into her house seemed the only option, except her words echoed in my head, *'I need more than an apology right now, I need space'* So I listened and practised restraint, for once in my life.

"About?" Liam asks, sitting on the bench pitch side and fastens the laces of his rugby boots.

I pick up the kit bags ready for our team and start walking out towards the grass, praying that talking to him isn't a bad idea. "A woman."

Liam grabs my arm, stopping me. "You need help with a woman? *You?*" His tone is teasing.

"Funny," I deadpan. He slaps my arm in jest, finding humour in my desperation, but I don't find it all that funny. "I'm serious. I need help."

"Let's start from the top, then," Liam suggests as we walk further onto the field.

"I, uh, I want to prove to her that I'm not a screw up and that I can do the whole commitment thing, but how the fuck do you woo someone?"

He laughs so loudly that it makes me want to low key punch him. "Firstly, never say you're wooing someone again. You're not eighty. Second," Liam pauses, assessing me by raising an eyebrow. "Do I know this woman?"

Fuck. This was a bad idea. "Uhhh, no, but that's not the point. The point is I'm trying to not fuck this up any more than I already have. She's important to me."

Jesus, I'm sweating.

"If she's important to you, are you bringing her to the wedding?" Honestly, Liam knows I know he knows. Or maybe he doesn't. The one and only message I've got from Nora was last night, telling me Jess knows everything. I tried to find out if Liam knew, but he said Jess was sleeping when he left this morning and he was already asleep last night when she got home.

He's my best friend and I want to be honest with him, but I don't know that I can just blurt out that I'm falling for his sister-in-law yet. Or that I may have broken her heart before telling her I'm falling for her.

"No, we hadn't talked about that exactly."

"Why not?" he asks.

"We're going off topic man I need help. Can you help me or not?"

I hadn't realised that our team had gathered around us at this point, all their wide, innocent eyes are on us, waiting to see what happens next in my sad little love life story. "Sorry boys, having girl problems."

They all groan as though they know exactly what that feels like. I hear Liam snigger under his breath.

"Like love problems?" Buddy asks, as he pushes his long dark hair out of his eyes. I nod honestly.

Our resident Mr fix-it, Giles, pipes up from the side of the group. "In my opinion, you've just got to love her man. Love finds you wherever you go. I've been hiding from girls who love me since I was five. They keep finding me, so just do it."

Solid advice from an eight-year-old.

"How do you even fall in love?" asks Buddy.

Shit, this conversation isn't exactly part of the rugby syllabus. I scratch my head hoping Liam will field some of these for me.

"I'm pretty sure someone has to get shot by a baby with an arrow or something, but I don't think the rest of it is so painful," answers Isaac, our wicked little runner. The smallest out of the bunch, but fast as a rocket on the field.

Jude, the best kicker of all these kids, narrows his bright green eyes, a dead serious look on his face as he says, "Just tell her you own all the sweet shops in London. She'll never leave you alone."

How these kids have any idea of love, or I guess, more of an idea about love than I do, a grown man, is terrifying. But what's more terrifying is that I might have to listen to them because my co-coach is too busy sniggering behind me.

"Alright, thanks fellas, you're all doing me a solid with the advice. Shall we start by doing two laps? Go, go, go," I shout and they all sprint like their lives depend on it. I turn to Liam. "It's a sad state of affairs when those eight-year-olds have better advice than you." I point my finger at him before storming away.

"Hey, all you need to do is buy that sweet shop, man." Liam catches up to me and slaps my back.

Guilt slams into me and I realise that I need to tell my best friend.

"It's Nora," I blurt. His eyes darken with several emotions, surprise being the one that seems to stick to him the most.

"Nora?" he confirms, his fists curling at his sides and I nod, mentally preparing myself for the punch that could very well follow. "As in Jess' Nora? My soon-to-be sister-in-law, Nora?"

I nod gingerly. "I'm... in love with her," I say out loud for the first time and it's freeing, releasing the pressure that's been sitting on my chest for weeks if not longer. I'm in love with her. Fuck, that's scary but it's a different kind of terrified from the other night, only because I want her to love me too.

Liam must remember where we are and composes himself slightly, but his fists still clench, so I keep myself on high alert, just in case. "You said you've messed it up already?" he snarls as he picks up a rugby ball and bowls it into my body much harder than he usually would, which fucking hurts.

"Yeah..." I wince, then cough, trying to clear the winded feeling in my stomach.

"So, tell me how you messed up. If Jess knows, you might want to watch your arse in my house because she'll kill you." *Yeah, I know.* "Second thought. I might kill you first."

I take a few measured steps away from him, not wanting to get another ball to the ribs. "I may have panicked about my feelings for her. I got caught up and fast, and I couldn't rationalise what I felt for her. I kept thinking about my parents and how fucked up they were and how my dad would tell me 'never get married'. Logically, I know we weren't getting married, but it didn't stop the panic. I was terrified, and I left her when she was asleep. Then after work on Friday, I..." I stop myself, feeling like a complete arsehole.

"Spit it out, will you?" His jaw ticks and I briefly fear for the next words out of my mouth.

"Two women started talking to me and I didn't stop it. At some point, even though I hated it, I just figured it would be easier, and she deserved more than me, but... everything was wrong. I couldn't get Nora out of my head. Then she was in the bar, and she saw me with them. Nothing... and I mean nothing happened, I realised I couldn't do that. But fuck... I've messed up." I deflate, the image of her crying still haunting me.

Liam's nose flares, and he exhales two heavy breaths. "Dude, Nora is like a sister to me and frankly, I don't ever want to see her hurt, and I kind of want to punch you right now." He twists his neck in frustration that he can't do just that.

"I'd like it if you didn't," I say honestly, hoping he won't.

Liam assesses me for a minute and places his hand on my shoulder, which makes me flinch. "What the fuck, though, man? Nora is good people, why?" His hazel eyes burn into mine.

"I don't fucking know. Like I said, I'm a fuck up. I fucked up. But I'm done using excuses. Help me. I want her more than anything." Desperation clings to my words, but I'm being honest because I finally realise this is how it needs to be.

He stares at the ground for what feels like an age. When he looks up, his mouth is set in a thin line. "You want to work things out with her?"

"I do." *So much.*

"My advice? And the only reason I'm giving it to you and not punching you right now is because I've never seen you hung up on anyone. But like I said—"

"If I hurt her again, I'm a dead man. Message received loud and clear, big guy."

Liam nods. "So, my advice. Women like being bothered by us. We think about them nonstop, so why not let them know? Jess eats it up every time I text her telling her I'm thinking about her, especially in the mornings after I leave for work so maybe try that to start with." Liam shrugs and I realise in that moment neither of us have a damn clue about women.

"Just text her?" I ask confused, feeling like this isn't enough.

"Well, text her yeah, but let her know that you're working on being better. Build her trust back in you."

Build her trust back. That seems like something I can do. But I know I've got to work through some things too. I don't want her to think that I'm just claiming her back and not listening to what she said. She was right. This is deeper than her. I have a fear of commitment that stems from my parents. But I want to be better, for her and for myself.

Liam points at me firmly. "But fuck up again and I will kill you and Jess will help me hide your body. M'kay pumpkin?" I'm slightly terrified by his wide, crazy smile right now.

"Did you just call me pumpkin?" I laugh, tossing him the rugby ball he threw at me.

"Go coach your team, dickhead." He points out to the kids still running laps.

"Okay, pumpkin," I retort, dodging yet another ball hurling my way while ideas begin to spill into my head.

I'm getting my girl back.

Chapter 31

Nora

Grayson: Nora, I know you asked for space, and I want to give you that. But I also want you to know that I will fight for you. There's no excuse for my actions the other night so I'll continue to tell you how sorry I am because it's genuine. I'll be here whenever you're ready to talk to me xx

This message is one of many. Grayson has been messaging me morning, noon, and night since last Friday. Sometimes, they're long messages, other times it's a simple, 'Good morning, shorty,' and my stupid, treacherous heart always leaps when I read that bloody nickname he gave me.

I've been a zombie, going through my usual daily routine. Work has been busy, thankfully, but it doesn't stop the ache in my chest when

I come home to an empty house. He's everywhere; in my kitchen, my bed, sitting at the side of my bathtub. Today is my last office day for the week, and I'm just about ready to collapse into a heap of exhaustion. It's been a hell of a week. After Jess and Zoey left me last Friday, I bolted the front door, and all but locked myself in my room with no sunlight, too much tequila and junk food, which wasn't my best way to set up a busy work week.

As I step outside my front door and feel a crunch under my trainer. Looking down, I see a single white sweet pea and I know immediately who left it there. My heart squeezes and my pulse hammers at the thought of him being so close.

Leaning down to pick up the flower, I bring it to my nose and inhale the sweet, earthy scent. I want to text him, I want to call him, but I refuse. I can't just give in because he's the first man to get me flowers. Where are my morals if I do? Plus, I have a new plan, a plan to get over my man—as *Monica Gellar* once said. Thankfully, I won't be making millions of jars of jam though.

Instead, I drop the flower back onto the floor and strut to work. My new mantra on repeat as I walk. *I do not need a man.*

By the time I get into work, I *feel* like a new woman. My mind is clearer than it has been all week and I'm ready to get back to helping people again. As I round the corner to my office, I stop immediately as I open the door, when I see another bunch of white sweet peas resting on my desk.

You've got to be fucking kidding me.

"Oh yeah, those were dropped off early this morning with strict instructions to leave them on your desk," the receptionist says, filing her nails, not looking up at me.

I feel like if I cross this threshold into my office, I'll be conceding something. One single flower I can handle. That goes in the bin. But a whole bunch? That's a waste and I hate that. But I also want to stomp on them, the way he stomped all over my feelings.

"Can you please remove them from my desk and donate them to another desk in the office?" I ask the receptionist politely. Her head slowly rises to meet my eye, obviously confused as to why I don't want this beautiful bunch of flowers, but I can't sit at work and stare at them all day. He's already in my head and my office was my sanctuary. And I will not be pushed out of my sanctuary by some flowers from a man.

Just as I step into my office, my client and first appointment of the day, Ella, rounds the corner. "Ooooh those are pretty," she says, giving the offending posey the biggest heart eyes.

"You want them?" I say without really thinking. Ella's nervous eyes flick between me and the flowers. "I'm not in the habit of giving out flowers, but I was going to donate those anyway." I'm trying to act nonchalant as I stand by the side of my desk, which, of course smells like the most beautiful fresh flowers.

Ella walks over to the bunch and plucks one out and then plonks herself onto her usual comfy seat opposite my desk. "So... do you hate flowers or just the person who sent them?"

I follow her to the seating area, pick up my tablet and notepad, and settle in my chair. "I like flowers. Those are my favourite," I say mindlessly.

"So, it's the person who sent them."

I silently huff. "Ella, we are not here to talk about me today. How was your weekend?"

She shifts, playing with the white flower head in her hand, assessing it like it's a complete anomaly to her. "My weekend was good. Mum and I went to get ice cream. I saw friends. It was the best in a while. No arguing."

"That's good," I smile, taking some notes. "Can you tell me how you felt after each day?"

She plucks a petal from the flower and squeezes it in her index finger and thumb, still not making eye contact with me. "Happy. Normal."

"Good."

"How was your weekend?" she asks.

I clear my throat. "My weekend was... good, thank you," I lie. That's when her eyes lift to mine.

"You're lying."

"Tell me what made you feel good, specifically this weekend."

She pauses, her big, wide eyes staring at me before she squashes the entire flower head in her hand. I can't help but smile a little because that was satisfying to watch. "Oh, he hurt you good if you're smiling at me destroying your flowers."

I lift my eyes to hers, which are laced with amusement. "Ella," I sigh. "I'm sorry, but talking about me won't be near as conducive to your treatment. Talking about you, however..."

Her eyes roll. "Yeah, yeah I get it. But just in case you think I'm a naïve kid, you know I've been through enough in my life for that not to be the case." The crushed petals fall from her hand onto the floor. "And for the record, he's an idiot if he hurt you."

I smile because the shy girl I met months ago wouldn't have dared be so open with me. But the blossoming young adult in front of me is growing in confidence and that's something to smile about.

We talk for the entirety of her appointment, and she doesn't revert to me again. When she leaves, she takes the flowers, offering them back to me once more just in case, but I want her to have them.

Around 2pm, my phone buzzes on my desk. I glance over, but it dims before I can catch the name. I'm too distracted by writing up client notes that I don't check it for another hour.

Grayson: I hope your morning has been good x

It's a text that he's sent before and one that I didn't think much about. But I can't stop the silly flutters that are trying to take flight inside my chest. I need to talk to him, but I need to get through today at the very least. I turn it onto silent and place it inside my drawer for now.

Grayson

I've done a lot of thinking, and a lot of brooding over the last week. Most of it productive, too. It turns out when I'm trying to woo Nora—yes, I said it again. Liam can suck it—I'm the most productive person in all of London. I wake up and workout, then I head over to the florist, buy a few sweet peas and place them on her doorstep. I don't know if she takes them inside or puts them in the bin, but either way, I'm not going to stop. I get to work on time, blitz all my paperwork and show up early, again, to appointments with clients. And today I'm heading to my first therapy appointment.

During my brooding, I realised that I have some topics I want to discuss. I asked Jess and Liam to help me find someone local who wasn't Nora, and Jess recommended two—one of whom had an appointment free today and we've already had a brief zoom call. He seemed nice, which is why I'm here waiting in a reception for him to call my name.

An older man opens a door, scanning the empty room before he settles on me. "Grayson." He smiles kindly. "Please, come in."

My pulse speeds up because I've never actively sought help for anything before. I'm much more of a 'sort it myself' kind of guy, so all of this feels foreign. I shuffle in, not knowing what to do with my hands or if I should sit or wait for him to invite me to sit.

"I won't bite. You can sit," Dr Hobbs says. With the very big name sign on his desk, I'll surely never forget his name.

"Uhh, thanks." I move to the chair opposite him. Sitting awkwardly and adjusting myself a few times until I'm comfortable. He sits, tapping away on his tablet until I'm settled. "Okay, Doc, I'm ready."

His eyes lift to mine with mirth. "I'm glad you're comfortable. So, today I'd like to get to know you and why you're here. The more involved and collaborative you are, the sooner you'll see benefits from our sessions. We will also touch on treatment plans depending on how much we get through today. Does that sound good?"

I nod, confidently. "Sounds great."

"Okay, so tell me about yourself. Even if you think I know it from our zoom call, tell me anyway."

I run my hands down the length of my dark jeans and take a deep breath. *I can do this.*

"I'd like to jump straight in, since you know my name and all that already. I recently started seeing a woman, and it was good. No, it was fantastic. She's beautiful, smart, amazing... well you get the idea." I pause, feeling the pang of missing her in my chest. "But I got into my own head too much, let my past dictate my future. And I'm here now because I want to be better, for me... which will hopefully in turn let me be better for her one day."

Hobbs nods his head and takes notes. "Go on..."

So, I do, I tell him every detail about my parent's divorce and messed up marriage and we talk about how it affects me as an adult. When I leave, an hour later, I feel different, like something has shifted. I've spent a lot of time burying the bad feelings around my parents and opting for the good times only. But that's not enough anymore. I need more out of my life, and I need to be on my way to a clearer headspace to do that. I can't be everything for anyone if I'm not a hundred percent for myself and starting this process with Dr Hobbs is helping me understand that now.

As I walk to my car, I pull out my phone. She hasn't texted me back and I don't need her to, not until she's ready to talk. But I'll be damned if I let her continue to think I don't care about her.

> **Grayson:** Hey, shorty. I hope you're having a good day. I can't decide on dinner, we both know I can barely cook anything, so I guess I'm heading to get Thai food. I hope you're having a good night x

I know I won't get a response. I haven't yet, and it's been a week of me texting. But I need her to know that I'm not going anywhere and when she finally concedes and talks to me, maybe I can tell her how I'm trying to be better, but I only want to share if it's something she wants to hear.

Grayson: Or maybe on second thoughts, I'll cook my famous chicken pasta but mostly because that's all I can cook. What I'd do for some of your cake making skills tonight. Sleep well, shorty x

Nora

"Can you pass the pepper?" Jess asks.

When I do, her eyes give me the same look she's been giving me all night. Like she wants to tell me something but doesn't know how. "For the love of God, will you just tell me whatever it is you're hiding?"

Liam chuckles next to me. They invited me over for dinner—which seems to be a recurring weekly event now, well the two weeks since the whole Grayson thing anyway—and I never say no, because I miss the company.

Jess grinds the pepper shaker over her salmon, then sets it down and looks at me. "It's nothing, really."

"Well, that's a lie. It's clearly something because you've been giving me that look all night. Are Mum and Dad okay? Are you guys pregnant? Are you moving? Please feel free to pause my questions if I get one right."

"Mum and Dad are fine. You'd be one of the first to know if we were pregnant and we've just moved. I am not in a hurry to do that again."

"So, then…"

"Jess, you're torturing her," Liam laughs lightly.

"Thank you. Someone sees my pain." I gesture to Liam gratefully.

The inhale that Jess takes is directed at Liam, almost silently asking him if she should say whatever it is she's about to say. He nods and she brings her bright blue eyes to me. "I wanted to see how you're doing after the whole Grayson thing."

My eyes narrow. "That's not all. I can see it on your face."

Jess shifts uncomfortably. "Grayson seems like he's doing good. Liam said he's been at work early and keeping busy. I just wondered, have you spoken to him?"

Hearing that he's doing well makes me feel something hot and upset. How can he be good when I feel like I'm breaking apart some days?

"He won't like me telling you this, but I think you should know he's going to therapy. Twice a week. He's been a few times now." Liam says, keeping his eyes on me.

Something that feels a lot like guilt slams into me, making my eyes prickle and the hairs on the back of my neck stand up. I haven't spoken to him, but I have heard from him. I haven't been able to reply for two weeks because, well, it has a lot to do with my pride, but also because I don't know what to say anymore. I still have feelings for him and even though I know I should be dealing with them, I can't bring myself to deal with the pain.

"I haven't spoken to him, but he messages me every day. And leaves me flowers on my doorstep," I say softly.

Jess clutches her chest, her voice laced with emotion. "He does?"

I nod, pushing my food around my plate. Suddenly, I have this weird feeling in the pit of my stomach, like I need to talk to him to check if he's okay.

"I think he's trying to change, and I think you should talk, that's all," Jess suggests.

And I know she's right. I want to talk to him.

A couple hours later and I'm sitting on my bed, phone in my hand, my thumb hovering over his name. "Get a grip, Nora. Just call him," I mutter to myself. Closing my eyes, I press down on his name and bring the phone to my ear. My heart beats wildly, trying to escape its cage.

"Hey Nora." His raspy, deep voice affects me far more than I'd expected it to. "Nora?"

Shit, I haven't said anything and now I'm just a creep who pants down the phone. "Hey. I'm sorry, it's late. I just realised the time," I say shakily.

I hear shuffling noises. "No, it's not that late. It's good to hear your voice."

"Likewise,"

"Are you at home?"

"I am."

And then there's an awkward silence because how am I supposed to casually ask my ex-fuck buddy about his mental health? There's nothing casual about us. We're still wading through the aftermath of whatever we were, and that complicates things. I can't just come out and ask, but I'm the one who called him, so I need to think of something.

"How have you been?" he asks before I get the chance to say anything, and I'm grateful that he took charge.

"I've been..." *tired, emotional, lonely, frustrated.* "Busy with work." It's the truth. I've thrown myself into work, spending more time than I probably should reviewing old case files and completing online training.

"Busy is good," he replies.

"How have you been?"

"I've been okay, not great. I have been working plenty too." He pauses for a second, then takes a sharp inhale. "I'm taking your advice."

My heart picks up to a steady canter. "My advice?"

"I'm talking to a therapist. You were right. I need to do it. My head has been a mess for a while and dragging you into that just proved to me that I had some unresolved issues I need to work through." He exhales roughly and I imagine him dragging his hand over his face and rubbing his chin thoughtfully. "Nora, I'm really sorry. I know you probably don't want to hear it, but I want to say it. I need to. I never meant to hurt you, but you need to understand why I acted the way I did."

"I'm listening."

He sighs deeply and I feel it all the way through the phone. "I know I've mentioned my parents splitting up before, but growing up, they weren't all bad. It got worse when I turned ten. They argued constantly and would threaten to leave the other and take me with them like I was a suitcase and not a human being. Living in a constant state of fear that my parents would never be happy has impacted me more than I'd realised. I shut myself off. I never got attached to anyone and I worst of all, I didn't show you how I felt about you because of that.

"I struggled to see how any relationship I would have with someone would be different. I was a product of two people who, in the end, hated each other. So, when I started having feelings for you, fuck, I was terrified. I wanted to tell you how much you meant to me, but the fear inside, I let it choke me and I ran. I shouldn't have and I don't know what I was thinking because as soon as I left you, deep down, I knew I'd made the biggest mistake of my life.

"Nora, I can't lose you. I don't want to. You make me so happy. I'm not perfect, but I'm trying to be better for me, and for you. I want…"

I cough to clear the lump in my throat. "What?"

He takes a measured deep breath. "More than anything, I want you to let me back in, please, let me try and be better for you, for us."

Tears fall freely down my cheeks. I can *feel* he's sorry, and that just makes me feel more confused. I want to forgive him, jump into his arms again and feel that connection we'd built over the last few months. But I also want to hold him at arm's length because I'm scared too. But isn't falling in love about taking the risks too? Isn't that what I've been trying to achieve with my list? I put myself out there and he took me on a journey that I'm incredibly grateful for. In a few months, I've had more fun than my whole life.

"I'm scared, Grayson," I admit, emotion coating my voice.

"I know, shorty. I am too. If there was a guidebook I'd give it to you, but there isn't. Emotions are raw and real, and that shit is scary. But let me chase away those fears. Let me show you how good I can be for you."

My heart beats for those words he's saying. I do want more with him. I can feel it. Maybe we can build something that's real. We sit in silence for a few seconds, listening to each other breathe.

"I'm really proud of you for speaking to someone," I say, breaking the silence.

"Thank you. That means a lot."

"So how do I make the mixture?" Grayson asks through the phone. I can hear him fumbling around and probably making a mess in his kitchen. "All I can really remember is the egg cracking, which I have mastered, by the way. I'm taking your egg-cracking ninja title."

I stifle a laugh. "Is that a thing?"

"It is now."

"If you say so."

"So, back to the cake mix," he prompts.

I get up off my sofa and head into my kitchen. "How about if I make one at the same time then we can talk through the steps together."

"Sounds good. Could we..." He trails off.

"Could we what?"

"Nothing. Don't worry about it. Teach me your ways, *Mary Berry*."

I snort an unflattering laugh. "Have you been watching Bake Off?"

"Maybe a little, but only the old stuff with Mary in. It's addictive, okay?"

"Hey, no judgement here." I chuckle. "Okay, maybe a little bit, but I like that you're taking this seriously."

"Very seriously."

"So, tell me what you wanted to say a minute ago."

He pauses, the huff of his breath the only sound through the phone speaker. "I wanted to video call you, but I don't want to push you. So, I decided it wasn't a good idea to ask."

A flush spreads from my neck to my face. It's hot and itchy. We haven't seen each other in any capacity for three and a half weeks, not that I'm counting. I'm nervous but we've spoken almost every day for the last week or so. Things are changing for us. We're finding ways to communicate that don't involve intimacy. It's been good.

"Nora? I said it's fine. Let's make this cake."

Before I can talk myself out of it, I move the phone away from my face and hit the video call button. When his face comes into view, I stumble on my breath and end up coughing a lot to clear the sudden inhale that's trying to choke me.

"Two seconds," I say, placing the phone on the worktop and getting a glass of water. *God, he looks good. Too good.* I forgot that magnetism I felt for him. His hair looks messy and wild, and his eyes are my exact shade of kryptonite. I need to pick the phone back up, but somehow, looking at him from a distance without him looking at me feels easier for a second, whilst I try and focus on swallowing my water.

"You okay over there? Need me to come over and perform mouth to mouth?" He smiles, amused but wearily. This cheeky side of him is also something I missed. I'm usually serious where he isn't, and I like that about him. I miss that about him.

I move over to the counter and pick the phone back up. When our eyes connect, he slowly releases a deep breath.

"Nora, fuck." I feel my pulse beating in my throat. "I know this might make me sound like a loser but seeing you just then... you made my heart stumble. You're so beautiful."

I'm radioactive now, uncontrollably hot and bothered because I haven't had a single compliment since he gave them to me. He shifts closer to the phone, as though he can gain access to me that way. I smile and he smiles back. It's heady having his attention. I'd forgotten how much I enjoy it.

"Thank you. You look good too, I guess."

He pulls the camera back, clutching his chest. "Be still my heart. I've missed your sass."

My hands tingle holding the phone, as I let my mind wonder what else he's missed. I press my lips tightly together to keep from smiling like a schoolgirl.

"I've missed *you*," he says, rubbing the back of his neck.

My insides heat to molten lava. The way his grey eyes take me in, even virtually, make me want to physically tremble. "So, the cake," remembering the reason we are video calling, desperately trying to distract from the moment we were slipping into.

He swallows and pushes his untamed hair from his forehead. "Right, the cake."

"You know that movie you suggested?" Grayson says sleepily through the video call that we've been on for over an hour.

"Which one?"

"The one where the dad is super highly strung, and his daughter gets married to a guy called Brian?"

I smile. "*Father of the bride*?"

"Yes, that's the one."

"You didn't like it?" I ask, wondering why he's still insistent on listening to my recommendations when his favourites include all the *Fast and Furious* films.

"I cried. Like a baby."

I sit up, my legs protesting at the stretch of my hamstrings from the speed I flung myself upright. "You cried?"

He nods but looks away briefly. "It was the wedding. When he was reflecting on his time with his baby girl. It just got me." I see his throat swallow and he exhales a long breath. "I'm going to be a mess at Jess and Liam's wedding next weekend."

I want to hug him, to feel whatever emotion he's feeling right now. These nightly video calls are becoming more and more like torture because I want more connection with him. I see him; all his flaws and his perfections and I'm beginning to want it all.

The fact that I'll see him at the wedding next week just makes me wish it would come sooner.

"Hey Grayson," I say, needing to tell him the truth about something I've been feeling for a while now. He turns his head to look at me, smiling softly. "I need you to know that I don't hate you for what happened. I had so many feelings for you that I ignored, and I should've been honest, too. I'm sorry."

His grey eyes widen, then immediately soften again. "You don't have to apologise. I never ever meant to hurt you, and I know I did. I should've never—"

"Stop. There's no point in 'shoulda woulda coulda'. Maybe we both hurt each other. I've done a lot of reflection too and I've stopped putting so much pressure on being this perfect version of myself, and that includes the desperation I felt when we were together, trying to label whatever it was or wasn't. I've also realised that it doesn't matter if I have a list. The truth of it all is that I'm happy with being who I am, and I'll take things as they come, instead of forcing things to happen. I'm sorry if you ever felt like I forced you into helping me with the list. It was never meant to be a shackling experience."

"I never felt that way, Nora. I told you once before, your list wasn't the reason I wanted to be around you."

I shrug off the building emotion lodging in my throat. "Even so. I would've become far less interesting once that list had ended and so I've removed the pressure of it."

His head shakes in apparent disbelief. "Nora, listen to me. You're the most interesting person in every room."

My heart melts in my chest, beating a gruelling rhythm. Any concerns I had about him not caring or not taking anything seriously melt away. It just took him a beat to get there.

"Can I ask you something?" His voice filters through my phone's speaker, raspy and sexy, just like it always was.

"Of course."

"A minute a go you said you had feelings for me, past tense. Does that... do you no longer have those feelings for me?" The layer of vulnerability in his voice has my throat constricting. We've been talking and for the last couple of weeks and frankly, I think I'm ready to talk about how we really feel too.

"I do have feelings for you. Big ones and they're not past tense," I admit, because although I was scared, he's made me see that I don't need to be scared all the time and neither does he.

He smiles, running his hand across his lips, drawing my attention to them. "That's really good to hear. I'm glad because I have some pretty big feelings for you too, shorty."

Grayson

"Dude, how you feeling?" I look at Liam who is packing to leave for the wedding venue tonight. I'm already packed and driving us both there, although we are staying off site—the venue is relatively small, and the bridal party needed all the rooms they had.

"Surprisingly calm," he replies.

"Yeah? That's good. You've got nothing to worry about. It's going to be a beautiful day."

He turns to face me, a question forming on his lips. "And how will things be between you and Nora tomorrow?"

I want to answer him honestly and say that I think it'll all be fine. Nora and I have been talking for the last month. At first, on the phone then video calls. And I've been leaving her flowers, which she told me she now takes inside rather than puts them in the bin, which is progress. I want to tell him that it won't be awkward, but it might be. We haven't been in the same room this whole time, both using the safety of the phone as a protective barrier.

I'm nervous, I'm excited and I'm a big ball of anxiety because what if she changes her mind when she sees me?

Therapy has helped more than I could have imagined. I've come to terms with some things from my past and am working towards letting some fears go, which I've been talking to Nora about. It turns out, a good few sessions under my belt and my doc was able to give me some much needed perspective. Dr Hobbs said this week that he thinks I've been living in a 'battle zone' state for a while, which explains why I pushed away ninety-eight per cent of human connections and kept everyone at surface level. I've never fully dealt with my parents' divorce and constant arguing, hence the fucked up state of mind.

The minute he explained it, I felt like a weight had been shifted from my shoulders. He saw me and he understood something I was feeling but couldn't quite verbalise. He didn't judge or make me feel like I'd done something wrong. He's teaching me how to accept and move on from things I had no control over and that alone has changed my mindset.

At some point, I know it's going to get more difficult because I'll be connecting with both my parents in the future which I'm hoping will be with Nora by my side. But I don't know exactly where we stand, despite me dying to tell her on a daily basis exactly how much I love everything about her. The way she laughs, the way she scowls at me when I call her shorty, her gorgeous body that I miss so much, her need to have everything done a certain way and to the best of her ability. She's easily the most amazing person I know and I'm a fool for not seeing it sooner… or at least not telling her how I felt sooner.

I didn't really know what this feeling was until her and yeah, it's scary but it's also incredible. Now I'm beginning to understand it more, I want to shout from the rooftops just how much I love her. It's killing me not telling her every day.

"I think it might be awkward to begin with, but things are going well," I reply to Liam, offering him as much reassurance as I can. I had some things delivered to Nora's hotel room today that I'm hoping will get her talking to me before the wedding tomorrow, and things won't be as awkward when we see each other.

He nods. "I'm glad. And the therapy is still going well?"

"It is. I'm working through things and feeling good." Not all my sessions have been productive, thanks to my stubborn arse trying to avoid the difficult parts, but even after a handful of sessions I feel better just talking to someone who doesn't judge. I'm getting better at sharing and being open.

Liam surprises me and slaps my back, pulling me into a hug. "Proud of you, man."

I return his embrace. "Thanks, dude. That means a lot."

We both awkwardly clear our throats, not usually opting for such deep topic of conversations or hugs for that matter. "Let's get you married."

Chapter 32

Nora

A rriving at the hotel, I slowly drive up the gravelled road until I see the beautiful brownstone building covered in winding ivy on the one side. It's a manor house that's been converted into a boutique hotel. It's very 'Jess' and it gives me a thrill of excitement that this day is finally here.

Gathering my bags and bridesmaid dress, I walk through the ornate arch doorway and push open the heavy door with a grunt.

As I approach the reception area, I adjust my bag on my shoulder and stand up straighter. "Hi, I'm part of the Scott-Taylor wedding party. My name is Nora Scott," I tell the receptionist.

He clicks a few times on his computer. "Ah yes, Miss Scott. Your room is ready if you'd like to check in now."

"Yes, please." I nod. "Can I also have the key to the bride's room? I'm her maid of honour and I have some surprises to set up for her."

"Of course." He taps the keys on his computer quickly before handing me two sets of keys. "The rooms are a floor apart, yours is room 52, which is on floor three and the bridal suite is 65, on floor four. Do you need help with anything?"

I shake my head. "I'm good, thank you."

I walk to the lifts. The usual pit I'd feel in my stomach thinking about travelling up in this death trap isn't there. It's replaced by memories of Grayson's lips on mine. My hand wanders to my mouth. I trace over my bottom lip and think about the way he would always suck and kiss it, distracting me until the lift doors opened. A weight settles on my chest at the thought of seeing him tomorrow. Excitement and anticipation swirling in my mind. We've been video calling for the last month, but this will be the ultimate test for me. For us.

As the lift opens on Jess' floor, I find her room and set up the few items I picked for her; prosecco, a bride-to-be silk robe, fluffy slippers, and some new cosy PJs. Then I text Jess to meet me at my room before dinner.

When I get to my room on the lower floor, I see something on the ground outside my door. As I get closer, I realise it's a white sweet pea. On top of a book. I pick them both up, smiling to myself and inhaling the sweet floral scent.

I open the door with my key card, making sure to leave the door on the latch for Jess, and I amble inside. Placing my luggage on the rack near the wardrobe, I hang my dress in the bathroom as I feel my phone buzzing in my back pocket. When I see the caller ID, my heart does a little dance.

"Hey," I answer breathlessly.

"Hey, shorty. How was the drive to the venue?"

"Good. Quick. I've just got to my room." I exhale, trying to even out my breathing. "Then I'm going downstairs for dinner with Jess in an hour."

"Oh yeah? How's your room?"

"It's good. A usual hotel room."

"Cool." I don't think I've ever heard him say that word. "So, was there anything interesting about your room?"

"Oh, you know the usual. Bathroom, nice white bed linen, balcony..." I trail off, listening to him hum in acknowledgement. "Oh, and there was a book and flower outside my door."

"Huh, interesting. Must've been a really awesome person to leave you gifts," he says, his voice laced with humour.

I look down at the book he left for me and my brows furrow. I'm only just realising now it's a crossword book. I hadn't looked at it properly before. Before I can open it and inspect it further, he speaks, gaining my attention.

"Okay, well. I'll see you tomorrow, shorty. Enjoy your crosswords and dinner. I can't wait to see you," he says with a little buzz in his voice that's echoed in the energy buzzing through me right now.

We hang up and I run my fingers over the black and white squares on the front cover. Opening the book, I start flicking through the pages when it falls open onto a page with a folded piece of paper inside. When I unfold it, my eyes widen and my heart catapults. It's a personalised crossword puzzle.

Grabbing a pen from the side table, I sit on the bed and begin decoding my puzzle.

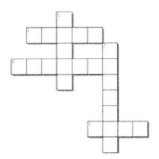

Across

2. Your last name
4. The amount of time I want to be with you
5. Your first name

Down

1. The way I feel about you
3. My full name

When you're done, flip the page over.

If I thought my heart was beating loudly before, I was wrong. Now it's a thunderstorm, a hurricane and a 4.9 earthquake on the Richter scale.

I read the completed words from the crossword back to myself.

GRAYSON LOVES NORA SCOTT FOREVER

Over the page I see more.

On your list you wrote 'Fall in love for the first time' and I'm pretty sure I wrote something like 'You're on your own with this one.' I didn't expect to be the one to admit to falling in love but it felt inevitable when I think about it.

You're the best surprise I've ever had in my life, and I don't want to live without you,

Nora. If I had a list, falling in love would be ticked off because of you.

I raise my hand to my mouth covering a sob, a happy sob, one filled with elation and joy. My heart soars out of my chest. My fingers are numb and tingling. There it is in black and white in front of me. He loves me.

I never wanted easy love with the white picket fences. What I wanted was for someone to come and knock that stereotype out of the window and replace it with something *we* created. I don't want a preconceived notion of what my life should look like. I want him. I want him raw, vulnerable, snarky and difficult. I want all of him. Underneath all his bravado, his heart is his best quality, and I want it all to myself.

"Hey, you." Jess opens the door to my room, startling me for a second. She pauses when she sees my tear tracks on my face. "Woah, what's going on?"

Just as I open my mouth, she looks down at the crossword on the bed in front of me. Her eyes widen and then they flit between me and the paper, reading what's written on the page. "This is from Grayson?"

"No, this is from another guy," I joke. Jess balks for a second and recovers quickly when she sees my unamused eyebrow quirked. "Of course, it's from Grayson."

"He loves you. I just got butterflies for you. This is so adorable." Jess swoons and I fight a smile.

"I guess he does."

"Do you love him?"

I nod shyly. "I do."

"Then we have loads to celebrate tonight."

An hour later, we're in the restaurant for dinner when I quickly fire off a text to Grayson.

> **Nora:** So... you love me?

> **Grayson:** Where are you?

> **Nora:** At the venue, just about to have dinner with Jess. You didn't answer my question.

A few minutes go by, and I think he might not reply when Zoey joins us, and I tuck my phone away to be with the girls.

My eyes are heavy as I lay on my bed in the hotel. The high thread count has me sinking into clouds. I made sure Jess didn't drink too much tonight, and Zoey for that matter, which left me feeling like I'd been herding cattle because those two are complete menaces. An hour after settling them both in their rooms and I'm back in mine.

A soft rattle startles me from my impending sleep. I bolt upright in bed, but I hear nothing, so I presume it must've been the ivy at my window. I close my eyes again and snuggle into my pillow.

Tap tap tap.

Now that definitely wasn't the ivy. I sit up, realising that someone is knocking on my door. I'm guessing it's Jess because she hates sleeping alone and I should've pre-empted this and just shared a room.

I drag myself out of my cosy cocoon, hating the way the cool air bites at my skin when I stand. Covering my oversized t-shirt I put on for bed, with my arms I open the door and there stands the last person I thought I'd see tonight.

His dark hair hangs messily over his forehead, his eyes are wild the way his gaze roams over my body, leaving hot embers in its wake. It's almost too much to bear the weight of his gaze. It's heady and delicious and something I haven't done in person for over a month.

God, I've missed him.

He closes the door behind him, and we say nothing, standing in my doorway, both suddenly panting with desire. He steps forward, towering a good foot above me, and I relish the way my neck strains to look up at him. My pulse quickens, my palms twitch to touch him, to run my fingers underneath his t-shirt and feel every ridge of his abs that I know are hiding there.

"Hi," he whispers. I'm unable to speak, unable to move before his hot mouth is on me, devouring me.

When we break apart, he's frowning and my fingers instantly move to smooth over the lines in his brow as he holds me against his body. "You're here," I whisper.

"Like I could stay away any longer," he sighs, my head drifting up and down with the movement. I need to ask you something. A few weeks ago, you said something that has been on my mind. You said you can't lose something you never had." He pauses, making my throat prickle with emotion. "I refuse to believe that. I know you. I know how big your heart is and how much you give it to people you care about. You show love in everything you do, and I know now that I felt that with you. Please tell me I have you because I can't go another second believing that you weren't mine all along."

I take in all of his words, dropping my gaze and closing my eyes for a second. When I look up and our eyes connect again, he's looking at me like I've stolen something of his and it guts me. This man is soft and gentle, hiding behind a façade of fear and a past that he couldn't escape, but he's trying. He's here, he's been here for me for the last month, talking to me, leaving me gifts, telling me he loves me.

And I love him. The memory of earlier, how my soul sprang into action from reading his crossword for me. I love him.

My hands cup his face, grazing against his dark stubble. "Grayson, I'm sorry I said that. I was angry and hurt, but only because I felt like you were mine even when I believed you weren't. The truth is, I wanted to be yours."

"You need to tell me if you don't want this anymore. If I'm not enough," he murmurs as his forehead lowers to mine.

Frogs leap into my throat, and I try to swallow to clear the feeling. "Grayson, you are enough. I want to be yours. I want you to be mine. I love you."

I don't have a chance to take another breath before he's back on my lips, searing kisses onto my lips. "Say it again," he mumbles softly in between kisses.

"I love you. I love you. I love you." I smile as he dives back in to take what's his.

We break apart briefly, our eyes to lock in a gaze that feels like a million words are being said, when really only our silence is speaking to one another. He brings his hands to brush my face and I lean into his touch. His hands move quickly down my body before he lifts my legs and wraps them around his waist as he comes crashing into my lips again. "I love you so fucking much," he says against my mouth, not letting me go.

And I don't want him to let me go.

When you've been starved of something, the feeling of having it again is like a comet crashing to earth. My whole body sparks to life as his mouth demands my attention and his tongue seeks mine. The feel of his hands gripping me possessively around my hips is spine-tinglingly good. My moan breaks the kiss that is consuming every inch of me. Grayson's eyes darken at the noise as he pushes me against the wall.

I whimper, silently begging him to touch me more. Needing him to. He hums in approval when he dips his hand between us and he discovers I'm not wearing underwear. His fingers find my clit as he applies the perfect amount of pressure and dips his fingers inside me.

God, I love it when he touches me. All too soon, he withdraws from me, leaving me needy again as he licks his fingers clean.

"I want to make you feel good, Nora. I've missed you so fucking much," he pleads before biting into my neck and immediately kissing it better. The sensation makes me crazy, my breathing completely surrendering to a staccato rhythm as his hands slip back into my sex, his fingers expertly working me into a glorious state of hysteria as my body tingles with my release.

His eyes roll back in his head when two fingers slide inside me, and I bite my bottom lip to stop from shouting out. "So fucking sexy," he growls. The deep gravel of his voice hits me right in between my legs, my body seeking friction as I push into his fingers further.

"Grayson," I whisper into his neck, feeling his hard cock against me. I need him, I want him, I've missed him so much. Reaching my hand between us, I palm his hard length over his jeans, and he thrusts further into my hand.

"Fuuuuck, that feels good," he hisses.

His thick fingers work me until I'm shaking in his arms. "I'm so close," I rasp. He increases the pressure on my clit, moving in circles, working me up higher and higher. My hand grips the outline of his cock harder, and he mumbles incoherently into my neck.

The echoes of my arousal fill my quiet hotel room along with soft whimpers that are slowly climbing towards loud moans from both of us. His head moves up to look at my face, his cheeks flushed with desire. "Let go for me. I need to hear you." Like the good girl I am, I let it go. The fastest orgasm I've ever had spirals from my core, tiny explosions going off inside me from where his fingers work me into a frenzy.

"Oh... my... God..." I scream as the pulsing pleasure rips its way through my body. I squeeze my eyes closed, riding the waves.

The soft open mouth kisses he sweeps across my collarbone make me shiver as I come down from my high. He keeps me against him, as though I might disappear if he lets me go, his grip not punishing anymore but soft, yielding.

He nuzzles his face into my neck, resting his lips on my pulse point as it hammers away under him.

"I can't stay away from you. I couldn't wait to see you tomorrow." He doesn't lift his head from my neck as he speaks, his words absorbing into my skin with his hot breath. I tangle my fingers into his hair rewarded with a groan when I reach the back of his neck and his head lifts to push against my hand.

I take in his face, inches away from mine. The angle of his sharp yet soft jaw, his irritatingly perfectly fanned eyelashes as they stay flush against his cheeks, the slope of his nose and the tiny imperfection in the bridge of it, the stubble that is decorating half of his face framing it perfectly. The man is a fucking masterpiece.

"You're staring," he whispers, and I melt.

"You make it hard not to, besides I've not been able to do it for a while." I stroke the side of his face, savouring the softness of his cheek before his stubble grazes my fingers.

His gaze cloaks me, encasing me in a vault of his energy. Waves of his emotions hit me like the tide, crashing into my own emotions like a mirror. I love him.

"Come, lay with me for a minute." He links our hands and pulls me towards my bed. He perches on the end of the mattress and lifts me onto his lap. His large hands wrap around me, his head resting on my chest. I push him backwards to lie down and softly rest over him, letting my body relax into his.

My head is laying over his left pec when I feel something soft and spongy, "What's this?" I poke it and he winces. "Oh my God, are you hurt?"

"Not exactly," he muses, "sit up for me a second," he asks and when I do, he reaches to the back of his neck and swiftly removes his t-shirt over his head. My eyes zone in on a small piece of gauze covering a part of his chest.

My fingers run over the tape. "What happened?"

"Take it off," he says, a smirk playing on his lips.

My frown deepens as I stare at him, wondering exactly what I'm going to find underneath. I carefully remove the tape and when the white padding is gone, I'm met with... Oh. My. God.

I stare at his chest and then his eyes, which are twinkling with mischief.

"Grayson, what the fuck?" I force the words out.

"Do you like it?"

My mouth hangs open as I take in the tattoo that says 'Shorty' over his left pec. It's my handwriting too. "How... how did you get my handwriting?"

"The list, obviously. I kept it and used it as a transfer for this. Stand up." I'm convinced my legs won't work if I try and stand right now, but he pushes me backwards until I'm plopped onto my feet that feel like dead weights. He stands to his full height and his hand brushes the top of my head, smoothing towards his body to directly where my nickname is etched into his skin. "This is where you always come up to when you hug me it's branded into my body, so I took a rough guess from memory and I'm glad I got it right."

"Wh... Wh..." My eyes fill with tears as his hands cup my face, tilting me so I can stare up at this man who continues to surprise me.

His thumb brushes over my cheeks, swiping away tears. "Are these good tears or bad ones?"

"G-good," I stutter on a sob. I throw my arms around his neck. "Grayson, no one has ever done anything like that for me. Ever. I don't... I don't know what to say," I mumble into his neck because there aren't any words to convey how I feel about him right now.

"You don't have to say anything. I just wanted you to know that you're important to me. I love you, shorty. You have my writing on your skin, now I have yours. Forever."

My heart flies out of my chest and straight into my throat at the nickname I once hated, but now has a completely different meaning for me. "Grayson..."

He loosens his grip on me a little as I tilt my head towards him so I can look him in the eyes. "I love you too."

His thumb brushes over my cheek. "You don't have to say it just because I did."

I grip his face between my hands. "Shut up and kiss me," I say, before crashing his pillow soft lips to mine.

He inhales, breaking the kiss, as he moves the tips of his fingers to trace over my lower lip and then my cupid's bow. "I want you more than I've ever wanted anyone, Nora, and that scares me. It also makes me feel like I'm fucking flying half the time. I know this is new, and we haven't planned for this, but I want you to think about us because I want you to be my girl... out loud, in the real world."

I tug his hair, needing to feel him against me. When his lips collide with mine, everything feels like it slots into place; the world, the universe, everything that's led me to this point and I'm not afraid anymore.

We break apart and his stormy eyes to lock onto mine like a honing beacon. "Are you sure you're ready to be mine?"

I take a deep breath and smile.

"I've been yours longer than you realise."

Chapter 33

Nora

"Good morning," I singsong whilst throwing open Jess' door. I'm met with a very dishevelled version of Jess. Her hair is sticking up in varying directions and she's naked or at least topless under her bedsheets. "Ah, I see I couldn't keep the lover boy away, even for one night then."

"I'm not sure you're one to talk. If Tweedle Dee was here with me, that means Tweedle Dumb was in your room." Her eyes glitter when I don't answer. "Don't try and deny it, Nora Scott."

I laugh, almost incredulously at how easily she reads me, "fine, I won't deny it."

Jess grabs a discarded t-shirt from her crumpled sheets and throws it on before sitting on the end of her bed excitedly. "Tell me everything."

"I don't think you want to know everything. The same way, I'd rather gouge my eyes out with a plastic fork than listen to your sex life."

She shrugs. "Maybe you're right, but still, give me something. Are you two okay?"

"We are okay. Better than okay." I get butterflies thinking about finding his tattoo for me, but I want to keep that to myself. Jess stands and wraps her arms around me as my nose wrinkles. "You absolutely cannot get married smelling like sex, Jessica. Shower, now."

Jess giggles and wanders into the shower. I set out the prosecco ready for a toast and call down and ask them to bring breakfast to the room. This day feels like it's been a long time coming, but at the same time it's strange for it be over soon.

The sound of an incoming text distracts me. I smile at the name on the screen, I knew Liam would text me this morning.

> **Liam:** How's the future Mrs Taylor this morning? No cold feet?

> **Nora:** Thoroughly fucked, thanks to you. Currently showering you off her. Her toes are going to stay toasty for you, I promise.

> **Liam:** Glad to hear it. I don't think you can complain about any of the midnight visitors last night, though.

My eyes squeeze shut. Nope.

Nora: Nope, not talking about this with you. If you carry on, I'll sabotage your wedding. Consider yourself warned.

Liam: You wouldn't.

Nora: Try me.

Liam: Grayson says 'Hi' by the way.

Nora: Well played. You're both evil and going to hell for being wicked.

Liam replies with a simple devil emoji. Jess emerges fresh as a daisy from her shower just as room service knocks with our breakfast. I go to answer the door and as it opens in barrels Zoey in true style, dragging her bridesmaid's dress behind her. The woman is a whirlwind 24/7.

"Sorry I know I'm like five minutes late, but that's actually good for me. Happy wedding day, Jess." Her arms throw around a towel wearing Jess as they both chuckle.

The door knocks again and this time it is our breakfasts. We get to work eating everything in sight as the hair and makeup team arrive to primp and preen us all. The room is awash with misty hairspray, powder, and dresses as my mum arrives to have her hair done as well, cooing over Jess as she should. It's a whirlwind of a morning, and before we know it, we have thirty minutes to get Jess in her dress.

It takes all of us to make sure Jess is securely in it. Every button has given us callouses and we've all sweated off our make up by now, but when we see how truly beautiful she looks in her blush pink wedding dress we collectively gasp in awe. She looks like a princess, a princess who is about to marry her prince.

My mum fans her face, trying to delay the inevitable tears. "Oh God, Jess, you're going to make me cry so much today."

"Don't, because then I'll cry, and we all know I'm an ugly crier. Imagine the horror of the pictures."

We're all ready when another knock sounds out through the room, and in walks my dad. The look on his face when he sees Jess is something that will forever play on a loop in my memories. He looks so proud, his eye filling with tears as he whips the hanky out of his breast pocket and dabs his eyes. He sniffs and smiles, regaining his composure whilst the rest of us quietly sob at the interaction.

"You ready, kiddo?" he asks Jess as she nods through glassy eyes.

When we reach the door downstairs to the wedding room, Jess starts to flap. My dad holds her hand tightly as I grab her face. "Jessica, you are about to marry the person who loves you the most in the whole world. That man is waiting for you behind these doors, and he can't wait to call you his wife. Go get him."

Her expression softens as all the panic disappears from her eyes. She nods her head and I nod to Dad that she's good to go. The music softly floats through the room, and we know that's our cue.

Zoey walks first, practically strutting down the aisle, then me and as I lock eyes with Liam, I give him a reassuring smile. He looks as white as a ghost though, so I mime to him that he needs to breathe, and I see him inhale at my words and smile back at me.

Grayson stands next to Liam, both boys matching in their almost dark midnight suits with black shirts that are contrasted with a single white rose attached to their lapels. I let my eyes drink in Grayson; the way his suit makes his eyes look impossibly deep, like a never-ending sea of grey, he looks... edible.

I can't help but lap up the coy smirk on his face or the devastating wink he gives me as I pass him. I stifle a smile as he licks his lips never taking his eyes off me. Silently I mouth *stop*, but that only spurs him on more, the heat radiating from him directly blazing into me.

Then the song changes to *Dandelions by Ruth B.* and all our attention snaps to the top of the aisle where Jess appears. I watch as Liam melts and simultaneously fills with emotion at the sight of his favourite person.

My eyes flick over to Grayson, and I realise he's looking at me in the same way. His eyes are soft and bewitching as he mimes, *I'm so fucking in love with you*. I look around and point to my chest, faking ignorance, and ask *me?* He suppresses a laugh, showing me a smile so bright that I might just die right here right now when he points to me silently saying, *only you, shorty.*

Chapter 34

Grayson

She looks stunning. Breath-taking. Like a goddess among mere mortals in that bridesmaid dress. The way it skims over her curves and dips at the back. *Fuck, I can't with her.* Her dark hair is tumbling around her face in waves, and she glows as she looks at Jess and Liam, but I can't take my eyes off her. Her deep caramel eyes have stolen every breath from my lungs. I'm so far gone for her, and I wasn't afraid to tell her while Jess walked down the aisle.

After the ceremony, we are whisked away for pictures in groups. I catch glimpses of Nora here and there laughing with people, smiling, but I can never pin her down and after last night, my body is desperate for her. An hour later and we're all sat waiting for the new Mr and Mrs Taylor to enter the main hall for their wedding breakfast.

Nora breezes in and sits on my table. Just as I lean over to tell her she looks beautiful the MC announces the newlyweds and I'm all but drowned out. We clap and cheer for the happy couple, but I still can't take my eyes off the woman with midnight hair and creamy skin, even as I stand and applaud the happy couple.

I asked Liam if I could do my speech before the food arrives, otherwise the nerves might kill me off, that or I'll be far too drunk to speak.

As I stand, a few eyes fall onto me and when I clock my favourite pair staring back at me, I relax and clear my throat.

"Hi everyone, I'm Grayson, the best man. I hope you don't mind me holding up your dinner for a minute because I've got a few things to say. I want to thank Liam for being the best friend any bloke could ask for; I owe you a lot, man, and to be standing here with you today is a great honour." I slap his shoulder and he fakes wiping a tear before winking at me. Fucker.

"Well, now that I've confessed my love for the groom, shall we carry on?" Laughter rumbles through the crowd as I turn to the bride.

"Jessica, you look absolutely breath-taking today. The way you and Liam are perfect for one another is beyond anything I've ever witnessed in my life. You are two halves of the same soul, and that's truly something special." My eyes flick to Nora sitting next to Jess. Her eyes are filled with unshed tears and all I want to do is run over to her and claim her in front of everyone and announce that I think I found my person too.

"You know, I had all these jokes and awful, really truly awful stories about Liam, but I'm feeling melancholy, so you're getting off scot-free mate." As the crowd laughs and boos at the same time, hoping I would've embarrassed the groom, I take a deep breath for my next move.

"I've always wondered what it would be like to find a love like Jess and Liam's, it's something you can see and feel simultaneously. The way they share a look, the way Liam knows exactly when Jess is on the verge of being hangry, the way Jess calms Liam down when he's stressed. There's something to be said for closeness and that tangible feeling of love. I've never been in love. Or I hadn't, not until I met someone recently and finally I got it. I started to love the attitude she gave me, the fact she made me want to be better for her but for me too, to chase away her fears, to be the person she turned to when she was scared. Suddenly, this life I didn't know I wanted was staring back at me in the form of this woman. So, Jess, Liam, I get it now. I get love and I want to thank you for being such a shining example of what a soul mate is. To the bride and groom."

People clap and Liam pats my back, bringing me into a hug. I chance a glance at Nora as she wipes her eyes before sipping her champagne. I angle my head towards the hallway hoping that she'll accept my invitation to follow me. I need to be alone with her more than I need my next breath. The room fills with chatter again as the starters begin to filter out from the kitchen. I nervously make my way from the room and two seconds later she's there.

"Hi."

"Grayson..." Her head buries into her hands, but she stills and when she looks up, her eyes are open and clear, burning into my soul. "I need to say this because what you just said... it was... perfect."

I tilt my head at her, hoping this is going to be a good declaration, but judging by her jittering, I'm really unsure.

"Bear with me, because I've got a lot to say." She shakes her hands out between us. "I've had a lot of firsts. The ones that everyone expects you to have. The first time you have sex, the first time you ride a bike, get a job, move out. But you... you have given me more firsts than anyone. You took my list and owned every single thing on it. All of those firsts belong to you. The big firsts? They don't matter to me. It's all these little first moments we've had together. They matter the most. You matter the most. You've shown me your big heart and I won't let it go. I love you, Grayson."

My heart is in my throat, pounding, trying to escape from my body. I haul her into me without a second thought, her familiar scent surrounding me. Smashing our lips together, needing to taste her and fill all of her. She kisses me back fiercely. Nothing about this kiss is gentle. It's claiming and God, do I want to be claimed by her.

"Do you have any idea what you're getting yourself in for?" I ask, breaking our kiss.

Her head shakes as she smiles at me. "No, but I'm in. I'm all in."

"Me too, shorty. Me fucking too."

I push her towards the wall and kiss her like I can't get enough, because the truth is, I can't. I've never wanted someone as much as I want Nora. I want to own every single part of her. I want everyone to know that she is mine and I am hers. It's taking all my strength not to walk back into the wedding and announce it right now, but I know she would hate that.

We walk back into the wedding reception, Jess and Liam eyeing our hands clasped together. I pull Nora in for a long and firm kiss in front of her chair before she sits down breathless, just as Jess squeals with excitement next to her.

Over the next few hours, we watch Jess and Liam dance, cut cake, and generally have a blast at their wedding. Exactly how it should be. Nora hasn't left my side. Our hands firmly grasped together, swaying to slow songs and singing our hearts out to others. It's been a hell of a day, but if I don't get Nora alone soon, I might just explode.

Chapter 35

Nora

H e's somewhere between heaven and hell, and I'm stuck in some sort of limbo, unable to decide if I want to be obedient or disobey him to get his punishments. I guess right now I chose heaven, because the man is on his knees in the bathroom of the hotel, devouring every inch of me.

"Fuck, fuck, I'm coming. Grayson..." My orgasm explodes like fireworks, a Catherine wheel of colour, spinning around my body as I feel him hum against me, dipping his tongue deep inside, as every sensitive nerve on my body is on fire and dancing like a Disney parade.

"I fucking love hearing those noises." He looks up and his lips shine with my arousal as I come down from my high. He unbuckles his suit belt and pulls his trousers and boxers down enough to free himself. I lower my hand, running my hand over the length of him and relishing his velvet skin, smearing the precum from his tip down his shaft. I pump him a few more times before he pins me with a stare. "Lift your leg for me, shorty," he demands, his voice full of need. I release his cock and lift my leg and wrap it around his waist whilst using the sink behind me to balance. He lines himself to my entrance, jaw slack and breathing shallow, before he pushes inside me, giving me that perfect burn of pleasure. "Fuck, you feel good. Now come again all over my cock. I want to feel you and then I'm going to send you back out there knowing that my cum will be dripping down your legs."

One other thing I'll never get used to is his dirty mouth. Jesus, this man can bring me to near combustion.

My body sags against him as he exhales. The heat from his hands sear into my back and my hips, making me delirious. He doesn't give me any time to adjust before he pushes into me again and again and again.

He hisses when I push us closer together, opening my legs more for him. "Fuck Nora." His hips drive harder into me as his pace increases, the tell-tale sign of my orgasm building in my lower stomach as I stifle a scream. "Yes, shorty. Scream my name when you come. I want everyone to know who owns you."

"Oh God, Grayson, that feels... you're hitting my... oh, my God. Gonna come."

I come with such a force that it sends Grayson over the edge too. "Yes, I'm coming fuck, I'm coming," he growls pushing into me harder before I feel him release inside me. His body falls against mine as we both gasp for air.

He moves from me, grabbing paper towels to clean himself. Since he said he wanted me to be dripping, the smirk on his face whilst he does this only serves to remind me why I hated him mere months ago.

His grin widens. "God, I fucking love you."

My heart skips, leaps, kicking up the biggest ruckus in my chest, knocking down walls of doubt and fear until all that is left is him.

A smile parts my lips. "I'm all yours."

In a flash, he hauls me back into his body, wrapping his big arms around me. "I'm not sure how I managed to convince you to love me, but you need to know that you're it for me and one day I'm going to make sure you don't go anywhere."

My eyes sparkle. "You're going to tie me up?"

He winks. "You'd like that, wouldn't you, shorty?"

Yes, sir. I would very much like that.

I raise an eyebrow at him, not fully understanding all too distracted from his comment about actually tying me up. We should circle back around to that soon.

Once we're fully clothed again, he tugs my hand and guides me out of the bathroom.

"Come with me a second," he says, pulling me towards the venue's exit. My legs struggle to keep up as he strides a steady pace across the foyer.

"Where are we going?" I ask with no reply.

We pass the reception, heading through the ornate front doors until we are outside on the front lawn, surrounded by the cool night air. "Grayson..." I start, but he places a finger over my lips, shushing me.

"Look up," he whispers as we stand close enough that our toes are touching. I stare at him for a second, wondering what is going on but I admit defeat and tilt my head towards the night sky.

Immediately, the shining bright orbs blink at me. Thousands of them scattered above me like a dream. There isn't a cloud in sight, only a pure dark blue blanket with diamonds glittering. "It's so beautiful," I marvel. I feel Grayson's hand grip mine as he brings them both to his chest. The wind picks up around us like a soft melody dancing around us.

"Nora?" he says, gaining my attention. When I look at him, the light from the stars reflects in his eyes, making him look ethereal. I move closer, trapping our connected hand between us, so close that I can feel his thrashing heart against my wrist.

He leans down, slowly at first, letting his warm breath mix with mine, until our lips touch. I open for him, letting our tongues meet, deepening the kiss gently.

When we break apart, I'm completely breathless and my hands, at some point, moved to grip the lapels of his suit jacket. "Look up again." I frown at his instruction but look anyway.

"They're stars," I say, laughing lightly, not really sure what he thinks I'm supposed to say.

"There's another thing ticked off that list of yours."

My eyes fill with emotion, the memory flooding back to me as look at my man. "I thought you said kissing under the stars was cliché?"

He pulls me into his chest, so I'm resting my face against him, inhaling my favourite scent as he kisses the top of my head, "It is, but it turns out, I'd do just about anything to make you happy."

Chapter 36

Grayson – One year, four months later

These boxes get heavier the more I lift. I swear moving house in August was our worst idea ever. Especially as London decided to have a heatwave on the same day that we hired the moving vans.

Things have been incredible between Nora and me. I still go to therapy every week, and Nora and I talk about any issues we have. I never thought I'd be the person to talk about my feelings, but it's addicting... freeing and I'm the happiest I've ever been.

"Don't forget the box that you need to donate to charity." Nora's voice travels from my now old hallway. I think somewhere over the last year we realised that we spent all our time at her house, which suited me fine, so I pretty much told her I'd be moving in because she wasn't getting rid of me anytime soon. We completed her list and made more of our own. Going to Glastonbury and seeing Foo Fighters was her favourite thing, and I got plenty of thanks for that one. I reinstated the sex in the limo since it was a bust the first time. It was arguably the most exciting. Nora was terrified, but it made it even hotter when she finally surrendered to me on her knees in the back of that limo. That's a core memory for me.

I swipe the sweat from my brow, the heat as well as that memory is stifling me right now and since we've packed everything there are no fans circulating air in my apartment. It's just fucking hot everywhere.

Nora comes into view and what a fucking view it is. She's wearing pink cycling shorts that show every ripple of her perfect peachy bum, and a crop top that leaves nothing to the imagination. "Hey, shorty. Come here often?" I wolf whistle as she bends over, picking up a few stray books from the floor.

"Don't even think about getting me all dick-stracted Grayson King. Not going to happen." She waggles a finger my way.

"But you love my dick," I say playfully as I rush up behind her, wrapping my arms around her waist. "And look, he loves you just as much." I push my now rock-hard length into her arse, and she arches her back into me, whimpering softly as I dig my fingertips into her hips. Then she slaps my hands away, jumping a foot away from me. "No, we have too much to get done, and it's a thousand degrees in here." She fans herself, her cheeks flushing red.

"You blushing for me, shorty? You know how weak it makes me when you get all flustered over me." I move closer to her again and her lips roll over her teeth, stifling a smile or a laugh as I haul her into my body once more and press our lips together. *Fuck, she feels like home, and I never want to let her go.*

"We're never going to get you moved in if you keep kissing me like that," she rasps, breaking our kiss.

"I don't know if I care right at this moment. All I want is you, always." The words fall from my lips with ease because it's the truth.

I want her forever. This overwhelming feeling to claim her courses through my veins. *Mine, mine, mine,* my brain chants. I've never had that before with anyone, and I'm not scared. I'm ready.

"You okay?" she says, sweat glistening on her beautiful face from the muggy heat, and I don't know how, but she steals another piece of my heart just by looking at me like I'm her whole world. Because she is mine, and I am hers.

"I'm good. I'm really fucking happy."

"Oh yeah? Who got you smiling like that, ponyboy?" She winks, knowing exactly who.

"You."

"Hmm, seems you're obsessed with me." She grins cheekily.

"Completely." *Kiss.* "Utterly." *Lick.* "Obsessed." *Kiss.* I hum into her neck, inhaling her sweet scent. "Fuck, you smell good."

"I do not. I'm sweating."

"I don't fucking care. You turn me on just by existing. A little sweat doesn't scare me," I reply between kissing her neck, lapping up the heat from her skin.

"Okay, we have to stop," she says, trying to push me backwards, but I won't let her go. I'll never let her go.

"Do we though, because all I can think about is fucking you right here." I smile at her, pushing myself into her hips.

"Down, you horn dog," she laughs, finally breaking free of me, her dark hair whipping around her as she moves.

Groaning from the loss of her heat against me, I huff. "Fine. We need to get me moved into your place because I need to fuck you, and I need it to be an all-night thing."

"Funny, that sounds a lot like what I've been saying." She taps the side of her mouth and I whip my hand across her arse as she turns from me.

"Sassy mouths get fucked, Nora."

Her head turns back to me with a grin that's borderline illegal it's so hot. "I'd better be a good girl from now on then, huh?"

I bite my bottom lip, ready to rip her shorts down and bend her over when Liam walks in through the door with Jess. *Fuck, I'd forgotten they were downstairs.*

"Whatever you just said, I'm erasing it from my memory. I do not need to know anything about your sex life," Liam says flatly, brushing past us both as Nora blushes fiercely from being caught.

Jess chuckles as she walks by us too. "Personally, I can't imagine Nora being anything *but* a good girl."

"Oh, you have no idea—" I begin, but am abruptly cut off by Nora's hand clamping over my mouth, her caramel eyes burning a glare.

"That's enough of that," she snaps. I push my tongue forwards and let it connect with her hand and she squeals, removing it instantly. "Eurghhh," she yelps, wiping her hand on my chest. "Boys are gross."

"That's not what you were saying last night," I say, smirking at my girl.

"Shut it," Nora says, zipping her lips and swaying her gorgeous hips as she walks away, bending to pick up a box as she goes, giving me a full view of her arse again. God, she kills me.

A few gruelling hours later and we've donated, tidied, and moved me into the townhouse. The humidity hasn't let up, but at least the sun is going down now.

I flop my exhausted body onto the sofa. "I'm never moving again." I exhale a loud grunt as I stretch out my tired body when I feel my girl land gently on my lap. The euphoria that fills my veins is like nothing I've ever felt before. My heart feels too big for my chest, when she's near me it's like sitting in direct sunlight, and I'll never get enough of her. My hands move to her hips as I shift her closer to me, so our chests are flush and she's straddling me now.

"Hi, baby," she coos, placing her hands around my neck and pressing her petite frame into my chest.

I angle my head so I can see her on my chest, and I stay that way for a while, just listening to her heart beating, feeling so fucking grateful that she belongs to me. I let out a deep, content sigh, because that's exactly how I feel. Content. And I feel like I've spent my whole life trying to *be* content and never fully achieving it until this moment with her, in *our* house.

"You okay?" she asks, absently stroking my hair on the back of my neck.

I look up at her, those deep caramel eyes glowing at me, wisps of amber sparking to life as soon as my hands drift up to her back and my fingertips dust over the exposed skin on her back. "More than okay. I feel like I'm exactly where I'm meant to be."

Epilogue – Four years later

Nora

I make my way home for the day and when I walk through the familiar dark front door of our house in Victoria Park, I'm greeted with the most wonderful sounds of my boys playing together.

My boys. I'm not sure I'll ever get used to that. We had our beautiful baby boy fourteen months ago. His full name is Oscar Grayson King, but we call him Ozzy for short. Once Jess had Poppy, our niece, Grayson got all googly eyed. It took him a whole month to admit that he wanted to try for a baby. He told me he wanted to make sure that I wanted it too and we were ready before he said anything. This man I share my life with has spent the last four years surprising me. He's so committed and the best father I could ever ask for our baby boy.

Sneaking into the living area to see them playing with dinosaurs, I'm not sure who is having the most fun. Probably Grayson. Watching them together fills my heart with so much joy I get tingles in my throat.

Two big blue-grey eyes spot me and shout, "Mama," as Ozzy comes barrelling into my open arms.

His tiny arms wrap around my neck, making my eyes close in bliss. He pats me and says my name over and over. Grayson smiles and walks towards us. I'm not sure I'll ever get over how fucking hot he is and how I ended up being so lucky.

His dark hair is more unkept these days, and he usually has stubble that feels absolutely divine when he's between my legs. I've told him he isn't allowed to be clean shaven anymore as I'm addicted. He's still my biggest crush; the person who kicks up my body temperature when I see him.

He tilts my chin as I shift Ozzy onto my hip and places an all too swift kiss on my lips. His eyes darken at my whimper, and he mouths *later* to me.

"Aren't you glad Mama's home, Oz?" Grayson coos as he walks around me grabbing a handful of my bum and squeezing whilst growling in my ear. I slap him away a tell him no fair if I can't touch, neither can he.

"Dinner is almost done. I've been home an hour or so playing with our boy, so I let Dora go early. She made us lasagne whilst Ozzy napped, so I figured she deserved an early finish."

"Of course, that sounds perfect. Dora texted me at lunch because she couldn't find Oz's bunny he sleeps with, but it was in our bed."

Dora has been our nanny for the last year, since I started part time back at work and she's a godsend. We couldn't live without her. Her lasagnes are amazing, but more than that, Ozzy adores her. She's like his surrogate grandmother. Not that his actual grandparents don't adore him, because they do. Ozzy and Poppy are the most spoiled grandchildren ever.

We amble into the kitchen to sit together at the dinner table and eat Dora's famous lasagne. Ozzy claps his hands gleefully when I sit him in his chair. He's such a foodie, exactly like his daddy.

When we've finished dinner, Grayson leans into Ozzy and lifts him out of his chair. "We'll be right back, Mama. Stay there," he says as my brows meet in confusion. But I sit and listen, staying where I am, wondering what is going on.

A few minutes later, Ozzy waddles back in without Grayson and I scoop him up when he gets to me, sitting him on my lap. "Hi, baby boy. Where's Daddy gone?" I ask. Ozzy points behind me to Grayson, who has an amused look on his face. "Okay, what's that face for? What's going on? Am I missing something?"

Grayson takes two strides forward and bends to kiss me lightly. I feel dizzy from his touch. He pulls back, cheeky smirk firmly in place. "Ozzy, show Mama what you have."

I look down at our baby, who isn't really a baby anymore. He started walking at ten months and he babbles nonstop. Ozzy smiles and pats his tummy, and that's when I notice he's wearing a t-shirt that says, '*Mama, will you marry Daddy?*' My breath catches in my throat as I look at Ozzy, who's smiling up at Grayson. Grayson drops to his knee and I'm staring at a ring that's got three diamonds sitting in a row.

"What do you say, shorty? Wanna marry me?" he says with so much confidence and adoration that my heart flips around acrobatically in my chest.

"Yes," I croak on a sob. "I want to marry you."

I stand, propping Ozzy on my hip as Grayson encases my face and pulls me into a kiss that steals my soul right out of my body. This man. He's shown me everything, his big heart, and he's loved me with it so fiercely. I never want to let him go.

Ozzy taps the sides of our connected faces, "Mama down," he demands, trying to wiggle free of my hold. I gently put him down and he waddles around our feet.

"I'm really lucky to have you both," Grayson says as I look up at him, his grey eyes shimmering and swirling with emotion.

"We're lucky to have you too. Now kiss me again, husband," I say with enough heat in my voice that he knows I need him.

His big hands wrap around my waist, pulling me flush to him with a growl. "Husband, mmm, I like that a lot."

A couple of hours later and Ozzy is finally asleep after a bubble bath. Honestly, I feel dead on my feet when I walk into our bedroom, but I'm also still buzzing from this evening. I'm someone's fiancé. Grayson King is going to be my husband. I'm giddy at the thought.

I find Grayson sitting on the edge of our bed. His eyes raise from his phone to meet mine, he smirks and crooks a finger for me to go to him.

My body isn't my own when he summons me like this. It's his to take and I'm not complaining one little bit. I slowly make my way to him as his hand leaps out to grab my wrist, dragging my body into his so I'm standing between his legs. His big hands roam over my bum, and he growls a feral noise when he squeezes me.

"I need you so fucking bad right now, shorty. If I don't get to be buried inside you in the next ten minutes, I'm going to fucking die, I swear."

"Oh, that sounds serious. I guess I could…"

He grips my leggings and rips them down my legs whilst stealing all the air from my lungs in the process. "I'm not fucking around shorty, I need that pussy and I need it now."

Well, if I wasn't wet before, I'm now sufficiently drenched and the look in Grayson's eyes tells me he knows it. His eyebrows raise as he slips his hands inside my underwear, and he hisses when he reaches my core. "Fuck, Nora." He tears the thin lace away from my body with one swift rip.

Bye bye panties.

"Lie down on the bed for me, Daddy needs his dessert," he says with a deep gruff voice, keeping his eyes trained on me.

When he goes all demanding and predatory like this, I can't deny him. Hell, I can barely form a thought, let alone defy him. Plus, there's something about a man who is desperate for you, for your taste, to touch you and play with you. The fact that he is craving me right now makes my whole body come to life in a way he only knows how to do.

As I position myself open for him, his eyes darken, he raises his fist to his mouth and bites as another growl creeps out from his chest. I can't stop the whimper that escapes my mouth either because he lunges forward, gripping his tattooed hands into my hip bones and drags me down the bed until I'm almost hanging off. The slight burn on my back from the duvet covers, alongside his possessive touch, is intoxicating. He drops to his knees, skating his hands across my apex, missing the exact place I need him to touch, and caressing my inner thighs. "There she is," he murmurs almost to himself. He skilfully parts my lips with feather light touch, and I realise I'm holding my breath, desperate for him to touch me. To take me like I know he wants to.

"Baby, please, I need you to touch me," I beg as our eyes connect. He drapes one of my legs over his shoulder and smirks before he dives towards my open pussy. Flattening his tongue and dragging it from back to front, he swirls when he reaches my clit. The sensation of his stubble grazing my skin has my hips bucking, but he stops me, pinning me to the bed, keeping my knees open for him.

"Uh-uh, shorty. I want you open so I can enjoy every fucking drop of you." He drags his finger down my slit torturously before he pushes one finger inside me. I tense around him, and he rumbles out curse words as he inserts another finger, while he massages my clit with his other hand. My head snaps up to look at him from the contact.

His tongue and his fingers work me into a frenzy. In between his growling and his groping of my skin, it takes me mere seconds for my orgasm to build like a fucking rocket zapping around my body. "Give it to me, Nora. I want all of it, right fucking now." He taps my clit once more and then sucks it into his mouth as I scream his name, coming apart. My entire body shakes its own earthquake of desire and need for more from my husband to be.

Not waiting for my orgasm to stop, I grab Grayson's shoulders and pull him towards me. His lips are glistening, and I lick off the evidence of my arousal as I push his boxers down his legs. A chuckle rumbles from him. "So needy. Tell me how badly you want my dick, Nora."

My words escape on a shudder of excitement. "So fucking much."

The smirk on his face is devilish, and it makes me hotter than I already am. "You want me to fuck you?" he asks whilst tapping the tip of his cock on my sensitive clit. My head throws back in a moan.

"Yes, I want you to fuck me." I blink up at him, licking my lips as I watch his eyes follow the trail of my tongue.

Grayson's eyes darken into a shade of midnight as he lines himself up at my entrance, his lips so close to my ear his hot breath feels like popping candy on my skin. "Scream for Daddy, baby girl," he whispers before thrusting into me unapologetically.

Grayson sets a relentless pace that has me screaming and clawing at his back. He mutters out curse words as he fucks me, taking my nipple into his mouth and biting to make me scream louder for him. It's a good job Ozzy is a decent sleeper because I'm almost positive our neighbours can hear me if they were paying attention.

"Fuck, Nora, you feel so fucking good." He moves his hand down between us and finds my clit, setting my whole world into a spin as his cock hits my G-spot and his fingers send me into actual oblivion.

My orgasm hits in waves. The first being little whimpers of pleasure escaping my mouth, then it's a scream that builds as Grayson pumps into me until he reaches his peak. We climb and climb until we fall, both of us panting and coming down from a high that we are both addicted to. The world begins to even out again with his soft kisses to my collarbone and my hands in his hair.

Our eyes meet, still hazy with lust. "I'm never going to get enough of you." He leans into my mouth and takes my bottom lip between his teeth and gently nips. When he pulls back to look at me again, I stroke the side of his stubble that so deliciously aided an orgasm earlier. "I love you," he purrs, his voice stated and quiet.

"Eh, you're okay, I guess," I joke as a laugh threatens to escape my lips. He fakes shock and pushes back into me, his cock still slightly hard as I whimper from the soreness that he left in his wake.

"You're going to earn yourself a spanking, Mrs King."

My eyes widen in delight. "Don't threaten me with something I'll enjoy, Mr King."

Grayson smirks as he bends down, taking my nipple into his mouth and biting again as he drags his body away from mine, leaving me more needy than I was before all of this started.

"You don't play fair," I pout.

"You don't think two orgasms is fair?" He cocks his head to the side as he saunters into the bathroom to get a washcloth. When he returns to clean me, he takes his time. "I fucking love watching my cum drip out of you," he hums.

"I fucking love *you*."

Grayson's eyes light up when I tell him that and watching him feel bathed in my love is something I'll never get used to.

"I fucking love you too, shorty. Now turn over. Let me see what I can do about that spanking."

Afterword

Thank you for reading my second book – I'm incredibly grateful for everyone who takes the time to read my work. Without you, I wouldn't be able to do what I love so THANK YOU!!

If you haven't read the first book in the series – All of My Lasts – you can find it here: https://books2read.com/u/4jNjG2

Coming in Autumn 2023 is Zoey's story – she's a wild ride so buckle up for the final instalment of The Ladies of London!

Acknowledgements

My readers – Thank you for sticking around for book two. It means the world to me. My incredible ARC readers, thank you for all the love for both books when you care about my work it makes me feel like all of the stress is worth it. I hope you're ready for Zoey's book, it's going to be wild!

Anna P. – Thank you for beta reading this and putting up with my chaotic brain all the time. I'm so glad to be on this author journey alongside you my dear friend.

Tash – Thank you as always for listening to my voice notes and brainstorming with me, checking in on me when you know I'm quiet. You always seem to just know when I need a little pick me up!

Vari Scott – How would I have gotten through this without you? Simple. I wouldn't have. If I don't hear from you daily, I panic haha. I'm grateful for you beyond words.

Anyone and everyone who has listened to me complain about this book. **Adi, Debbie, Emma** (who never judged the earliest copy of this book – I love you my little Welshie), the RARE chat. It's finally done and now you can all listen to me complain about book three – lucky you!

About Author

Meghan lives in rural England with her family – husband, two children and a yappy dog!

She works in Education by day but writes smutty romances by night.

There are lots of plans for Meghan to write more books so if you enjoyed this one there are more on the way!

Follow Meghan Hollie on Facebook, Instagram, TikTok and Goodreads.

If you enjoyed this book, please consider leaving a review on amazon and you'll be thanked in virtual hugs forever!

Printed in Great Britain
by Amazon

27927159R00189